INTO THE EBB

Other works by the same author include:

Peace Comes Dropping Slow (Ramsay Head Press)
A Resurrection of a Kind (AUP)
A Twelvemonth and a Day (AUP)
Two Christmas Stories (AUP)
Venus Peter (with Ian Sellar)
(screenplay: Christopher Young Films Ltd)

AUP Titles of related interest

Full Score: short stories
Fred Urquhart
edited by Graeme Roberts

The Laird of Drammochdyle
William Alexander
Introduction by William Donaldson

Grampian Hairst
An Anthology of North-East Prose
edited by William Donaldson and Douglas Young

Glimmer of Cold Brine
A Scottish Sea Anthology
edited by Alistair Lawrie, Hellen Matthews, Douglas Ritchie

INTO THE EBB

a new collection of
East Neuk stories

Christopher Rush

ABERDEEN UNIVERSITY PRESS

First published 1989
Aberdeen University Press
A member of the Pergamon Group

© Christopher Rush 1989

The publishers acknowledges subsidy
from the Scottish Arts Council
towards the publication of this volume.

British Library Cataloguing in Publication Data

Rush, Christopher, *1944–*
    Into the ebb.
    I. Title
    823'.914 [F]
    ISBN 0 08 036590 6

PRINTED IN GREAT BRITAIN
THE UNIVERSITY PRESS
ABERDEEN

for the two Patricias

Contents

A Winter's Tale

The flakes were drifting thickly up the firth from the northeast by the time the wandering figure reached Crail. The bundle on his shoulders was large, flattish, and seemingly heavy.

A lone fisherman hurried away from his shrouded boat. The bunch of haddocks swung numbly from his fist like dumb winter bells.

The wanderer's shout arrested him briefly as he stooped to enter his low cottage. He put his shoulder to the stiffness of the door. The house leaked yellow lamplight. A girl ran to him, a bright collection of rags, out of the shadows.

'What's the big house up there, friend—the one with the towers?'

The fisherman half turned in the dim doorway. It was growing dark and his features were sculpted bronze. He looked curiously at the other man's luggage, mysterious under its sacking.

'Is that your tombstone on your back, gaberlunzie man?'

The figure in the snow stood and laughed. This was the usual East Neuk trick of answering one question with another.

'You'll need your stone with you if you go begging up there, man. Balcomie House that is.'

Snowflakes turned to beads on the bronze cheek.

'Thank you for the information, fisherman.'

Now the little girl started to tug impatiently at her father's sleeve and a woman's voice tinkled like a bell from inside. He put his hand on the girl's head, ruffling her curls, and stayed on in the doorway. He seemed content, with his fisherman's patience, to prolong that satisfying moment of crossing the threshold between two worlds: the cold works of winds and waves and the red hours of rest by the fireside.

'I tell you you won't get any favours up there, man. Not from the great folks—their bellies are as pinched as mine these days—and certainly not at this time of night.'

There was a warning in the coarse salty voice that was not unfriendly.

'You'll march a mile for nothing,' he added, turning to go in. 'They won't have a haddock's head to give away as much.'

1

'I'm not a begging man,' shouted the wanderer as the door thudded shut.

He thrust his head down into the whitening night and made for the big hall.

His knuckles froze on the nail-studded doors.

There was no answer to his thin knocking so he picked up a stone. He stared, fascinated for a moment, at its cold white mantle of fur. Then he skimmed it off slowly with one finger and rapped smartly three times.

The snowflakes stung his ears.

Down towards Fifeness the sea was roaring on the sands. He heard it, and envied the fisherman sitting at his supper, that blithe bundle of rags gladdening his knee.

'Come on, come on.'

He bent to pick up the stone again. As he did so the door swung open.

'Get off,' came the thorny voice of the porter, 'we want no begging scum here.'

The wanderer stood upright in the snow. He approached the doorway through the swirling flurries, unlacing his single item of baggage from his back and removing its cover.

He held it out with a smile.

'That's different,' humphed the doorman. 'Step inside and I'll say that you're here.'

The wanderer stood out of the night. At once the snow melted from him, resolved itself into a pool at his feet.

'You're to go in.'

The porter was back, marshalling him the way.

'If it was up to me, mind,' he grumbled, 'I'd still send you packing. I won't be less hungry after you're done.'

The travelling man sighed.

'Man cannot live by bread alone, so we're told.'

'First I've heard of it,' muttered the flunkey. 'In you go.'

He found himself standing in the great hall. A second wave of warmth washed over him and more snow water glittered about his feet. Shivering, he set down his load carefully, out of the wet.

The torchlight brightened on the sweeping golden curves of a harp.

'Well, minstrel,' said the lord of the gathering, 'let us hear your skill.'

He spoke from a distance. Dinner was over, the flagstones swept and strewn. At the far end of the hall, in the huge grate, a stack of peats pulsed with heat. Torches along the walls were crackling islands of light in a sea of shadows. Some ladies sat proudly on benches, stiff-backed. Others and their men-friends lay loosely by the fire on scatterings of straw.

The minstrel took up the centre of the floor, where a stool was set for him. He sat down facing the lord and his lady.

'Some strong drink, if you please, good people,' he said.

'Strong enough to reach my frozen fingertips and free them to play and please.'

A cup was placed in his hands, brimming with deep dark wine-light.

'Play well on the strength of it, poet,' the lord said. 'In these uncertain times some of us have been known to crawl inside the empty butts and get drunk on the mere memory of wine.'

There was a low laughter from the benches.

It was mouth laughter, not from the belly.

The minstrel tilted his chin, his eyes tight shut. The light from the cup drained into him.

'Thank you,' he said. 'In spite of what a Crail fisherman told me, you pour with a generous hand.'

'Doubtless the fisherman was right,' said his host. 'But with you it's different. Poets have the faculty of giving us back our dreams, when even the wine-strength fails. So let us see what you can perform for us.'

The guest bowed his head, brought it up close to the strings of the harp, raised his eyes to the rafters.

'A new poem,' he proclaimed. 'You shall be the first to hear it.'

And he struck the strings and sang.

> *Quhen Alexander our kynge was deid*
> *That Scotland led in lauche and le,*
> *Away was sons of ale and breid,*
> *Of wyne and wax, of gamyn and gle.*
> *Our gold was changit into leid,*
> *Christ, born into virgynyte,*
> *Succoure Scotland and remeid*
> *That stade is in perplexite.*

The spell was cast at once, from the first clang of the string.

He sang to them of the past, of the long and palmy days of Alexander. Ah, then, he said, there was wine in the drinking place, and bread in the eating place, and laughter and love in the long halls. Thus he harped and sang, giving them back the illusion of their youth, their country's confidence and strength. He did so with the accomplishment of the master.

The notes came out sharp and bitter sweet, like elderflowers on a summer night, the maddening fragrance of mortality and love.

So he played. And sang.

And the harp shivered like the sea. The tide of grief gathered, heightened, swelled, to flood the hearts of the listeners, and the harp itself went out on that sea of its own making. Its proud curve was a ship's prow, the harpist the helmsman, riding the surge.

Yes, he was skilled, this navigator of notes. His two hands were the sun and the moon, pulling on the rippling strings, drawing out the sea of music to its floodtide.

Secretly, as he played, the wall tapestries stirred and the faded scenes came to life. The huntsman's arrow flashed after so long an aim and the deer sank dead in the dell. The young lover at last caught and kissed the girl he had been pursuing since the day the tapestry was made. His arm snaked round her girdle and he drew her down among the leaves.

In the flickering hall the two silent dancers, light and shadow, circled hand in hand to the poet's song. Now they suddenly swung together on the golden waves.

They entwined. A moment of poise, togetherness.

The harp-ship hove to, unloaded its cargo, the fulfilment of dreams.

With a final flourish of his arm the skipper smote his ship into silence.

It was once more a harp.

The captain was a man of rags. His face a face of stone.

But the host remembered what he had just done.

'Well sung, poet,' he said. 'You have gladdened us and saddened us and taught us to see life anew, and that is the business of the singer. Now put away your harp and be a storyteller among us. The blizzard is blowing long and hard. Shorten the winter's night for us with a tale.'

The minstrel stood up and bowed low.

'I am at your disposal, lords and ladies. What story shall you choose?'

'Give us the story of King Alexander,' replied the host, 'the subject of your latest poetic lament. Tell us the story of how he came to die.'

'Ah.'

The poet, now the storyteller, pondered the pale lamps of faces, bobbing in the shadows and silence and flames.

'Ah,' he said, 'that story is even older than Alexander himself, good people. But if you will be patient, I will tell it to you.'

He allowed the silence to gather again.

Then he sat down, thought for a space, and spoke.

'Put back your minds a hundred years, lords and ladies. A hundred years. Thirty-six thousand five hundred and twenty-five days.

How many of you were alive then?

None.

I see an octogenarian or two sitting in this goodly gathering, but no centurions. Nobody with a hundred years under his command.

A hundred years, I say—and the year of our Lord twelve hundred and fourteen.

Then was born, not thirty miles from here, the notorious Michael Scot, the wizard of Balwearie.

Picture the birth-weary mother and the proud father looking down together on that pink, sucking thing. Do you think if that moment had extended itself to a millenium, they could ever have come to believe that this blind little blob of life would become infamous in his time? I can tell you that even as I speak, the wizard of Balwearie has been cited up by the great poet Dante, in his *Inferno*, as one of the world's most fearful enchanters. But little did that infant's parents imagine their son's dark doings as they adored him then in his first hour of life.

Maybe as he grew up they realised that he was not going to bear the curse of ordinariness.

The young Michael Scot went first to Oxford. And though many go to Oxford and return home none the wiser, Balwearie soon knew everything that there was to be known. There he studied with Roger Bacon, another expert in forbidden books.

He denuded the orchards of Oxford: mathematics, music, medicine, science, philosophy, law.

He approached the accursed tree and plucked its various fruits: divination, demonology, the dark spells of stars.

But could Oxford and Roger Bacon satisfy that deep alchemical thirst? He travelled on to Padua, Toledo, to the mysteries of the Orient and the Moors; he attended the schools of magic at Salamanca and Seville; he became court astrologer to Frederick the Second at Bologna.

He predicted Frederick's death. He foretold the decline and fall of many a great city.

And Dante remembered him.

At last he came back to Scotland, to stand on the old tower at Balwearie, conversing with constellations in his age. He dimmed the dog-star's winter brightness, watched the stars of the Navigator's Line go out one by one, discovered the secret of how to tie up the Pleiades, how to loose Orion's belt.

He stared out Aldebaran, unwinking.

After that he grew a little tired, as old men do.

But he was never allowed to rest for long. A work-mad spirit began haunting him for employment.

Among a million brain-boggling tasks, he had this spirit build a dam-head across the Tweed at Kelso, but it was back the very next morning, having finished off this assignment in one night's working. He told it to divide the single cone of the Eildon Hill into three. Again, it was done in a night.

It carved the Bass Rock into a bear, counted the birds on the May Island, sunk the peat-bogs to keep Fife burning for a thousand years. The Bog of Star, and Our Lady's Bog of Lindores—these go down to the centre of the earth.

Finally he set it to the hopeless chore of making ropes out of sea-sand.

That was a clever move. The spirit is still at it, endlessly, to this very day, and always will be; never to be worn out by the nature of his work, but never to complete it either. Walk down to the shore in the morning when the tide has withdrawn, and you will see his night's work—the sandbars on the beach, wetly reflecting the sky. A weave of white rope that stretches all the way from Kingsbarns to St Andrews and from Fifeness to Aberdour. And it will all be washed away by the next sea.

He was no fool, Michael Scot of Balwearie.

No sooner had he chained up this demon to his task than his sovereign required him for affairs of state: special ambassador to France.

'The French pirates are giving our sailors too much trouble,' Alexander told him. 'Go and tell this king of theirs that I require satisfaction. Take what ships and retinue you will.'

'Certainly, my liege lord,' said Balwearie, 'I'll go as you command. But none of that cumbersome court nonsense will be necessary, I think.'

He conjured up a fiend in the shape of a black charger and he rode this thing through the air to France. Nobody knew he was coming.

Anyway, they were high over the white surge when the horse started pawing the clouds. The Devil was in its ear.

'Michael,' buzzed the insidious questioner, 'what is it, do you think, that the old women of Scotland mutter into their gums at bed-time?'

A less wary wizard would have answered right away, 'Pater-Noster', and that would have given the Adversary the power to hurl him from the horse's back into the foaming chasms far below. But he only said, 'What is that to you? Mount, Diabolus, and fly!' And he dug in the spurs.

When he reached France he tethered the horse to the palace gates and strolled in.

A most unconventional ambassador.

'Your pirates are getting up our Scots king's nostrils,' he yapped unceremoniously. 'You'd better let me have some concessions back with me before the red lion starts to roar.'

'And what if he does?' asked the French monarch, amazed at this irruption into his stately afternoon.

'If he does, you'll hear him at your breakfast tables next morning from a long way off. But you'll find him an unwelcome guest for supper, he'll be here so fast.'

The French king laughed. All his courtiers in their fine French fripperies laughed. Even the poodles grinned a bit.

'So this is what you Scots offer in the way of courtliness and diplomacy, is it? This is the extent of your statecraft, this honest, rustic plain speaking? Very well then, I consider that the sharp edge of the axe will somewhat improve your bluntness.'

Balwearie decided not to fall in with that arrangement.

'I tell you what,' he said, 'my horse at the gates out there likes your concessions so badly that he is going to stamp three times, to encourage you to better them. You'll hear him if you listen, for he is no ordinary horse.'

On which there was an almighty pounding and every steeple in Paris shook its bells. Notre Dame herself broke out in an iron flowering, the like of which had never been heard before.

Balwearie addressed the ranks of open mouths.

'That was for fun. Here is the second caper.'

Instantly three of the palace towers toppled into the courtyard. The noise was sudden and deafening. Through the windows everybody could see a mountain of rubble sunk in a sea of dust.

The French weren't laughing any more.

'Now for the third.'

'Wait!'

The king interrupted him with a white face.

'All right, have what concessions you will, you monster—only take yourself and your fiend of hell away!'

'Oh, well done, your majesty,' Balwearie said. 'I'm glad you've decided to dispense with all that flowery French talk. I'll go and tell the lion how sorry you were about your seamen's depredations, and how direct and accommodating you have been.'

He was a powerful persuader. You can see why Alexander liked to use him, though doubtless we minstrels have put a little varnish on his deeds.

In his extreme old age he grew bored with politics, as most wise men do. He practised all kinds of pranks to cheer himself up—he sold his shadow, for instance. Can you imagine? He made a harp with invisible strings, for the wind's invisible fingers to play upon.

In the end his Books of Power had to be interred with him, so deadly would they have proved in the world had they been opened by the ignorant. Yet only six feet of earth holds them—what a thought!

Yes, he was the greatest of magicians, greater even than true Thomas of Ercildoune, he who had passed into the halls of faeryland itself and had received from its Queen the gift of the tongue that can never lie.

So as Thomas lay in the Castle of Dunbar, the prescience of that great disaster came upon him, the calamity that was to devastate our kingdom.

His prophecy would soon be fulfilled, everybody was to see that. Here is how it happened.

The king married again, she who had crossed the sea, throwing off a nun's habit for a bride's veil, the lovely Yolande de Dreux. It was said that when their wedding nuptials were held in Jedburgh Abbey, every barrel in the land was broached, every belfry blossomed, every harp clanged. The drinking and dancing went on long into the night.

Ah, but that is how Death comes, isn't it—just when we look for him least?

Into that glad hall there slunk a malignant figure, a pale skeletal phantom gliding among the dancers, turning their steps to marble. The harp strings faltered, the laughter froze on every face.

Without a sound, its feet not seeming to touch the floor, the phantom approached the royal chair, pointed to the king. Alexander, candle-cheeked, managed to smile, and held out his cup. The shade lifted the jug nearest the king and dealt him his measure.

There was a great gasp. It was pure blood. The pitcher spouted forth an unending torrent, splashing into the king's lap and running the length of the great table, causing the guests to stumble backwards among their stools in horror and confusion. Yolande screamed. The phantom vanished. The king looked at his bride.

When he heard all that, the wizard Michael Scot took to the top of the Balwearie Tower. The Tiel ran blackly beneath his feet. His eyes were fixed on the stars.

By this time, of course, he was incredibly old.

See him in his eastern robes, constellated with occult signs, his white hair a winter waterfall, streaming from his stone head—only his eyes afire with what he sees.

And what does he see?

Far above him, hidden in the heavens, a riderless horse of bones, the stars winking in its ribs.

He came down from the tower and travelled to meet the king.

He found him along the Kinghorn cliffs and prophesied to him immediately.

'My lord, I saw last night the cause of your death, written in the pages of the stars.'

'You are a powerful seer,' said Alexander. 'Tell me what you saw.'

The sea boiled beneath them. Balwearie licked a spike of spray from his white moustache.

'I saw your favourite charger,' he replid, 'the one you are riding now. It is he who will kill you.'

He looked straight into the king's eyes and added:

'There is no more to be done.'

Alexander dismounted.

'Isn't there?' he challenged.

The blood of his race coursed through him in spate.

'This is my answer to Jedburgh, then!'

Without a pause for thought he drew out his dirk and stabbed the beast where it stood. One fatal thrust. Its hooves pranced skywards, scattering red streamers.

It died on the very edge of the cliffs.

'Lie there and rot!' shouted the king.

And he thrashed on along the cliffs, his anger smouldering.

Balwearie went back to his tower, looked at the stars and shook his bewintered head. Not even kings could unwrite the Book of Fate.

Alexander took another horse.

Winter storms whipped up the firth, then spring squalls. The faithful fared on fish for the crabbed time of Lent.

The king did not force that on his flesh that year, however. He was dining well in Edinburgh in mid-March. It was his understandable opinion that being without his lovely Yolande was Lenten fast enough.

She lay in Kinghorn Castle, the girl on the blue headland, loverless in bed.

But wine creates a stirring in the flesh. The thought of her suddenly maddened the impulsive king. He rose from the banqueting board, flushed with the grape, and galloped to the firth.

The boatman was not keen. But even good sailors have to be loyal subjects.

He landed at St Margaret's Ferry.

It was a filthy night.

But his guides were not spurred by love's alarms, as he was. At Inverkeithing they lost him—all but one, who did his best to keep pace, shouting on him all the time through the fog-banks to slow down.

The king was fey.

The sweating guide just caught a corner of what happened, out of his bedrizzled eye.

A patch of misty moonlight glimmering on the waves as the clouds came apart.

A white gleaming of bones at the cliff's edge—the grinning skeleton of the horse he had killed the previous year.

The charger went wild under him. He tossed the king like a doomed ship from an angry wave, high into the air. Alexander went straight over the edge and broke his neck on the hard, sea-wet rocks.

It was daylight till the spectacle emerged that spoke the woes of Scotland.

A riderless horse standing by a pile of bones, and a king lying dead at the bottom of the cliffs.

From Lindores and Dunfermline, from Balmerino and St Andrews, from Pittenweem Priory and the Isle of May the masses went up for the dead king's soul.

So Death is the end of every story.'

The listeners sat like ghosts in the shadows. The peats in the grate were a sunken wreck, a fire-ship gone out. Nobody moved.

At last the lord spoke.

'You yourself are something of a magician, sir,' he said. 'Sleep here tonight, and take this for your enchantment.'

The storyteller accepted the coin with a theatrical bow.

'It's not much, wordwright,' he added, 'but when did poems ever make a man rich?'

'I told you last night you'd get precious little up there,' the fisherman laughed when he saw him the next morning. 'You look just as poor to me as you did before.'

He was scraping the snow from the boat's shroud. The minstrel helped him push out the prow onto the waves. They caught the rest of the boat at once and started rocking it about. The fisherman jumped in.

'Well, shipfloater, I'll live another day, I reckon.'

He felt the coin in his pocket. It was like a warm little fire in the cold grate of his hand.

'How about you? Are you going to make your fortune on the firth this morning?'

The fisherman grunted.

'When did fishing ever make a man rich?'

That made the minstrel laugh.

'When did anything ever?' he said. 'Maybe de Brus will do something for us all this year.'

'Him?'

The fisherman put his hand to the tiller and waved the other arm in derision.

'He'll never be another Alexander, that Frenchman,' he shouted.

'He'll be dead by the summer, you'll see—King Edward will put paid to him!'

'Ah,' cried the minstrel, 'then I see I'll have to compose another lament.'

'You still won't get rich!' came the far cry from the waves.

Tutti Frutti

Tutti Frutti, the boys called her.

It suited her, somehow; though once you thought about it for a moment it was clearly ridiculous and didn't apply to her in the least. She was totally without frills.

He vividly recalled the first time he ever saw her. She was kneeling down on the grass in her back garden, stroking Shakespeare, who had gone through the hole in the fence, exploring. He fell desperately in love with her at once. The time was out of joint: she was sixteen, he was fourteen. He was captivated, transfixed.

Naturally, he realised, he must have seen her without thinking about it, hundreds—no, thousands of times before. They had always been neighbours, his folks and hers, divided by nothing more than an old wooden paling.

And by religion.

They were Close Brethren, the Cargills.

That meant they would have nothing to do with the god of the Old Kirk, or the Congregational Kirk; or the noisy god of the Salvation Army, who marched down the pier, sounding brass and clad in scarlet and black. For that matter they had no truck with any of the other cells and sects in the salt-sprayed honeycomb of St Monans. They were on speaking terms with no god but their own. In Virgin Square Close Brethren meant what it said. Their god was a secret god, a god of whispers. You couldn't tell if he wore a cassock or a trench-coat. They went into their Meeting Place every Sunday and saw him privately, like the doctor. Then they came out and turned the key on him. Leaving him behind a blistered door and under a corrugated iron roof.

So when Sunday came Elizabeth disappeared for the whole day. That was the day she turned into a flower, pressed by the hushed pages of the big black book. Her sweetness was hidden away among sermons and texts, locked up in chapter and verse.

That at least was how he put it to himself, after a little fanciful consideration. He was learning to be a poet.

Somewhere between Genesis and Revelation lay his love.

Genesis: at a quarter to eleven every Sabbath the Cargill front door opened, and she—the beginning of all things—stepped out among the sparrows and seagulls. A parent on either arm. Her father was out of his yellow oilskins for Sunday and into black, the only colour suitable for this day of the week. Mrs Cargill wore black also. They were both grey-headed—douce, decent folk, quiet and gentle in their ways. Her mother was not one of those vultures that stood at corners and closes, stabbing at the remains of a reputation. Mr Cargill sailed with a religious crew, not with one of the drunken boats. She, their only child, had come to them late in life. A gift from God, certainly. Elizabeth.

Revelation: at twelve-thirty they came back along Shore Street, a sedate trinity, arm in arm. And if it was a warm day with a brightness on the waves, then she—the end of all things—would be wearing a white dress. He saw how closely they bound her to themselves, even to the front door; she, the white flower, pressed between the two black covers, the Lord's own script. The word of God. Elizabeth.

She was not allowed out on Sundays except to go to the Meeting. Sundays were strictly for church-going and bible-reading. During the week there was school, but she was in her fifth year at the Academy, and he was only in third. Their two orbits never intersected and she seldom appeared at nights. Saturdays were more hopeful. On Saturdays she helped her mother with the washing and the messages.

It was on a Saturday that he saw her—really saw her—for the first time, with the eyes of the poet-lover.

He saw Shakespeare go slinking under the paling. One of the boards had rotted at the bottom, leaving a spiky tunnel for him to pass freely from the one garden to the other. An irresistible means of feline ingress and egress. Following him, and hunkering down at the foot of the high fence, he found himself staring through a knot hole at eye level. He put his face close to the aperture—and there she was.

Stroking Shakespeare.

She was bent over the cat with her head on one side and one hand extended. Puss was primed for play and for adoration. He nosed her knuckles, cupped his paws around her waist and pretended to fall ineptly onto his back. Four legs and tail splayed absurdly wide, a furry starfish, so that his belly was vulnerable to tickles.

She tickled him. He squirmed. Clearly he was going to adopt her.

But it was the girl's face that mattered that morning. It was the first time in his life that he had actually studied a girl—and studied her without her having any awareness of it. She was ecstatic. Her lips were parted in a wide, almost pained smile. Her teeth were so white.

She stroked the cat slowly, worshipfully, wordlessly. And he allowed her to manipulate him; he granted her the illusion of command. He was a living thing that she could caress as her own, not a fixed dogma, freezing her every gesture. She abandoned herself utterly to the cat.

She was not allowed pets.

That was how it happened: how he, who had never given girls a second thought, fell in love that Saturday morning. And to make the certainty absolute he went inside and confided it breathlessly to his diary. Yes, she was his Genesis and his Revelation, his alpha and omega; the first and the last. For fourteen years he had been living next door to a miracle of creation and he had never known it. His hand shook as he wrote.

> *Since first I saw your face I resolved*
> *To honour and renown you.*
> *If now I be disdained I wish*
> *My heart had never known you.*
>
> *What I that loved and you so liked*
> *Shall we begin to wrangle?*
> *No, no, no, my heart is fast*
> *And cannot disentangle.*

What was he to do? This business was entirely new to him. And no matter what he wrote or thought or said or did, she would never know how wildly he loved her and how fanatically devoted to her he was. Not even after he had courted and married her, she would never know.

But that was in the future. The immediate thing to do was to attract her attention and to please her at the same time. In both missions his dumb accomplice, willing or unwilling, he decided, would be Shakespeare.

No sooner do you conceive a revolution, he discovered, than something happens to frustrate and delay your bringing it off. The next day was Sunday, when she made her usual appearance: like a beautiful saying caught up between two black quotation marks, mysterious, untouchable, remote. The new minted image went down into the diary.

Monday began a week of the wickedest weather imaginable for May. Spring squalls in the morning shook the sea roughly and most of the boats bided their time. The sun appeared in bright bursts, but the winds worsened and rain hissed into the sun-streaked harbour so fiercely it seemed to be on fire.

He saw no sign of her at school. Mr Leslie launched himself tediously into Caesar.

> *For once upon a raw and gusty day,*
> *The troubled Tiber chafing with his shores.*

'Just such a day as this, wouldn't you agree, boy, or do you have troubles of your own? Whatever you are dreaming about, it certainly isn't Shakespeare!'

Of course, it was. Partly.

The sun went in for the rest of the week, crawling out stickily like a dismal slug. Every night after school he entrenched himself at the back window, hoping to glimpse her. The wind drove the raindrops grimly into the panes with sharp crackling sounds; he thought the glass would splinter. The back gardens glistened and streamed. Shakespeare sat by the fire like a cartoon cat and refused to acknowledge the back door.

Life was squalid. He closed his eyes and for hours on end he relived the scene of the previous Saturday: a girl stroking a cat, over and over, just behind his eyebrows.

'It's looking fairer,' his mother said to him, when Saturday came round again, 'and I haven't an egg in the house. Run down to Agnes Meldrum's and get me half a dozen.'

He was coming back past the west pier, clutching the eggs in a brown paper bag, when the loudest voice he had ever heard came clattering out over the harbour.

> *One o' clock two o' clock, three o' clock rock,*
> *Four o' clock five o' clock, six o' clock rock,*
> *Seven o' clock eight o' clock, nine o' clock rock,*
> *We're going to rock around the clock tonight . . .*

Provost Brand had opened his new café on Shore Street.

Having been kept in all week, many of the boats were ready to take the tide even though it was a Saturday. Some fishermen stopped what they were doing—battening hatches and stowing nets—to listen and stare. Most of them carried on with their chores, ignoring the alien racket. On the *Shepherd Lad* he could see Mr Cargill quietly coiling a rope, his grey head bent deeply into his work.

Fascinated, he drifted back to the café to look through the big plate-glass frontage. Frantic arms beckoned him. He went in. Some of his friends had put on long coats, drainpipe trousers and thick-soled shoes. They had slicked their hair, and one or two of them wore bootlaces for ties. The girls were in flared skirts with waspy belts; they were all polka dots and bobby socks and pony tails.

'Here, come and listen to this—it's great, man!'

He sat down at one of the tables. Everybody was drinking Cocoa Cola. All eyes were riveted on two constructions that squatted like buddhas against the far wall. One was a fat red refrigerator, a complex of chromium, levers and slots.

'Try it out, go on.'

He bought a Coke with the change from the eggs and placed his purchase in a cavity moulded to the bottle's fancy shape. A penny in a slot, a pull on a metal bar, and a cold Coke shot out from a chute at the other end, now a bronzed ingot of ice that burned his fingers.

The other god in the temple was the juke box. He had never seen such a monster. It was as big as a boat's wheelhouse. Behind the glitter and the glass were stacked all the latest musical hits. For a sixpence and the jab of a button a plastic arm swung out and brought in the selected record. The tables of teenagers listened in ecstasy. They looked at one another and grinned, and looked away in embarrassment.

Cigarette smoke misted the pounding air, a blue acrid haar; he shifted his seat to the window. Out in the harbour, and beyond that, in the firth, their fathers and grandfathers, their uncles and great-uncles, carried on the works and ways of the old days. In here the teenagers worshipped their new idols, thanked them that they no longer dressed and talked like *that*—not to mention listening to Jimmy Shand and Abide With Me.

And sitting on the harbour wall, poised between the two traditions was—Tutti Frutti. A wave of panic went through him.

Yes, there she was, her message basket on her arm, talking to some of her classmates. They were all dolled up in their finery; the fifties had reached them right at the end of the decade. She had on a print frock and ankle socks and a navy blue donkey jacket; that was all. But she had her hair in a pony tail. Had it been like that last Saturday? He couldn't remember. It suited her, though, suited her large glasses and her open, honest face. Plain as she was beside all those birds of plumage, she was rarer than any of them.

Another wave hit him. Supposing she flew off and he never saw her again? Supposing he failed to capture her heart. Or what if one of the older boys came along right now and took her in hand? One of the boys in her year. Surely hc couldn't be the only one in the universe to think her so beyond the epithets of beauty.

A knot of youngsters got up to leave and he sidled out with them over to the harbour wall, near to where she sat. Her friends were trying to tempt her inside.

'Oh, come on, Elizabeth, come in and listen. Just the one record.'

'I can listen out here. I'm not allowed.'

'Well have a coke then. There's nothing wrong with a coke, is there?'

'No, I can't, I can't. I'm not allowed.'

She wasn't allowed into Brand's new cafe. But that stood to reason. She was Close Brethren.

She wasn't allowed jewellery, make-up, scent; she didn't wear bangles or rings; she couldn't go to the Regal or the Empire in Anstruther, or to the pictures in Pittenweem; she wasn't permitted to go to the sixpenny hops or the dancing on the pier. There would be no radio in her house, no record player, and certainly no television set. The Close Brethren didn't even buy newspapers, and they gave house room to precious few books apart from the bible. Tutti Frutti wore no bobby socks, no bright scarves, no ribbons in her hair.

And she had no boy friend.

Suddenly he felt a wash of gratitude towards her parents, those two black bookends. If it had not been for their strict ways she would by this time be inside Brand's café and would be the property of some lounger with a long jacket and greasy hair. She would be sitting on his knee and he would be holding her hand. No: this was the way it was meant to be. She had been saved—for him.

He stole a side glance at her. She waved once to that quiet grey man, her father. The *Shepherd Lad* was purring out of port. She left her friends and started for home. He followed her discreetly, locked to her in longing. In love.

Another Sunday. And nothing happened all day, except for that one bright sentence, briefly appearing between the black quotation marks, lingering poignantly in his memory like the smell of new-cut grass. Everywhere was so still. All the kirk bells boomed sadly, sullenly, at eleven o' clock, not just from the Old Kirk and the Cong, but from Elie and Pittenweem, even Anster three miles away. He could hear them all along the coast.

At school that week they'd been reading with Mr Leslie Charles Lamb's essay, 'The Superannuated Man'. He picked out one sentence from it—

Those eternal bells depress me

and entered it into his diary. He decided that from now on he was going to keep a Commonplace Book, like a real writer.

Halfway through another week, with dry weather, and still no sign of her. Then Mr Leslie said:

'I am trying—only trying, mind you—to lay the foundations for your Higher English, which you'll be sitting in two years time, like that cannon fodder down in the exam hall right now. Food for powder, I'm afraid, most of 'em, food for powder!'

So that was it. She'd be inside studying every night of the week. The Fifth Year were all taking their Highers. No wonder he'd seen nothing of her.

'Yes, that's right, boy, dream about it, dream about it, do. But you won't dream up a pass, I can tell you that, if you pay this little attention to your lessons.'

'Sorry, sir.'

'Yes. Dreaming of Glaramara's inmost caves. Or something.'

May slipped over into June.

The sea slid back over the weeded rocks, so far, it became little more than a blue lane running the length of the skyline, and the seaweeds popped and hissed and steamed. The sun simply forgot to leave the sky; the corn stood stalk still, breathless, expectant. At nights the Milky Way drooped its great branches low over the earth, dripping stars thickly onto the roofs. Out in the far firth the seals whooed and cooed like siren ghosts. His hands and face burned. Magic had returned to the old earth, myths were being spawned in the glitter of waves, faces appearing in the skellies and cliffs, new constellations flung up into space. Sleep was impossible by night, and concentration by day evaporated easily. Mr Leslie began to lose all patience.

'Write me a poem, dreamer. Write a whole cycle if you must. I am for whole volumes in folio, if necessary. But get it out of your system, whatever it is, and then get back to your English!'

He sat at the back window that evening and wrote in a hardback science notebook.

The sun whose beams most glorious are
Rejecteth no beholder,
And your sweet beauty past compare
Made my poor eyes the bolder.

Where beauty moves and wit delights
And signs of kindness bind me,
There, oh there, where'er I go,
I leave my heart behind me.

He was about to pen the next stanza when she stepped out of the back door. This was what he'd been waiting a lifetime for. He vaulted the banister and sped into the garden, snatching an astonished Shakespeare from the vestigial pleasures of a blue saucer. He bundled the cat, squirming, over to the fence, shoved it through its tunnel, and applied his eye to the knot-hole.

She was coming over to the fence already. Shakespeare was still standing there, his tail twitching, somewhat outraged at this unceremonious treatment meted out to a cat of his distinction. Closer she came, and closer. Dare he remain where he was? She might see his eye. But if he moved now she'd be more likely to spy a shadow. He held his breath and shut his eyes.

When he opened them again she was eighteen inches away, maybe less, he calculated. Nearer, nearer than he had ever been before. And so intent was she on the cat that she would have scarcely been aware of him even had the partition never existed. Though his heartbeats hurt and his head pounded, he was at liberty to make a cool study of her. She was his, just as the cat was hers. No-one had looked at her like this before. Yes, she was his, uniquely. He could see the china blue eyes, the flush of her complexion, pink over paleness, the two or three freckles on one cheek. Again her lips parted in that smile of abandonment, that ecstasy, as she stroked and stroked.

Shakespeare accepted this adoration as his due. He presented every curve and arch of his furred person to her reverential touch. Then, when she had catalogued his excellences from whiskers to tail, he leapt into her lap—she had on a sleeveless blue check pinafore—and stretched his front paws up onto her shoulders. She clasped him between her breasts and rocked him backwards and forwards in a smiling silence, her eyes tight shut.

The cat, with all the arbitrariness of his race, decided he'd had enough. He sprang over her shoulder, slashed at a stray galaxy of thistledown floating by, and streaked round the side of her house. Tutti Frutti lay on her back and communed with the sky.

That night as he lay awake he mentally charted her freckles. Were there three, or was there a fourth one just above the cheekbone? The question set him on edge with remembered excitement. He rose and put on his clothes.

It was strange to go padding about the house at this late hour of the night, when everyone else was asleep. Objects took on a curious new life of their own: his diary seemed to be listening and alive, his new Commonplace Book reading his thoughts; his various bindings looked out at him from their shelves, waiting to be read, sharing his secret. The conspiratorial thickness of the silence sent a shiver through his groin; he stood and tingled. He had never done this before, not in this way. Perhaps he was the only person in the village up at this hour.

Except for the fishermen, hauling somewhere out there on the watery world. He tiptoed to the back door and went out into the night, shivering through the dew-drenched grass, as far as the fence. He hauled himself up on one of the stobs and dropped down soundlessly on the other side. This was where she had been; she had occupied this very space that he was taking up. Right now he was inside her. At one.

A cold wetness on the back of his hand made him leap out of her skin. Shakespeare had followed him from the house. He sniffed and twitched for a minute. What was all this about?

Every house was darkened, every window containing a sleeper. The whole seatown was asleep. Strange, when you thought about it, that you couldn't actually hear anything of that combined rise and fall of many breaths. Maybe you could in one of the upland hamlets, with only cows and owls to break the heavy silences of fields and sky. But here everything was dominated by the huge hush of the sea, only yards away. Beyond the firth the ocean slurped slowly over the globe. Boats were working it even now, part of its cold poundings: his grandfather, his uncle.

Rocked on the bosom of the deep

Yes, they would be sweating at the nets, miles away, at the Dogger Bank or Peterhead. But only a few feet from where he stood, separated from him by a little night air, a few bricks and mortar, was the gently rising and falling bosom of Tutti Frutti.

Shakespeare had been rocked on that bosom. He had lain between her breasts. *Rocked on the bosom of the deep.* But then she'd had her dress on . . .

He looked up at her window. Vega burned like a torch over the fields.

Bright star, would I were steadfast as thou art—

He breathed the words quietly, religiously. Mr Leslie had begun Keats with them yesterday.

> *No—yet still steadfast, still unchangeable.*
> *Pillow'd upon my fair love's ripening breast,*
> *To feel for ever its soft fall and swell,*
> *Awake for ever in a sweet unrest,*
> *Still, still to hear her tender-taken breath,*
> *And so live ever—or else swoon to death.*

The sonnet was already down in his notebook. He longed to quote it to her. And so he would, he would—

Emprison her soft hand, and let her rave,
And feed deep, deep upon her peerless eyes.

But what if one night he should come out here and see her in her own bedroom, privately, the curtains undrawn, taking off her clothes?

Half-hidden, like a mermaid in seaweed.

What if he should see the very parts of which Tutti Frutti was composed?

No.

Ravished by that thought, he swung himself back across the fence. Shakespeare hurried in at his feet, with dew-wet fur.

Once in bed he regretted his vision of a naked Tutti Frutti. She was a goddess. To hold her hand all day long would be enough. And at the end of the day, to remove her spectacles alone, and be granted a kiss.

On those chaste lips.

He spun himself into a wild web of dreams.

Next morning he slept late.

In the belfry of his head bells were booming, bells that sounded so far away. He was drifting past a foreign shore, out of reach of his own head. He stretched out his arm and woke.

He had been cast up on Sunday. And she would be at the Meeting. Shirt flapping over his jeans, he ran out, a disreputable wreck, onto the holy sands of the Sabbath. Overtaking the late stragglers, he arrived, panting, at the Meeting Place. He stopped outside its tarred bricks, sobered a little by the cold breezes that always blew round Virgin Square. A seagull sat on the funnel, listening to the holy din.

Wide, wide as the ocean,
High as the heavens above,
Deep, deep as the deepest sea
Is my Saviour's love.

Somewhere in the middle of that droning sea of voices was Tutti Frutti in her Sunday frock, singing palely between her mother and father. He stood and shivered outside her city walls throughout the length of the service. When the door finally opened he sprang away to a safe distance. Out she came, stepping stiffly between her bookends. He followed her home, a sly shadow in their religious wake. Saluting them as they passed the harbour were the strains of Buddy Holly from Brand's café.

Throughout the days
Our true love ways
Will bring us joys to share
With those who really care . . .

Once the Cargill door closed on her, he knew he would not see her again till the following week.

That Sunday was the longest he had ever known.

'It is midsummer's day today,' said Mr Leslie the next morning. 'Let us make shift to finish our *Midsummer Night's Dream*.'

The lunatic, the lover and the poet
Are of imagination all compact.

'Well, you'd have to be something of a lunatic, wouldn't you, to conduct a love affair through a wall?'

The Pyramus and Thisbe scene was duly completed.

'But it's as the poet said. Stone walls do not a prison make. Love has a way of overcoming obstacles. Read us the epilogue, boy.'

After school he tore a single sheet from an exercise jotter and wrote on it the three simple words, 'I love you'. He folded the page into a long strip, folded it again, then sought out Shakespeare. Tucking the missive tightly under the cat's collar, he waited by the back window. Soon after tea she came out. He took up the cat and carried it to the paling. As soon as it was through its tunnel he fled.

When Shakespeare returned he had nothing under his collar.

For the rest of that night he did not even dare go near the window. But when the house was asleep he rose up again from his bed and stole down to the harbour.

The tide was full, the sea calm, a few seine-netters lying quietly in their moorings; the harbour lamps, red and green, made trembling bridges across the water, from pier to pier; the boatyard was silent, the shops shut up. No old men at the corner, no conversationalists at the pier head; every house as tight and silent as a log. Only the stars and he were up and awake.

He shivered with the knowledge of it. And with the knowledge that only he understood the special holiness of this fishing village. Every slate, every stone, every boat and brick, every street she walked on, every wave that visited her shore—all were blessed by the fact that Tutti Frutti lived here. Asleep as she was, his consciousness of her overspread sea and earth.

And now she knew that somebody loved her—and she must surely know who that someone was. He had struck his blow. He took to his heels and raced madly along the sea front, Italian arias throbbing in his head.

The next day he sent her a Shakespeare sonnet, courtesy of Shakespeare.

> *Shall I compare thee to a summer's day?*
> *Thou art more lovely and more temperate.*

Puss returned with milk on his whiskers.
He sent her another.

> *O carve not with thy hours my love's fair brow*
> *Nor draw no lines there with thine antique pen.*

And another.

> *Being your slave, what should I do but tend*
> *Upon the hours and times of your desire?*

Shakespeare made the trips meekly and came back well contented. Sonnetless—but with the milk of paradise trembling on his wet whiskers.

He started to work his way through the sequence.

> *When in disgrace with Fortune and men's eyes . . .*
>
> *When to the sessions of sweet silent thought . . .*
>
> *When in the chronicle of wasted time . . .*
>
> *When I have seen by Time's fell hand defaced . . .*

Yet he could never bring himself to witness the moment of rapture. He fled from the knot-hole after each delivery. His mother began to tell him that he looked pale in the face.

'You're like a candle,' she said. 'Go and get yourself a fish supper!'

Shakespeare grew sleek.

'There are one hundred and fifty-four sonnets in the Shakespearean cycle,' said Mr Leslie at the start of the final week of session. 'No-one who has not read the whole of Shakespeare will ever be able to consider himself properly educated. Why not see to it over the summer? Vain hope!'

He calculated the number of trips Shakespeare would have to make. There were fifty-five days in the summer holidays.

But on the second last day of the term a policeman and a policewoman came to the Academy. And Tutti Frutti was driven away from the school.

In a police car.

Her friends stood in the playground, a white, shocked circle of faces. Their voices were hushed. Something had happened to Mr Cargill.

When he came home from the Academy at the end of the day, he found the Cargill curtains drawn. Out of respect, his mother had done the same, and so had some of the neighbours. The *Shepherd Lad* was on its way back from Peterhead. The word was all round the town.

After tea the west pier was crowded with folk, waiting. He could not bear to mix with them. He ran instead to the high kirkyard and stood at the dyke, looking out to sea.

He heard its engine before he saw the boat. It was a breathless evening, the sea laid out like a length of blue silk, only its hem rustling whitely.

Peering east, he saw the black speck off Pittenweem. Closer it buzzed, like an angry, ugly fly on the blue dress. Down on the pier the folk were pointing. Already they'd be saying it was the *Shepherd Lad* for sure, by the cut of its jib. It made a wide sweep, well past the May Island, before turning to starboard, as though unwilling to come into port.

It was a death ship.

Soon its engine was the only sound to be heard in the world, a harsh, dark drone, filling sea and sky. One or two gulls attended the death-boat. Bringing Mr Cargill home.

At the narrow harbour mouth the engine shut off and it glided through. The harbour accepted it quietly, like a soul to haven. Then the engine started up once more. The boat, a tormented heartbeat, churned its way to the west pier, hugging the old stones. He saw the mooring rope go snaking through the air to be caught by a hand somewhere in the crowd.

After that everything went quiet again. The awful cargo, tarpaulined, was brought out and transferred to the shore. Arms reached out. Hundreds of hands went up to heads and every cap came off. The village stood, the various sects, bareheaded under the one blue vault of the sky. They stood like that for one minute. Before the sound of many voices broke the stillness.

On his way home he passed groups of fishermen.

'No, it was his oilskins, caught in the winch. He was hauled in. You can picture the rest.'

'Picture it if you like. I'd forget about it if I were you.'

Forget about it.

How do you forget about it? A man had been pulled into the boat's winch and mangled. A grey-headed man of God. A bible-reading man.

He peered fearfully out of the back window. What was Tutti Frutti doing now in the dimness that lay behind these terrible curtains? They would be kept drawn now for three days, front and back. What was she thinking and feeling? Nothing of love, that was for sure. Nobody near and dear had died yet in his family, and he was fourteen. For years he had wondered what it would be like to be on the inside of one of these stricken houses, marked out by their shrouded windows.

The school broke up the next day. A generation of black and red blazers swarmed out of the building and broke up with shrieks and loud halloos. They were demented with joy. Everybody piled into Brand's café.

Got myself a cryin', walkin',
Sleepin' talkin', livin' doll . . .

Two days later the big black car hummed quietly up to the Cargill front door. The Close Brethren drifted in. There was no minister. Nobody knew in advance who would conduct the service, except that it would be some chosen person so moved by the Holy Spirit. One of their number would be saying the words right now.

Blessed are they that mourn: for they shall be
comforted.

The souls of the righteous are in the hands of God,
and there shall no torment touch them. They are in peace.

The door opened and out came the box, borne on a black wave that drowned the sun. And the black snake of mourners gathered, arranged itself, shuffled its feet, and moved off, drawn by that gleaming black head, the hearse. A head crowned with flowers. Neither Tutti Frutti nor her mother were there. Women did not go to funerals. The last they ever saw of their menfolk was when they were carried out of the door.

But at every corner stood knots of men. When the hearse passed them they put their hats and bonnets to their chests and bowed their bare heads, like actors at the end of a melodrama. Then they joined the cortege at the tail end. So, at every turning point, the snake increased its length, grew more tramping feet. The sound of polished boots crackled against the wash of the water. Brand had shut off the juke box for the afternoon.

He raced over the barley field to reach the kirkyard by the back way, well before the mourners. The inevitable gull stood sentinel on the kirk steeple, a gleaming white sea-angel. It watched the black snake toiling up the kirkyard hill and breaking into pieces at the graveside. The snake's head opened and its mystery was removed: the polished box with the dark shine and the coldly glittering name plate. Mr Cargill was lowered into his fathom of earth, underneath the turf.

Silence.

And like a cracked bell came the words—familiar, dreary, comforting as the tides.

> *I am the Resurrection and the Life, saith the Lord;*
> *he that believeth in Me, though he were dead, yet shall*
> *he live: and whosoever liveth and believeth in Me*
> *shall never die.*

The words were heavy as clay, but they glinted like newly turned clods after the rain.

> *I heard a voice from heaven saying unto me,*
> *Blessed are the dead which die in the Lord*
> *from henceforth: yea, saith the Spirit, that*
> *they may rest from their labours; and their works*
> *do follow them.*

A voice inside him sneered, But they don't rest from their labours, they just die and are forgotten.

'No!' he shouted out loud. 'That's not true!'

Some of the mourners raised their heads in his direction. He ducked down behind the dyke.

A new breeze rustled the barley.

The gull left the steeple then and winged its way east. Out in the bright firth the fishermen carried on with their labours. Except for the crew of the *Shepherd Lad*. And a cloud of white birds followed them.

He went back home through the barley, and he sat down and wrote in his Commonplace Book.

> *Only Love and Death change all things.*

The barley turned with the season.

Tutti Frutti did not return for her Sixth Year. She left school and went up to the Art College in Dundee.

The barley-wave was yellowed, stubbled, darkened by the plough, whitened by winter, pricked by spring, greened over again by summer.

A boy from his class took a berth on the *Shepherd Lad* following the death of another of its crew. He was not a Brethren worshipper; he worshipped in Brand's café every Sunday. But his folks at least were members of the Old Kirk. And the boat needed a cook.

'You are all in it up to your necks,' snapped Mr Leslie. 'The Highers will not go away like a bad dream. And time marches on!'

He sat at his table by the back window night after night, bent over his books. Down in the garden Shakespeare lazed about without a care in his belly. The little tunnel to Tutti Frutti's house was overgrown by now, and in any case he preferred the opposite garden these days. There was a fluffy creature called Samantha on that side.

By the time he sat his Higher English Samantha had had kittens.

Twice.

'You could do a degree in English,' Mr Leslie said to him at the start of his last session. 'You have a fine feeling for literature.'

The field-wave undulated once more under the wind of the seasons.

St Andrews University accepted him for an Honours course in Mr Leslie's subject.

He was lying reading in the hot grasses of August, waiting for the long communion to pass, when he saw her for the last time. She was wearing a mini-skirt and a cutaway blouse that left her brown midriff bare. The pony tail was still with her, and the glasses. She was walking west the braes towards the kirkyard, hand in hand with her boyfriend. He was one of the Jesus boys—all beads and beard and sandals and hair. They had a transistor with them that was playing fuzzily.

She'll switch it off, surely, he thought, when they go into the kirkyard.

But they didn't go into the kirkyard, where Mr Cargill lay. They walked right past, and as they reached the crest of the hill, the transistor cleared.

A smash hit single, announced the strident voice of the disc jockey—by an exciting new group called The Beatles.

Love, love me do,
You know I love you,
I'll always be true,
So ple-e-e-ease
Love me do.

The sounds died away as the twisting, laughing couple disappeared over the shoulder of the hill, holding hands. He stared down into his well thumbed copy of The Works of Shakespeare. Then he shut the fluttering pages, got up stiffly, and walked away.

Outside Brand's café he stopped. The same single was playing in there. He went inside, bought a coffee, put money into the juke box, and sat down with his book.

His song came on.

You go your way and I'll go mine,
Now and forever till the end of time,
I'll find somebody new, and baby,
We'll say we're through,
And you won't matter any more . . .

'Buddy Holly!' the girl in the corner muttered to her friend. 'Can you credit it?'

Her lip lifted.

He put his chin on his book and stared out to sea.

The two of them looked at him in disgust.

The Frithfield Tragedy

It was William Pitbladdo of the farm of Leys who first made discovery of the dead infant, and thereupon informed the Reverend Beatson at Kilrenny.

He was on his way to the plough at first light, he said, when he stopped to wet his beard at the Daffodil Burn, having a night's thirst on him at the time.

MR BEATSON Describe to me what happened, William, just as you remember it.

PITBLADDO My heid was fair thick wi' the last nicht's drinking. I dooned a good pint o' clear cauld watter, and I had just stopped to tak breath when I saw the drookit bairn, adrift amang the daffodils.

MR BEATSON When you say 'drookit', William, tell me precisely what you mean. That is to say, tell me what you saw.

PITBLADDO I say what I saw, sir. A bairn, drookit deid.

MR BEATSON Dead, you say?

PITBLADDO Droont and deid, Mr Beatson, droont and deid.

MR BEATSON That will do then, William. I have made a note of your words. You will be required to testify to this under oath before the Session, and before the Presbytery, doubtless. Aye, and wha kens, in front of the entire panoply of the law, up at Cupar. Do you understand?

PITBLADDO I understand I saw a deid bairn, sir.

MR BEATSON Aye, well. Leave the rest to me.

The next day following being the Sabbath, the minister called the Session into conclave after church, and acquainted them with Pitbladdo's discovery. There was much dissension among them as to how they should proceed, but the minister declared that, the child's being laid up in the Tolbooth of Cellardyke, and there being no marks found on its corpse, according to William Pitbladdo's testimony, it should straightaway be buried and the Presbytery apprised of these unfortunate events.

In the meantime it was agreed upon that all proper inquiries be carried out towards the uncovering of the murderer's identity.

But when John Middleton, chief elder, arrived home from the
Session in the latter part of the day, he found his twisted stick of a wife
in an exceeding foul temper and not one whit impressed by their
deliberations. A good dinner destroyed and not fit to set before a
swine—and all, she avowed, for the doings of some filthy slut who
had committed child murder.

JOHN MIDDLETON That's as yet unproven, mistress.

MISTRESS MIDDLETON Unproven my arse. It's as plain as the nose on
your face, man. And what are you men o' the kirk proposing to do
aboot it, may I mak inquiry?

Her spouse informed her that the Session intended to catechise all
young women in the parish on the following morning, and in the
presence of an officer of the law.

MISTRESS MIDDLETON Officer o' the law indeed, you poor dumb brutes
o' men, you havena the wit to find a cock in a midden. But you will
tak me along on your roonds the morn's morning, and I shall discover
your slut for you withoot the need for catechism. Now eat your ruined
meat.

The subsequent morning there went out John Middleton and his
spouse and some members of the Session, together with Mr Beatson,
and also the keeper of the Tolbooth at Cellardyke, Andrew Watson,
who was Mistress Middleton's brother.

Under Mistress Middleton's guidance they were to search the
breasts of all the unmarried young women in the parish, starting their
itinerary at the westermost of the fisherhouses, and so working eastwards and up to the farms, Rennie Hill, the Leys, Frithfield and Blacklaws. At each house they caused each unmarried girl to submit to
having her breasts examined by Mistress Middleton.

This caused much bad blood by the time they reached Frithfield.

At Frithfield they found James Morres, widower, sore laid up in his
bed, unable to put his hand to the plough.

MR BEATSON Where's your daughter, man?

JAMES MORRES She'll be oot amang the young barley, picking stanes.
What's to do?

Then was Isobel Morres sent for and brought at once into the
house.

ISOBEL What is it that they want, faither?

JAMES MORRES Just do what they tell you, lass, and answer what they
speir at you.

She was then escorted into the adjoining chamber by Mistress
Middleton, while the gentlemen waited by the bed with old James.

MR BEATSON How long have you been thus, James?

JAMES MORRES The best part o' a year. The last spring sowing near broke my back in twa. By the time I'd taen in the hairst I was good for nocht but the auld box bed here.

MR BEATSON You do not seem to look at me properly, man. Is your sight impaired in any way?

JAMES MORRES My een hae failed me sair this past twelvemonth. I hae lain here aa winter wi' nocht but my lass to see to my needs. She's a good lass, sirs.

JOHN MIDDLETON Aye, but wha did your ploughing for you this spring? I see the mark o' a man's hand on your field oot there.

Before the old man could make reply there was a shrieking from within, and Mistress Middleton came flying through with triumph lighting her face.

MISTRESS MIDDLETON I have her, sirs, aye sirs, I have the foul bitch on the hip! Look, here's the slut's milk dreeping fae my fingers!

MR BEATSON I am afraid this will hardly stand as evidence, mistress. We shall have to see for ourselves.

Upon this all the men followed Mistress Middleton into the next chamber, where Isobel Morres was compelled to remove her bodice and expose her breasts to the eyes of kirk and state.

MR BEATSON You need have no fear, Isobel. Just let us see if what Mistress Middleton says be true. If it be not true, then no harm shall come to your door.

Mistress Middleton then took one of Isobel Morres's paps between her fingers and squeezed so long and so hard that the girl cried out in some pain. But there was no milk forthcoming. She did the like with the other pap, and to no apparent purpose, pressing with such vigour and determination as to make the girl beg her to desist.

MR BEATSON Where is this milk you spoke of, Mistress Middleton? For shame, woman, cease your efforts, and let the lass do up her bodice and go about her business.

MISTRESS MIDDLETON But wait, sirs, gie me just one mair minute, if you will.

Thereupon she seized one of the girl's nipples into her wrinkled mouth and began working at it with a will. Isobel Morres tore herself off with a cry of anguish and disgust.

ISOBEL Tak this she-deil awa fae me, Master Beatson, I beseech you. My breists were made for the sucking o' a bairn and no the fangs o' an auld tigress like yon!

MR BEATSON I think we have seen enough, gentlemen.

ISOBEL (doing up her bodice) Aye, sirs, I've been exposed to your een to satisfy the spite o' a thrawn bitch that's been as barren as a boulder aa her days, and hates the sicht o' mithers and bairns, as aabody kens!

When she heard this, Mistress Middleton sprang at the girl, bellowing for her spouse and brother to hold her still; which they did, by her arms and legs and the hair of her head, she struggling and panting like a bird in their clutches. Mistress Middleton then locked herself on once more and worked away at the breast with increased venom, ignoring the girl's screams.

When John Middleton's spouse turned to face the Reverend Beatson it was at once evident that she could not utter a word for the fullness behind her lips.

MR BEATSON Well, let us see your mouthful, woman.

She made a cup with her hands and ejected into it a good half gill of warm white milk. Every person present looked at it in silence and looked again at Isobel. Gobbets of milk stood out brightly on her breast and spattered to the floor.

MISTRESS MIDDLETON Had she let the bairn suckle her, as nature had intended, she'd hae run like an udder. It was a long haul fae the well, sirs, but it cam up in the end. She's a whoor and a murderess and there's the guilt o't slap in her brazen een!

She flung the two handfuls of milk direct into the white face of Isobel Morres. The girl blenched, then looked up at the minister.

MR BEATSON Do yourself up, lass, for decency's sake. Yet I fear, Isobel, you will be examined after today in more than the breasts. For you are at the start of an auld familiar road. And God kens, you may have much to answer for.

After that she was taken to the Tolbooth at Cellardyke and held prisoner there until such time as the entire Session might be brought into conclave for the purpose of examining her. Which was fixed for two of the clock on the following day.

As she lay in the Tolbooth there came to her Andrew Watson, the keeper, with a dish of good wholesome meat.

ANDREW WATSON Now Isobel, lass, if you'll just unpreen your bodice a minute and gie to me the very same as you gied to Mistress Middleton the day afore, and that withoot let or hindrance either, then you shall fare weel aa the time that you bide here.

ISOBEL What kind o' a woman do you tak me for, man?

ANDREW WATSON Ane that murders her bairn, I'se warrant, and a sweet little whoor that'll dae just fine for me wi' her knees in the air.

ISOBEL (*spitting*) Tak your foul tongue to your sister that's worthy o't, you ill-minded man!

ANDREW WATSON Now Isobel, that's no the fashion to earn your meat, my lass. Dinna be sae thrawn. Just the ane sook at your sweit breist and this braw kitchen shall be yours.

ISOBEL I am no what you think, man, and you should think shame to tak advantage o' a woman under your key. I shall lay your sin afore Mr Beatson and ask to be taen oot o' your keep.

On the which Andrew Watson fell into a blind rage and gripped her by the thrapple with the one hand, while with the other he attempted to tear open her clothing. She clawed at him hard. He fell back at once, kicking over the plate of meats and retreating to the door, which he slammed and bolted. He thrust his faceful of red stripes to the grill and roared in at her. He was shrill with the pain and his anger.

ANDREW WATSON Do you think I'm nae better than the faither o' your deid bastard to lie wi' on the flair? Weel, you'll suffer sair for this, you murdering whoor, just you wait and see if you dinna!

Isobel Morres sat in the corner among the straw and wept quietly.

The day following the Session met after prayer at the second hour of the clock in the afternoon. Isobel Morres was brought out of prison and convened before the Session.

Extract from Kilrenny Kirk Session Register
At Cellardyke Aprile 28th 1694
Hora Secunda post meridiem

The minister having caused acquaint the said Isobel Morres of the occasion of the Session's meeting, he earnestly exhorted her to be ingenuous, and as in the sight of God to declare the truth freely in what was to be proposed to her.

Then she was interrogate first if this child was hers that had been found by William Pitbladdo of Leys in the burn known as the Daffodil Burn on the twenty-fifth day of the month.

She answered at once that it was hers.

Interrogate next who was the father of the child, she answered James Small, ploughman in Frithfield.

She was again interrogate as to when the child was begotten and when it was brought forth.

Answered that it was begotten in August last summer and that it was brought forth just before mid-March on St Monans Mercat day.

Interrogate how her father, James Morres, had received the information as to her being with child.

Answered that she had kept it from him for his peace of mind, he being too blind and bedridden of late to know or notice her condition.

Interrogate whether she had brought forth the child alone, or if she cried for help, or caused acquaint any of her neighbours with it.

Answered she brought forth the child at the house of Jennat Doig, widow of Blacklaws, she that had the art of midwifery at her command since long syne.

At this juncture Mistress Middleton interrupted the proceedings clamorously, saying that in her opinion the Blacklaws widow had more arts than that of midwifery at her command. Mr Beatson enjoined her to keep her silence but instructed an officer of the kirk to go straightaway to the widow Doig's house and bring her to Cellardyke against the time she could be cross-examined.

The Session continued with its interrogation.

Isobel Morres questioned next as to whether the child was born dead or alive, and exhorted by Mr Beatson before making reply to place her hand again on the great Book and to tell the truth freely before God.

Answered it was born dead.

Yet again Mr Beatson proposed the question to her as to whether it came into the world dead or alive, this time placing her left hand on the Bible and forcing her to raise her right hand to God and making a stern oath out of her answer.

Answered again it was born dead.

Mr Beatson urged her a third time to be sincere and not to hide any particle of her sin, yet she still persisted to refuse the guilt of the infant's blood.

Interrogate further why then she had cast the child into the burn, seeing she had not murdered it.

Refused to answer.

Asked if she had called upon a corroborative opinion concerning the infant's condition at its bringing forth.

Answered that the opinion of the widow of Blacklaws was sound and sufficient unto her. The child was a stillbirth.

Asked why she had kept the stillborn child to herself, witholding it from due process of medical scrutiny and the sacrament of burial.

Answered she was afraid.

Interrogate yet again why she had thrown the infant into the water, supposing she was guiltless of its death.

Gave no answer.

Interrogate whether she had informed the child's father of its bringing forth.

Answered she had.

Asked what the father had said.

Refused to answer.

Interrogate where James Small now was, and in what habitation or employment.

Said she did not know.

Mr Beatson ordered that an officer be sent out to inquire whether James Small was to be found in employ on any of the farms in the neighbouring parishes, and if he be so found, to be brought to the Tolbooth for interrogation.

Further Mr Beatson announced that, Isobel Morres remaining silent upon that most vital question concerning her disposal of the infant's corpse, and there being nothing more to be gained from the present proceedings until such time as both Jennat Doig and James Small be convened, the Session should conclude its meeting and Isobel Morres returned to the Tolbooth.

Thereupon Isobel Morres begged not to be returned to the Tolbooth but to be put in custody at any other secure place of the Session's choosing.

Asked what was her objection to her confinement at Cellardyke.

Answered that it was not the jail but the jailer she had objection to, Andrew Watson, keeper, having attempted to interfere with her privately and she having struggled with him and put marks on his face, he had since then offered her neither meat nor water. She begged a cup of water to be supplied to her before her return to custody.

Mr Beatson, much disturbed, ordered that food and drink be set before her, and ordered further that Andrew Watson be relieved of his duties at the Tolbooth until the allegations concerning him be taken up and assessed.

Sederunt concluded with prayer.

A bad day for kirk and country, said Mistress Middleton, when a loyal servant of the parish and her own kinsman forbye be dismissed his employ on the strength of the foul droppings from the tongue of a slut and a drowner of bairns. That whoor would rue the day, she said, when she had opened her filthy lips to slander her brother.

Andrew Watson being relieved of his civic duties in the meanwhiles took to frequenting the ale shop at the harbour head in Cellardyke. There he sat blackly among mugs of beer, drinking himself each day into a blind silent fury.

Jennat Doig was taken from Blacklaws and brought to the Tolbooth for private questioning preliminary to her hearing before the full Session.

Isobel Morres asked leave to return to her home so as to look to her bedridden father, but by order of the town magistrate she continued to suffer confinement at the Tolbooth.

James Small having disappeared from the parish, the Session could not at first get the three parties confronted. Indeed the bluebells were out among the trees at Wormiston until information was received that James Small was known to be working at the farm of Balkaithly, in the parish of Dunino, near St Andrews. An officer of the law was sent up with promptitude to bring him down to the Tolbooth. This was done without impediment and the Session prepared to reconvene for the purpose of probing the case further.

Extract from Kilrenny Kirk Session Register
At Cellardyke May 24th 1694
Hora Secunda post meridiem

The Session met after prayer.

Jennat Doig, widow, Blacklaws, brought before the Session and exhorted, after taking the oath to Almighty God, to be honest and sincere in giving her answers, whatsoever she might be asked.

Interrogate first whether she had acquaintance of Isobel Morres of Frithfield.

Said that she was approached by her in the third month of the year when the latter was exceedingly heavy with child and on the extreme verge of bringing forth.

Asked if the said Isobel Morres had brought forth at Blacklaws.

Agreed that this was so, and that Isobel Morres had been delivered of her child on her own bed, in the cottar house at Blacklaws.

Interrogate whether the child was born dead.

Said that this was the case; that the infant had come too soon to the doors of the womb, having been begotten in August of the preceding year according to its mother, and being little more than thirty weeks formed. Said moreover that had the child breathed at its bringing forth, it was not like to have continued so for long.

Asked how Isobel Morres had deported herself when she knew that her child was dead.

Answered that she had wept.

Interrogate whether she had inquired of Isobel Morres the paternity of the dead child.

Answered she had been informed that the father was a ploughman by the name of James Small.

Interrogate how she had parted from Isobel Morres.

Said the girl had left the house at Blacklaws in a weak condition, refusing all sustenance, and had taken the dead child with her, wrapped in a blanket.

Jennat Doig then asked to stand down, and James Small, ploughman, Balkaithly, admitted before the Session. He was likewise admonished to give a sincere and ingenuous account of the truth, in answer to what was to be proposed to him.

He was first interrogate if he was guilty of habitual uncleanness with Isobel Morres in Frithfield.

Answered that he was not.

Interrogate whether he had not been guilty of fornication with her at the beginning of August last year.

Answered that he had never been guilty with her even the once.

He was next asked if he knew anything of the said Isobel Morres as to her bringing forth a child in March last and casting it into the Daffodil Burn, but he positively refused both.

Asked if he knew anything whatever of her being with child, he replied he could see she grew heavy-footed but did not consider it his business to inquire into her condition. His business, he said, was to plough the land.

Interrogate why then he had left Frithfield upon report of the child's discovery and Isobel Morres's apprehension, which flight was looked upon as a shrewd presumption of his guilt and his being accessory to the infant's murder.

All his answer was that he had not fled the parish as being supposed but had gone to Boarhills to see his brother. There he was put in the way of a ploughman's position at Balkaithly, the which he took, on account of James Morres's prostrated condition, the old man being unable to render him any assistance whatever with the labour of the farm at Frithfield.

Asked whether he had not felt any dutifulness of compassion towards James Morres, he replied that this was none of his concern. His business was to earn his bread without having to sweat twice as much as any other man.

Thereafter he was removed and Isobel Morres brought before the Session.

Mr Beatson put to her that James Small, accused by her of being the father of her dead child, had within this hour denied all knowledge of it, whether of its conception or its bringing forth, and that she was now exhorted in the presence of God to speak freely and openly whatsoever she knew contrary to James Small's most adamant denial of the infant.

On hearing this the girl was much distressed and asked that James Small be brought to stand in front of her and reiterate his refusal with his hand on the Bible.

Here Mr Beatson said to her: 'You may take it from me, Isobel, that he gave this as his word to God. Only tell us the whole truth from hereon now.'

After further weeping she gave an indication that she was ready to answer all questions put to her, promising not to remain silent on any point.

Interrogate whether John Small was in truth the father of the dead infant.

Answered that he was, as surely as she was its mother.

Interrogate whether she had been unclean with him on more than one occasion.

Answered that he had often pressed her to lie with him and that she had persistently refused his advances, submitting to him but the once.

Asked what had caused her to alter her steadfastness in this respect.

She replied that he had threatened to abandon her without provision of manual labour upon the farm at the beginning of the harvest the previous year, her father being sickly and infirm at the time and incapable of work. Thereupon she had affected a complaisance to lie with him once the harvest was taken in. Accordingly, when the very last stook had been bound and set up, he had roughly demanded his due.

Interrogate why she had not put up any resistance to him, seeing that the promise she had given him was enforced upon her.

Answered that she was spent and weary with the labour of taking in the harvest and had lain down like a dumb thing while he had his desires.

Asked whether James Small had accosted her again in this respect.

Replied that he resented her passiveness and manifest loathing of the deed to the extent that he approached her no more after that day.

Interrogate whether she had acquainted James Small with her condition.

Said that she had.

What was his response?

Said that he had on several occasions brought her herbs, desiring her to make use of them in order to cause her part with the conception. Which she had each several time refused to do.

Interrogate next where she brought forth the child.

Answered at the house of Jennat Doig.

Interrogate where was James Small at that time.

Answered at that time he was at the plough.

Asked repeatedly if the child was born dead.

On each occasion that the question was put to her she said she took

It wrapped in a cloth from the widow Doig's house and carried it home, where she laid it in a secret place by her bed.

Questioned why she did this, she replied that she could not bear to part with it.

Interrogate how long she had kept the infant's corpse, she replied upwards of four weeks.

Asked if it had not begun to smell, she answered that her father in the room adjacent to hers had complained of an odour in the house, which for some time she disguised by burning candles and incense.

Interrogate where she had acquired such articles of popery.

Answered that these had lain in the house for upwards of seven years since the Killing Times in the reign of the last James.

Asked what they were for, she answered that the Session must know very well what purpose they served, it being a common enough ruse among country folk at that time to deflect the suspicions of the king's dragoons when they came into the remoter districts of the country to fall upon the Covenanters.

Mr Beatson allowed that such subterfuges were not unknown at that time.

She was next interrogate whether her father had not asked the reason of the fumigation.

Answered yes, that it had been evident to her that she could not keep the infant's corpse any longer, but that she had been near out of her wits with anguish for these past weeks since the child's delivery.

Whereupon being informed that one of her sheep was lying dead on Airdrie Lees, she went out early one morning to pull the wool of the beast, and took the corpse with her in her lap, meaning to bury it herself alongside the dead sheep.

Asked to go on, she said that she had first plucked the wool from the sheep, keeping the dead child by her all the time, still swathed in its blanket. She then laid the child in the midst of the pile of wool, while she dug the hole for the sheep. It had come into her mind, she said, as she looked upon it, to bury the child wrapped up in the wool, in place of the decencies of shrouding and other ceremony which were to be denied it. However that was, she went on, she could not bring herself when it came to the bit to lay the child to rest in a wild and unconsecrated place, without so much as the speaking of a word or a psalm, or a prayer, to give it godspeed unto that eternity to which we all come.

That being her state of mind, she took up the child again in the blanket and walked over the fields towards Kilrenny, meaning to acquaint the parish authorities of the child's bringing forth and stillbirth, and its witholding hitherto from bell and burial.

Interrogate why she had not done so according to this virtuous intention.

Answered that she came upon James Small in the fields, and, informing him what it was she intended to do, he begged her to bury the child there and then, keeping secret their sin of fornication. When she refused, he knocked her to the ground with a hard blow, from which she lay senseless how long she did not know.

Interrogate what she did on recovering her senses.

Answered that on coming to she had run back home to Frithfield, where John Small later told her that he had begun to bury the infant himself, but being put into a panic by the sight of persons approaching, he speedily hanged a stone about the infant's neck and threw it into the waters of the Daffodil Burn at the deepest part he could find. And there it had lain until William Pitbladdo came upon it the week following.

Isobel Morres asked if she had anything she desired to add to or subtract from her testimony and saying she had now confessed the whole truth, she was taken down and removed and James Small summoned to recompear.

He was interrogate if he had at any time brought herbs to Isobel Morres for the purpose of causing her part with the child's conception.

Answered that this was a false allegation of hers. He being a simple man of the plough, knew nothing of herbs, nor of Isobel Morres's child.

Probed again and again, he persistently refused its paternity.

Interrogate once more why he had left the parish the day the infant's corpse was discovered, he remained stubborn that he had gone to Boarhills to see about better work.

Interrogate if he had not prevented Isobel Morres from taking her dead infant before the parish: first by causing her to sustain a blow from which she was knocked senseless; second by removing from her the child's corpse and hanging a stone about its neck, afterwards casting it into the Daffodil Burn.

Answered all in the negative, insisting that these were false allegations of hers and obstinately denying that the child was ever his blood.

He was taken down and removed.

Mr Beatson, addressing the Session, then said he was persuaded beyond doubt that Isobel Morres was telling the truth before God, and that James Small was lying under oath.

Given the testimony of the widow of Blacklaws that the child came into the world before its time and was stillborn; given their own recollection of the smallness of the infant on examination of the same prior to burial, and the absence of marks on the child's corpse; and given James Small's unsatisfactory explanation of his disappearing the parish on the very day the infant was discovered, he was disposed to believe that James Small was guilty on several counts.

First, on having pressed Isobel Morres to lie with him, exerting upon her her father's enfeebled condition and her dependence upon his labour; second, on having committed the act of fornication itself; third, on having taken on himself no responsibility for the infant's paternity, and offering no succour whatever to its mother from the conception to the bringing forth; fourth, on having taken the child's corpse by force and unlawfully casting it away without the due rites of burying at the hands of the proper authority; and fifth, on persistently lying about all of this in spite of being under oath.

He therefore proposed that Isobel Morres be set free forthwith and be allowed to return home to see to her father, on condition that she appear in church on three successive Sabbaths for admonition before the congregation. He further proposed that James Small be referred to Presbytery.

All agreed, with the exception of John Middleton.

The three parties were then brought in together and confronted.

The widow of Blacklaws was first dismissed.

Next James Small was admonished for his wickedness and lies; and after it was intimated to him that there was no proof of substance against him and he could go free, he was notwithstanding summoned to compear before the Presbytery of St Andrews at their next meeting, which would be at St Andrews on the second Wednesday in June.

Isobel Morres was censured for her fornication, and ordered to appear before the congregation at Kilrenny on Sabbath next, 31st May, for correction on the penitential stool.

Sederunt concluded with prayer.

James Small went straight from the Session meeting to the aleshop in Cellardyke, where he fell in with Andrew Watson, the erstwhile keeper of the Tolbooth. He had made that place his second home, fulminating to all who would listen regarding the foul mouth and fingers of Isobel Morres, who had put marks on both his reputation and his face.

He found a ready enough listener in James Small. Together they fed one another's resentment to the point of a mutual intoxication which rendered each man legless. When they had regained the use of their limbs they staggered up to the house of Andrew Watson's sister, who sat at home fuming, on account of fornicating infanticides set free to murder other folks' bairns. John Middleton, isolated from the rest of the Session because of his uncharitable vote at the previous meeting, made no move to break up this unholy trinity, and indeed before too long made one of them.

These four spent many hours together in the days before James Small's appearance before the St Andrews Presbytery.

Extract from the Minutes of the Presbytery of St Andrews
At St Andrews Wednesday June 9th 1694
Hora decima ante meridiem

The Presbytery convened at ten of the clock, Dr Levack, Presbyter, presiding.

After prayer was brought in James Small, ploughman, Cornceres.

Examined as to how he answered the charge of Isobel Morres, spinster, Frithfield, that he had taken from her her dead infant and consigned it to a watery grave in the burn known as the Daffodil Burn, near the farm of Frithfield.

Answered that this was a foul and flagrant lie, conjured by the said Isobel Morres to hide from the representatives of the kirk her own condition of guilt.

Examined what condition of guilt he spoke of, he replied that this was not for him to guess at, whether she had herself laid the child in the water dead or alive.

The words of the Scripture were then recited to him by Dr Levack, that whosoever harmeth any one of these little ones, it were better for him that a millstone be hanged about his neck and he be cast into the sea.

Had he so hanged a stone about the neck of Isobel Morres's infant?

Answered that he had already refused that charge.

Did he so accuse Isobel Morres of hanging the stone about the infant's neck.

Answered again that this was not for him to guess at, as he had said already.

Examined whether he still refused the child's paternity, and made the reply that it was none of his.

Examined why then Isobel Morres so stubbornly would allow none but he to be the father of her child.

Answered he supposed that she said this out of spite after he had rejected her persuasions on him to lie with her uncleanly.

Laid before him the record that it was she who had accused him of wishing to lie with her. Why then had he not previously made any mention that it was the other way round according to his present testimony?

He replied that he had gone so far as he could at that time towards keeping Isobel Morres out of fault and ill favour, but he feared now he must speak the truth whole, or incur the displeasure of God through the instrumentality of the Presbytery.

Asked what was the whole truth, he said that Isobel Morres, having flaunted herself unto him without avail, had one day given him certain herbs mixed in with his dinner, and that afterwards he had been consumed with a desire to lie with her.

Examined whether he had then asked her to lie with him, he answered no, that she had herself led him to the hayfield at Frithfield, he following her like a man in a dream, as though his head had been torn off his shoulders, he felt so amazed and confounded at the time.

Examined what happened thereafter.

Answered she had lifted up her skirts and urged him to lie with her.

Examined if he had done so, he said he obeyed, still as one in a dream might do, but that he could not enter into her on account of his members would not obey their natural promptings.

Ordered to continue, he said that after that she wox angry and foul-tongued, shouting that if he could not be her paramour she would find one who would, be it man, beast or devil.

Dr Levack, presiding, much shocked, asked John Small how he had interpreted that remark.

The said John Small avowed he had not stopped to reason what was meant thereby but had fled from her in a panic.

Examined whether Isobel Morres had made any subsequent demands upon his person.

Said that she had several times accosted him at the plough, desiring him to have recourse to another concoction of herbs, which, she said, would have an altogether pleasanter effect upon his members.

Examined if he had complied.

He stoutly denied this, saying that, on the contrary, he had taken to having all his meat and drink away from the Frithfield table, for fear of the bewitchment of his vittles.

Examined next if he had any knowledge of where the said Isobel Morres obtained these herbs, he said that he had often seen her in the Gudeman's Acre in the late hours of the night, coming home from his work.

On requesting some elucidation on that point, Dr Levack was informed that the Gudeman's Acre, sometimes called the Gudeman's

Croft, in the parish of Kilrenny, lay contiguous to the farm of Blacklaws.

Examined if Isobel Morres was always alone on such occasions, James Small minded that he had seen her, under the moon, in the company of another person, on that wild patch of ground, and once more in the company of another two, none of whom he was able to identify.

Asked what construction he intended the Presbytery to place upon these remarks, he replied that their construction was none of his concern, he simply laying before them the facts to the best of his remembering. But, says he, he had one of these times seen her while he was walking in the company of Andrew Watson, who remembered his sister saying how she had seen Isobel Morres gathering herbs on the Gudeman's Croft.

After saying so he was asked to stand down.

Then said Dr Levack, the drift of James Small's evidence scarcely being lost upon the members of Presbytery, it behoved them now to probe Isobel Morres to the limit. If she were innocent of his insinuatory charges, he had no doubt that God would protect her, punish her defamer, and guide His servants of the Presbytery, who must now summon, indict and examine her according to the latest accusations against her.

Sederunt concluded.

There came to Isobel Morres at Frithfield Mr Beatson, Dr Levack, some several members of the Session of Kilrenny, with John and Mistress Middleton, and of the St Andrews Presbytery.

ISOBEL What do you seek wi' me? I was sent awa fae you an innocent woman, freed to look to my faither in his hour o' need.

DR LEVACK And a free woman you shall surely continue, Isobel, if you'll but answer our questions to our satisfaction, whatever it be we put to you.

ISOBEL Wha are you, sir? What questions can there be? I answered aa things afore.

DR LEVACK Aye, but there are fresh charges against you, Isobel.

ISOBEL What charges?

DR LEVACK Such as necessitate we first make a thorough search of this house.

ISOBEL I hae nothing to hide.

DR LEVACK Good. Then stand aside and let us be about our work.

She sat quiet by her father's bed, old James Morres all the while in a state of fear and agitation as to what they should do.

They searched a long time.

When at last they stood before her they were holding bundles of herbs, powders, ointments, candles and candlesticks such as had been referred to at the Session inquiry, a black gentleman's cloak of exceptionally fine quality, and various other domestic articles. They had also searched under the mattress on which James Morres lay prostrate and near blind, and removed from thereunder another armful of herbs.

Then Dr Levack addressed her.

DR LEVACK Isobel Morres, I charge and arraign thee with child murder and on suspicion of being a witch, and I order thee to come with us before a magistrate to answer these aforesaid charges.

ISOBEL (*kissing her father*) God help me.

She was taken from there to the Tolbooth, and then after the space of a week to the prison at St Andrews, where a room was prepared for her interrogation. Beside the magistrate there were present Mr Beatson, Dr Levack, members of the Session and Presbytery of Kilrenny and St Andrews, and certain officers of the law, together with an approved torturer and a witch pricker from Edinburgh.

MAGISTRATE Isobel Morres, you stand charged both with infanticide, a heinous enough offence in itself and repugnant to society, and with the graver and more terrible crime of witchcraft, for which today you must answer in your defence. First, I am to tell you that the Lords of the Privy Council of Scotland have instructed us to use whatever means of persuasion prove necessary in order to extract from you a full and unvarnished confession on the charge of witchcraft, be you innocent or guilty. Second, I am further to instruct you that such a confession cannot be deemed full and frank under the law until such persuasion of torture has been tried and adopted, however freely you may choose to answer at the first. Now speak. How do you answer.

ISOBEL I dinna understand. What is it that you desire me to say?

MAGISTRATE Dr Levack will speak for me from hereon now. Simply confess to the truth.

ISOBEL The truth o' what? You must tell me what you want to ken.

DR LEVACK Confess then that you are a witch.

She shook her head violently.

DR LEVACK Answer these questions truthfully then. Did you not murder your bairn?

ISOBEL No, my lords, the bairn was born deid, as I hae said ower and ower at the like proceedings.

DR LEVACK These proceedings will be somewhat different today, woman and will take an altogether different turn if you do not answer quickly and to the point. Who was the child's father?

ISOBEL I am heartily sick o' saying his name. It was James Small, the plooman in Frithfield.

DR LEVACK He says no.

ISOBEL He would say so, to cover his ain guiltiness.

DR LEVACK Say what guilt you mean, woman.

ISOBEL He made me lie doon wi' him, I hae telt you aa this afore.

DR LEVACK Did he coerce you then?

ISOBEL What do you mean?

MR BEATSON (*interposing*) Did he use any kind of physical force to make you lie with him, Isobel?

DR LEVACK Silence, sir. I am conducting this examination. Did he compel you by force to be guilty with him?

ISOBEL I lay doon wi' him only to mak him bide a bit longer on the ferm for the sake o' my faither, as I am weary o' repeating to you, sirs. Syne he tried to mak me scale the babe fae my womb, which I wouldna do. At the hinder end he took the bairn, deid as it was, and put it awa in the burn, and that was the last I saw o't. There's nothing mair I can tell you, gentlemen.

DR LEVACK Oh, I think you will be persuaded to tell us something more than that, before God, woman, but we shall come to that by and by. Tell me this, wasn't it you who tried to mislead the ploughman James Small into lying with you? And in citing him haven't you put the cart before the horse somewhat in order to mask your own filthy fornication that is unmentionable in its kind unto all decent folk?

ISOBEL I dinna ken what you say.

DR LEVACK He says he was terrified to come into your house after you gave him a dinner cooked with herbs that rendered him helpless before your wiles.

ISOBEL He's a shameful liar! It was he that brocht herbs to me, to scale awa my bairn. What is it he is trying to do to me?

DR LEVACK What is it you are trying to do to him, woman, but to lay at his door a common enough crime, God knows, to conceal from us gentlemen the altogether darker parentage of this ill-begotten bairn?

ISOBEL What in God's name do you mean?

DR LEVACK Confess that you are a witch.

ISOBEL I am no sic thing, sweet Jesus befreend me!

DR LEVACK Do you dare take the name of our Lord Jesus in vain in the presence of this gathering, you witch?

ISOBEL (*shouting*) I tell you I am nae witch, sirs, but you are sair misguided men, let me tell you that, and James Small shall surely rot in hell for the thing he has brocht upon me this day!

DR LEVACK (*rising*) Aha, do we see your true nature now begin to surface, with your talk of hell? Strip her down, if you please, Mistress Middleton, as you are here for the purposes of decency. And witch-pricker—let us see your skill.

Then were the clothes removed from the girl, every stitch, and she made to stand naked before the righteous and just assemblage of persons, exposed to all their censure. Thereupon she started to shiver.

DR LEVACK Aye, do you tremble already at what we are about to find, you lummer?

ISOBEL It is cauld.

DR LEVACK Then call on your infernal legions to warm you with their fires. Come away, witch-finder, and get about your business.

At the very first insertion of the probe, which the witch-pricker carried out secretely from behind, entering it into her left buttock, there was a loud gasp from those people grouped about her; for much blood was let out, the pricker having driven in his blade to a depth of two inches, yet Isobel Morres did not so much as by a whimper give forth any indication that she had experienced the least sensation of pain.

The wife of John Middleton shouted in triumph.

MISTRESS MIDDLETON There she stands, sirs, what need hae we to try her ony further?

She pointed to the floor. Isobel Morres, following her finger, looked round and saw the floor sprinkled with drops of her own blood, at which she shrieked and drew back in fear.

DR LEVACK Aye, aye, it is useless to put on a show of pain now, you deceitful misleader of men. It is clear you felt nothing at the first probe. This pricker, my masters, fairly kens his work!

Mr Beatson urged, however, that, the girl being greatly overwrought, fearful, and in a condition of acute shame at having to stand naked to the eyes of so many men, it was very like that shock had rendered her immune to the passage of the probe.

MISTRESS MIDDLETON What would a fornicating bitch like yon ken o' shame, do you think? And a servant of Satan as weel. She's as guilty as Lucifer!

Dr Levack agreed, but reluctantly bowed to Mr Beatson's request that further probes be made for the discovery on Isobel Morres's person of the Devil's Mark. The pricker then tried his probe into her legs, thighs, buttocks, breasts and belly, more than a dozen insertions, and each time she moaned and cried out in pain, so that Mr Beatson urged him to desist, as he was causing her much suffering to no purpose.

DR LEVACK Ah, sir, the Devil's Mark may be as small as the point of a pin, and how many points do you think there may be on an area as great as that of the human frame? Thousands upon thousands belike—nay, millions—invisible to sight, and only Satan's eyes can see the place he has marked out in token of the infernal compact between the witch and the Dark One himself. No sir, this subtle whore attempts to mislead us by thus crying out. Yet you all saw how insensitive she did remain to the first stroke that took her secretly and by surprise. I tell you therefore that God's hand guided the probe straight to the mark, and I declare myself satisfied that the mark of Satan has been identified on Isobel Morres. That being so, we must now search her further for the witch's mark. Let us proceed, if you please.

Isobel Morres was then examined, inch after inch, for the place at which her familiars came to receive suck of her blood. Dr Levack advised the examiners to be on the watch for any scar, birthmark, blemish, wart or mole that might lie hidden in a covert place. Accordingly they examined her armpits, ears, genitals, buttocks and tongue, and under her eyelids, inspecting her from her scalp to the soles of her feet, but without result.

After ordering a second examination to be carried out, Dr Levack professed himself satisfied on discovery of a small supernumerary existing under the fullness of her left breast. When this was found she was then blindfold and held still for a period, her breasts and legs prised apart, so that she had no knowledge of when or where the pricker would operate. He tried her in her belly, back and sides several times to her evident anguish before slowly inserting the point of his probe into the secretly positioned nipple, she lying the while white and rigid under their hands. Then he drew back, leaving the probe hanging by itself from the underside of the breast.

Dr Levack ordered the blindfold to be removed. When she saw the probe hanging from her pap, Isobel Morres cried out at once.

DR LEVACK Aye, too late, too late, thou witch! How long have you had hidden about you this secret mark?

ISOBEL It has been wi' me since the day I was born, as my mither would tell you if she were here.

DR LEVACK You are a liar, madam. Who taught you to make potions of herbs to lead men astray from the paths of righteousness? Was it your dark master?

ISOBEL James Small is the only dark ane when it comes to herbs. I learned my country skills fae Jennat Doig, my mither being deid since I was a bairn.

DR LEVACK I thought as much. Did she teach you such skills on the Gudeman's Croft, this Blacklaws widow?

ISOBEL What if she did?

DR LEVACK Don't be insolent woman, or it will go ill for you. Though God knows you could hardly be in a worse pickle. Why did you cull your simples from there, woman?

ISOBEL The field grows wild, as weel you ken. There is there a goodly gathering o' herbs for healing and for seasoning.

DR LEVACK A goodly field of damnation, O thou seed of Satan! What else did the witch of Blacklaws teach you besides the arts of cooking and healing with herbs?

ISOBEL She is no witch. What would you hae me say?

DR LEVACK (*holding up some leaves*) You can tell us for what purpose these were laid under your father's bed. Answer quickly.

ISOBEL These be nothing mair than bay and sweet chestnut, to help him wi' his sair limbs. It's a weel kent country cure, sirs, as mony a ane will tell you.

DR LEVACK (*holding up a phial*) And this?

ISOBEL The same, sir. It's the juice o' these leaves, to be rubbed into his back and legs.

DR LEVACK For what purpose?

ISOBEL To get him back his strength, to walk and work once mair. It's the auld belief, sir.

DR LEVACK Aye, old it may be, I have no doubt. And have you never applied such juices into your own naked skin? Speak at once.

ISOBEL Just the once, sir, when I was fashed wi' a woman's troubles, and then it was crushed thyme. But mony a lass does the like.

DR LEVACK But how many a lass finds the powers of flight thereby?

ISOBEL What do you mean?

DR LEVACK Never mind that. What do you call this?

Here he held up the black cloak that had been taken from the house at Frithfield.

ISOBEL That was gien to my faither by the auld laird, the day they put my mither below the sod. It was for mourning, he said, and he never wanted it back. He was a good man.

DR LEVACK Aye, a good man conveniently dead. I've seldom heard an unlikelier tale. What else did the Blacklaws witch instruct you in? Tell us that.

ISOBEL She helped me bring forth my bairn when I was in travail, and that's aa there was atween us. She succoured me as best she kent, but the poor bairn was deid when it cam into her hands.

DR LEVACK Liar. That bairn was born alive and well. You strangled it between you, didn't you?

ISOBEL I tell you ower and again, the bairn was early come, and was still as a stane at birth. Do you think I could strangle a new born bairn wi' my bare hands?

DR LEVACK Who said you used your bare hands? You used this (*holding up a woman's garter*).

ISOBEL What's this?

DR LEVACK You can see well enough what it is. Don't act the daft lassie with me. Where's the other garter?

ISOBEL What do you mean?

DR LEVACK When we searched your abode we found only the one garter. This one I am now exhibiting was later found by Mistress Middleton near the Daffodil Burn.

ISOBEL (*turning to look upon her*) You evil auld lummer that you are, you took a scunner at me fae the first. But you'll gan girning to hell for this, you barren auld bitch!

Upon this Mistress Middleton flew at Isobel Morres, and, spitting in her face, had to be restrained.

DR LEVACK Well gentlemen, it seems the fiend is now showing her claws. Torturer, I command you in the name of the Lords of the Privy Council, and of our Lord Jesus Christ, to do what you have to do, under our direction.

First the torturer applied the thumbscrews, and while she was under this rigour Dr Levack continually put these questions to her.

Who was the true father of her infant?

Was it not Satan himself, with whom she had been guilty of demoniality after failing to arouse James Small to an ardour sufficient to get her with child?

Had she not befuddled his wits with herbs on the instruction of Jennat Doig, but these same herbs had bewitched his organs of regeneration, making him incapable of intercourse with her?

Did not she and Jennat Doig eat of the flesh of the unbaptized infant subsequent to strangling it, and afterwards dropping it into the burn?

What were her familiars—were they not hares, toads, cats and spiders and the like?

The cracking of her joints tore sharp shrieks out of her, but no confession on any of these points. Dr Levack therefore commanded that the pincers be applied to her fingernails and that a fingernail be drawn forth for each failure to confess to a point of interrogation.

DR LEVACK Why did you put the marks on Andrew Watson's face? Was it not because he too refused to lie with you when he brought you your meat?

ISOBEL He's an evil liar. He was the ane that set upon me wi' his filthy embrace and his interfering fingers.

DR LEVACK You'll never claw again with these fingers of yours, witch, Draw forth the first nail, master torturer.

This was done, and she cried out loudly at the extraction, but would not satisfy her interrogator, either on that question or on any of these following.

When had she first entered into a pact with the Devil?

Was it Jennat Doig who had initiated her into the black arts?

Had not her father's disability caused him to curse his prosperous neighbours when he saw how he could not similarly thrive, and had he not, on account of this, become a servant of Satan?

How many boats had she caused to perish out of Cellardyke with the winds and waves she had raised?

What crops had she blighted, what milk curdled, and what cattle smitten with sterility and disease?

There had been fires and pestilence and civil disorder in diverse parts of the country. How many of these were attributable to her?

Did she not use to have incestuous dealings with her father, James Morres?

Had he not a succubus that collected his semen so as to inject it into her at a later stage in the incubus form of the demon?

To none of these questions would she supply the desired answer, by the conclusion of which she had lost every one of her nails, and her fingers hung from her like a cluster of white tentacles, tipped with red.

As no confession was yet forthcoming, Dr Levack warned those present that they must therefore steel themselves for yet sterner methods, putting out of their minds the image of a simple country lass, and seeing this as nothing more than the very front adopted by Satan for the insidious operations of his secret ministry. No, said Dr Levack, this was no innocent rustic girl but an instrument of hell, which only the greatest severities of persuasion might expose. To these horrors it was now necessary, in the name of the Lord, to proceed.

Isobel Morres was taken and her hands bound fast behind her with cords, which were passed through a pulley, so that she was suspended in this manner from the rafters, with great weights attached to her one to each of her ankles.

Each time she was hauled up to the roof, Dr Levack directed the same question at her as to whether she was a practiser of the damned arts. She refusing to answer to his contentment, he nodded to the torturer, whereupon she was caused to drop quickly from that height, the torturer stopping her short of the floor with a sudden jerk each time, so that those standing by heard the dislocation of her bones and the rending of her sinews even above the inhuman noises of her howling.

MR BEATSON (*intervening for the first time*) Stop it, for God sakes, man, stop it, stop it, I beg you! Had there been anything to confess she would surely have told you by now.

DR LEVACK Aye, does her wailing make you sweat, man? That's understandable. Yet what is that compared to the wailing of the damned in hell that goes on forever and forever and is a million times worse? As yet we stand not even on the threshold of damnation and its pains, and here you are unnerved by the screaming of a solitary reprobate, not yet cast into the lake that burneth forever. Think of the billions that will howl there in eternity! And remember, *In inferno nulla est consolatio.* The one consolation we can offer this miserable and accursed sinner is that she confessed her sin before she died.

MR BEATSON Talk you of her dying, sir? She is not yet found guilty.

DR LEVACK Guilty? In the name of God, man, how do you think she has withstood the suffering so far? No woman could conceivably hold out so long but for the diabolical assistance of her masters, making her adamantine heart harder still. They are here around us on every side, invisible and strong as the wind. But with Christ on our side we shall be stubborner yet than the very Devil himself. No sir, speak not of putting your hand to God's plough and then turning back. Such a one is not fit for the kingdom of heaven. Torturer, let her go!

Whereupon he released the cords altogether and Isobel Morres crashed to the floorboards, weights and all, with a loud shivering cry that made all but Dr Levack turn pale. In the merciful silence that signalled her loss of consciousness her head opened and a quantity of blood issued onto the floor.

Water was then thrown over her, and, shrieking and shivering, she was strapped to a chair while Dr Levack commanded the torturer to heat the pincers to a white-hot preparedness.

DR LEVACK (*motioning to the fellow to bring the pincers close to her eyes*) Now Isobel, you are in a sad and sorry condition. But I assure you that worse is yet to follow if you answer not speedily and truthfully. Was your infant born alive or dead?

ISOBEL (*in a low voice*) It was deid.

DR LEVACK (*to the torturer*) Take off her nipple.

MR BEATSON (*coming between them*) O for the love of God, Isobel, tell them it was alive whether it be true or no!

DR LEVACK For shame, sir! Stand aside! Now my masters, we'll have the whole breast off her till we have our answer.

The pincers had not quite touched the girl's breast when she screamed out the word loud and long that had been so many weeks in coming.

ISOBEL Alive! alive! alive! alive! alive!

The word flooded through her and the entire assembly over and over with a sob of sweet relief.

DR LEVACK Ah, Isobel, Christ hath broken through into thy heart and Satan is thrown from the door. How we have longed for this moment of joy! Now let me hear you say it just once more. What was the bairn now, alive or dead?

ISOBEL Aye, alive, sir, o aye, it was truly alive.

DR LEVACK And you killed it, you and Jennat Doig?

ISOBEL Aye, to be sure, we killed the bairn, just like you said afore.

DR LEVACK Now open your heart entirely, Isobel, and tell us the rest.

ISOBEL I will sir, I will, only dinna hurt me nae mair.

DR LEVACK Your hurts are over but one, Isobel, if your answers be true.

From that point on she confessed without further torture to every article of truth that Dr Levack demanded of her.

How she had first been learned in the black arts by Jennat Doig, who had conjured up Satan at midnight in the Gudeman's Acre.

How she had kissed his arse and organs, promising to hate God and all Christian kind, he sealing the compact by marking her on the left buttock.

How she, Isobel Morres, had presented herself obscenely to Satan, both belly and buttocks, and he had penetrated her private parts with his member, which, she recalled distinctly, was hard and painful and exceeding cold.

How, when she discovered that his dark seed had begun to blossom, she had tried to part with it, using concoctions of simples, moistened by moonlight, which had not, however, the power to banish the bairn, so invincible was the Devil's implantation.

How she had mapped out James Small as the likeliest candidate for blame, and had very near succeeded in her design. Aye, she had tempted James Small in the summer of the previous year, but the Devil himself had enchanted James Small's organs, intending that her womb would be reserved for the begetting of no offspring but his own infernal seed.

How she and Jennat Doig had strangled the misbegotten bairn with one of her garters, subsequently partaking of its unbaptised flesh and dropping it into the deepest part they could find in the Daffodil Burn, a stone about its neck.

How her father, struck by God in the back and legs, yea, even in the eyes, and unable to see to the managing of his own farm, had cunningly connived at all of this, jealously raging from his sickbed against his honest neighbours in vile and filthy fashion, and exhorting his devil-inspired daughter to blunt their ploughs and shred their nets so that they should never prosper more.

And how she, Isobel Morres, had had intercourse with demons, times without number, and given suck to her familiars in sundry forms, such as hares and hedgehogs, toads, bats, sucking pigs and crawling insects. Spirits in one shape or another had indeed been seldom from her bed, she having gathered unto herself semen in a thousand varying seeds over the space of the past eighteen months.

After she had made her mark on her confession, holding the pen in her teeth, for her hands were incapable, she was taken back to her cell and left to ponder her iniquities and the torments that awaited her in the next world.

Then were James Morres and Jennat Doig taken from their homes, and under torture of the like that was administered to Isobel Morres, they corroborated every word that she had said, adding even more, to the point where the good decent folk who heard their revelations and the things that they uttered, could be shocked no longer.

These two also were also in a sorry plight by the time they were done.

All three of these miserable wretches were brought to trial at Cupar, having been warned that if they dared deny the least syllable of what they had sworn to, they would be returned straightaway to the house of torture until their perverseness had once again been overcome.

All three pleaded guilty and were sentenced to suffer the full rigour of the law, as laid down in the Holy Scriptures, that Thou shalt not suffer an witch to live. They were then returned to separate confinements and it was decreed that they would not see one another again until their last day upon earth, and then only at the stake, when their hard hearts would be melted out of them by the punishing flames and their ashes scattered to the four winds. Thereafter their souls would meet forever in the hell that would be their portion for evermore.

On the night before her execution there came to Isobel Morres Mr Beatson, to read to her from God's Holy Word. He was much affected when he saw her, for they had earlier come to take away her hair, and her head had been shaved so cruelly that it resembled a turnip.

MR BEATSON Well, Isobel, you are in great misery, and I doubt that God will look on you now. It is not allowed by Scripture, and yet I hope in my heart that Christ will find one drop of His redeeming blood for you that has escaped our understanding of God's terrible law.

ISOBEL Alas, Mr Beatson, I am as guiltless as you, as my God weel kens, and Jesus will tak me to his bosom wi' forgiveness, I am sure, for I never hurt a flee in aa my days.

MR BEATSON (horrified) Weesht, weesht, lass, for pity's sake, hold your tongue! You must not say this to me and I must affect not to have heard these words. You have confessed to abominations unimaginable, and for you to retract one word of that now would mean a sure return to the torture room for an unrepentant witch. Aye, and they would deny you the mercy of strangulation before the fire. But I shall stay silent upon this on account of your great suffering. Simply tell me that you repent your sins.

ISOBEL Aye, sir, I repent me my sins, I do.

Then she said nothing more after that.

At dawn they put on her the long white shirt.

It was hard to think then that she had ever been a lass, with her blue turnip head wobbling at the top of her nightgown and her entire frame collapsed.

She could not walk because of her broken legs. Nor could James Morres nor Jennat Doig any the more. The three condemned were taken in a cart to the stakes which had been prepared for them on the East Green of Cellardyke. To these stakes they were bound with shrieks, their own legs being unable to support them.

John Middleton, wood merchant, had arranged for the faggots for their burning, which were exceedingly green wood, to lengthen the spectacle for the benefit of the crowd. Mr Beatson, however, having made previous note of this, had already paid out of his own pocket for tar barrels to be placed beneath their feet, to quicken the flames.

When Mistress Middleton saw this she was much angered against Mr Beatson. Moreover when she saw the executioner go up to each one of them and attach the cord around their necks, she raged to all around that they ought to be caused to suffer the full affliction of the flames.

She could scarcely be heard above the noise of that crowd. They had gathered from all the farms and fishing ports from Leven to St Andrews. Mr Beatson shouted to her above the gale of jeers and jests that as they had all confessed their crimes they were all allowed the mercy of the cord.

So the executioner went up to James Morres and strangled him first. He never seemed to notice. Then the widow of Blacklaws was dispatched with a quick shrug.

Yet before he could approach Isobel Morres, who lay huddled against her stake, Mistress Middleton ran up to her and pointed her finger into her face, leering and laughing thus.

MISTRESS MIDDLETON You may well escape this burning, you lummer, but no the red fires o' eternity that await you!

The girl shouted back at her with all the spirit that was left in her.

ISOBEL You are as evil a woman as ever disgraced the inside o' a kirk, but I gan to dwell in the hoose o' the Lord forevermair!

MISTRESS MIDDLETON Wi' these crimes on your back, my lady, your dirt will never reek in the coorts o' the Lord!

ISOBEL I tell you I'm mair innocent nor you, you wicked auld wife, for I was convicted by lees and compulsion and pain—and by your ain evil slanders!

Here she spat from on high full into the wild face that gnashed its teeth at her bare feet. Mr Beatson, with a mouth of horror, had come up close to the stake in an effort to drown out what she was saying, but some of the folk standing by had heard what she said. The word went round like quicksilver and a great roar went up that Isobel Morres had recanted her guilt. By this time the executioner had placed the cord around her neck and Mr Beatson urged him to be brief, but the folk would not have it so.

CROWD Remove the cord! Remove the cord!

This was done.

Mr Beatson fell to his knees at the foot of the stake and bowed his head in prayer.

So James Morres and Jennat Doig died, uncomplaining corpses, in their fires, But Isobel Morres expired in the flames, her blue turnip head turning to a black cinder before it finally stopped screaming.

A north wind was blowing up the firth when the ashes were scattered by the beadle to the four points of the compass.

Extract from Kilrenny Kirk Session Register
At Cellardyke August 22nd 1694
Hora Secunda post meridiem

It was reported to the Session that James Small, ploughman, Cornceres, was discovered dead in the hayfield at Cornceres, with his own scythe struck through his belly and out at the back.

Considered likely that, being given to excess, he stumbled in his drunkenness while sharpening the blade of the implement, and so died.

Suicide ruled out of consideration, it is proposed that he be buried at the expense of the parish in the pauper's portion of the kirkyard at Kilrenny.

This same day Mistress Middleton, spouse to our chief elder, John Middleton was laid to rest following a stroke.

Jock

'It's no any use,' the women would say, peering at the brand new guernsey that had just come off the pins for one of the fisherboys. 'It's like it had been made for Jock Buckie.'

Or if a jacket had been picked up for a tanner at the kirk rowp, and brought home for trying on, one of them would throw up her hands in a wailing wall of despair, and cry:

'Oh, tak it aff now, for peety's sake, can you no see it's ten sizes ower big for you?'

Then she'd add, 'It's surely a cast-aff fae Caiplie, that ane—and fit just for Jock Buckie!'

When the boats were in on a winter herring day, and a white net of gulls fluttered over the harbour, the boys liked to stand on the pier watching the fish come on shore.

It was then that the biggest man on the Fife fleet, Star Jeems, knowing that he was on show, and scorning the use of rope and hoist, would tackle the cargo single-handedly. Cran barrels of herring and sodden tangles of nets. If his strength failed, or he baulked at one of the great white mountains of the winter nets, all the men stopped what they were doing, showed their teeth at one another, and lit up their cigarettes.

Somebody then, leaning a scarred arm against the wheelhouse door, would be sure to blow a smoky grin across the noise, and grin and shout:

'Aye, Jeems, it'd tak Jock Buckie, I doot, to bring that ane on shore!'

Jeems's brow would darken. The sweat on him glistening like tar, he'd bristle hugely among all the fish and funnels, and shout back:

'Dinna speak aboot the fermer to me—he'll sink the boat!'

A bairn would be restless under the blankets on a summer's night, and mother's head full of sleep under the stars.

'Wheesht now, wheesht,' she whispered wearily. 'If you dinna wheest, the giant o' the Coves will surely come and tak you.'

The wee thing's mouth grew as round as its eye.

'Wha's the giant o' the Coves?'

'Jock Buckie, of course,' came the answer.

Through the caves of its sleep lumbered an incredible giant. His torso was shapeless with the baggiest guernsey ever knitted on a set of masts, and his jacket flapped like a foresail. He carried a cran barrel of herring under his oxter. Among the glittering green herring scales and the dull dead beads of fish-eyes peeped a white little face. The wild eyes of a sleepless bairn, alive alive-o, among all those eyes of glass.

On Sunday morning Miss Teena Wilson, the Sunday School teacher, asked her five year-old captives for the faith:

'Who can name the strongest man in the Bible?'

That was an easy one.

'Jock Buckie, Miss Wilson.'

The gulls screeched derision on the corrugated iron roof.

And when no bookmark was awarded for that one, it came as a painful surprise to somebody that Jock, for all his strength, was not catalogued in the Bible along with leviathan and the like.

So God and his recording angel did not after all see everything. How on earth could they have missed somebody the size of Jock?

Not that any bairn could ever claim actually to have set eyes on him. All along the coast, from Leven to Crail, he simply lived in folks' mouths, like a proverb, and like the byword he was, the man was surely immortal.

But one day the impossible happened.

'Jock Buckie's dead,' was the word.

Armageddon had arrived. Bairns grew up in a single day.

'But whatever made you think that the man wisna real?'

So astonished mothers spoke to their grave-faced offspring. Jock had simply been a legend in his own lifetime, that was all.

When the hearse moved along the road from Caiplie to Crail, folk could get a good idea of the size of the coffin even through the smoked glass windows. Jock seemed even bigger dead than he had been alive. And when they arrived at the kirkyard, and the box was eased down onto the turf, they found it took ten men to get him into his grave.

A voice among the mourners said:

'It would hae needed Jock Buckie himsel to lift that box!'

'Eh, what a peety,' an old wife girned under her shawl.' Jock's dead—and never the once did he preach fae a pulpit.'

'He would hae made a grand minister,' another white head lamented.

And their crow-black companion, standing at the graveyard dyke, mumbled through her gums:

'Weel, weel, he's awa—him and his theories aboot Mons Graupius. For a' the good they ever did the poor man.'
Old Rob Mair said afterwards that it was Jock's theories about the battle of Mons Graupius that had put him to his grave. And that was sufficient proof for him of the dangers of education.

But that was only part of it, of course, as Rob liked to point out.

Jock's folks were tinks.

They had come to Caiplie from the Highlands with nothing but Gaelic in their mouths and middens at their feet.

His mother was a short but strapping enough quine; a slattern, kindly in her ways. His father was a shrivelled radish of a man. It was a wonder how a colossus like Jock ever sprang from the mating of such a pair of loins.

The old worthies of Cellardyke, whose understanding of genes came from lectures delivered on the pier by Rob, reckoned it was because they'd saved it up for so long.

For thirty years old Buckie worked the tiny envelope of land between the Caiplie Coves and Willie Gray's dyke, without any remarkable results whatever. Once a tink always a tink, the Dykers said. His woman saw to the hens, baked her soda scones and grew fat. The middens multiplied around them. A nice quiet life.

'Quiet life be damned!' thundered Rob at the pierhead. 'That was the noisest hell-hole in the East Neuk afore Jock took ower. What wi' a hunder hens and the sea-maws roond their middens—and the pair o' them skirlan awa in Gaelic. I've never heard the like!'

He rammed his unlit pipe back into his mouth for effect. The old men nodded and pulled on theirs.

'She was anchored aff fifty by the time she had Jock,' Rob said. 'I'm no just sure what side o't, the north or the sooth!'

South was younger and stronger in Rob's language; north was older and colder.

He flourished his stem, sucked baccy air, waved to the ageless sea, and carried on.

After thirty years on the croft at Caiplie old Buckie had never got a Scots tongue in his head. But he must have suddenly learned English. For he started reading the Bible—the heathen. That was how he came to understand that all his life he'd been breaking God's earliest commandment to fallen man.

Be fruitful and multiply.

It came to him during the Spring ploughing. He left the plough halfway down a dreel, ran inside and started to till the old woman.

Jock was the result. The giant of Caiplie.

And that was how all the genes for bigness, that should have been parcelled out piece-meal over a generation, came together in one stupendous lump. By rights the effort should have killed the old wife. But between them they went on from there to develop a taste for breeding.

'Late flowerers they were,' pronounced Rob with mock solemnity.

There were three more births.

Jessie, Euphemia and Agnes arrived on the doorstep of the Caiplie croft. As ugly, Rob said, as though a muckle cormorant had done the job of the stork.

That was the best bit of the story as far as Rob was concerned. After that the storyteller in him faded somewhat into the harbour wall. Into the line of jackets and jumpers and grey heads. He became little more than a breath in an empty pipe.

Everybody knew the rest of the story anyway.

Jock sat dutifully through all his Primary schooling, as quiet and inoffensive as a blotch of sunlight on the desk. Nobody thought twice about him.

But he shone at the Secondary School. The Waid Academy in Anster was a place that prided itself on recognising talent.

The other pupils battered their brains against the cruel lines and angles of geometry, and came away bruised and demented at the end of the first day. Jock fitted together all the hard shards like pieces of stained glass.

'Geometry is the measuring of the earth,' said Mr Watt on the first day of the session.

By the end of the year Jock Buckie saw the earth through an entire window of beautiful angles. And he saw it steadily and whole. The window was a rainbowed arch over the world. Three hundred and sixty degrees measured eternity.

'You could be a master navigator,' Mr Watt said, looking at Jock's trigonometry jotter. 'I've never seen such flair.'

Jock bit the end of his pencil. He contemplated a voyage on a tideless sea. His charts were pressed between black covers. There was gold lettering on the spine.

The class went on to algebra, statistics, graphs. Some of the girls did pretty neat work. Even one or two of the boys made a fair stab into these departments of mathematics, that is after a great many nights toiling over the homework, and a great number of alterations and erasures.

Jock's curves had the grace of a seabird. His hand felt the beauty of the line; he conveyed the meaning with a softness and a truth that made Mr Watt marvel.

'All things are numbers, John, as Pythagoras said. And rightly said. You have all things at your disposal, my boy. Numbers is the key that will unlock your world.'

That was arrant nonsense, said the French teacher, Mrs Anderson, praising Jock's prose translations. Languages were the key to the modern world—the real, practical world, that is to say, where people live and work and talk.

'And by that I don't mean dead languages,' she smirked, looking meaningfully out of her window in the direction of the Classics Department.

Mr Hay summoned Jock to his room.

'John,' he said, 'you have more than mere understanding of the language.' I have never come across a pupil who could compose poems of his own in Latin—and poems of such sensitivity and originality—*ad astra sublimis feror*— Horace would not have been ashamed of this. You introduce fresh life—sap, if I may so use the metaphor, into what some of my benighted colleagues would regard as the dry timbers of a dead language.'

Jock stood in the faded Latin classroom. He felt like a ghost. The dark benches were a mass of ink-stained signatures and sayings, carved into the varnished oak.

Requiescat in pace Robert Fyall—died of boredom

Jock saw a tree of knowledge, its roots in an eternal garden, its leaves and branches spreading into time.

'As I was saying, John, leave the German tongue to the barbarians who speak it, and teach it. That race is spoiling for war, believe you me, You shall do Greek with me in the Third Form.'

The boy heard a hundred tongues clattering around Babel. Atoms were what life was really all about. History was our only hope—the single subject we could hope to learn from and so avoid the disasters of the past. The next war might involve the whole of Europe, maybe the entire world. Literature alone could teach us how to be more human; to be re-united with our better selves; how to attain to the best that had been thought, written and said.

'He could be a draughtsman,' said Mr Lees, the Art teacher. 'Or an architect. He could design ships.'

'Or aeroplanes,' suggested Mr Mason mildly. 'Improve communications by land, sea or air. Or by wireless.'

'In other words,' said the rector, Mr Robin, looking round the table at his staff, 'there is no end, it seems, to the things that John Buchan could be. Anything from a fluent linguist to an ingenious inventor or designer. But on the one matter we are all agreed. And that is that whatever the boy does he will be brilliant at it.'

Everybody was agreed upon that score.

'Very well then. Plainly the time has come when we'd better find out what the boy actually wants to do. Has anybody asked him?'

There was consternation among the teachers when Jock announced his decision.

'A genius in our midst,' said Mr Robin, 'and he wants to be a minister. A minister.'

A dozen pedagogues watched every one of Jock's multifarious talents go gurgling down a vestry plughole.

'Still,' the rector said to Jock, 'a sense of vocation is as important as the use of any one particular talent. And as you have such a bewildering variety of talents, perhaps in the end to follow your vocation would be no bad thing.'

As an afterthought he added, 'And the ministry, of course, is a good calling. Oh, yes.'

It was put to old Mr Buckie that Jock had better stay on at school till he was eighteen and then sit the scholarship exam at St Andrews. To his credit old Buckie agreed at once. He still had a good few years of work left in him, he said, and could manage the bit farm without the help of his sixteen year-old son. Though anyone could have seen what a help young Jock would have been to him, his height and strength being what they were.

Events took a different turn.

Mrs Buckie had grown overweight in recent years. The doctor had warned her either to lose six stones or to take life easy. She did neither. So one fine spring morning, while feeding the hens, she dropped like a stone into her own field.

Old Buckie came round the gable end of the house to find her flat on her back; a burly effigy surrounded by a hundred hens. Her white fists were still shut on a quarter pound of meal, and the maddened hens were pecking at the grains trapped behind the stilled gates of her fingers.

Her man never recovered from the shock. Thin as a peeled stick to start with, he shrank to a reed, then to a hair. Finally he faded out altogether.

By that time Jock had been neglecting his studies so much, what with doing the work of the farm and taking days off school, that it cushioned the blow of not being able to stay on for the bursary exam and proceed to university.

Not that he failed. His Highers came out as a brilliant set of results, with a special commendation written to the rector by the Examination Board. Mr Robin showed Jock the letter.

'A remarkable mind you have, John,' he said. 'Your Leaving Certificate reveals a most astounding display of all round ability, especially in the light of your recent troubles. And the letter says here that the quality of some of your answers simply transcends the examination questions themselves. I don't know what to say, except that you must stay on into the Sixth Form and sit the scholarship exam.'

Jock said there would be no point in that now. As his parents were both dead, things needed looking after at home.

'But John,' said Mr Robin, 'I'm sure in a case like yours certain provisions can be made. Let me write a few letters. Why, I shall go so far as to say that Mrs Robin, my good lady, would welcome you into our home as a free boarder. Our own children have all flown the nest some time ago, and—'

'It's no use sir,' Jock interrupted him. Thank you *very* much indeed, sir, it's most kind of you. But no. My parents may be dead but they're still alive in me. The old place at Caiplie may not be much, but it meant a lot to my father. You see—'

Jock paused, looking hard at the spines of Mr Robin's books, glittering round the walls. He cleared his throat and went on.

'You see, it stood between him and—and his past.'

'You mean his vagrant days, when he was a . . . when he . . .'

'Was a tinker.'

Jock finished the sentence.

'Yes, sir. The point is I feel I owe it to his memory to keep the place going. At least for just now. I'm sure to get to university soon.'

'Yes, I see, John, I see. But surely your father would have treasured the building of your academic future more than the—shall we say the more mundane edifices of Caiplie?'

'There's more to it than that, sir. My sisters. All young girls. They'll be leaving school in the not too distant future, I expect. If I can see them through first, see them on their feet. Then maybe I could apply to sit the scholarship exam in a few years from now. I'll still be fairly young.'

The rector looked down through his sad white moustache. He inspected his polished brown brogues.

'Not so easy, once you've left school, John,' he said sorrowfully. The system doesn't cater for it. You might have to pay your own way. And what will have happened to your brain by then—your impetus?'

Each of them listened to the inexorable tick of the pendulum in Mr Robin's dark study.

'I'm sorry, sir,' Jock said at last.

'Yes, yes, of course. I'm sorry too,' Mr Robin murmured. 'More sorry than I can say. You are without a doubt the most brilliant scholar I have encountered in my entire career.'

They shook hands.

Jock soon changed the way of the croft.

He smartened everything up, house and barn, and his hand on the plough soon made its mark on the land. The seasons turned over like water.

His first harvest was almost in when Jessie came to him through the stooks.

'Jock,' she said, 'I want to go back to the school next year and take the exams. I want to go to Moray House College of Education and learn to be a teacher.'

Jock screwed up his eyes. He watched the sun westering behind Kellie Law.

'You'll be a fine teacher, Jessie,' he said.

He had made a small profit out of his first year's crofting, which he had put into the bank against the day when he would go to university. With the income from the harvest, he calculated, it would suffice to start Jessie off on her three-year course at Moray House.

The waves went over the croft: the russet wave of autumn, the white wave of winter, the green wave of spring, the golden wave of summer. Then again: autumn, winter, spring, summer, the sea rolled over the land.

Once more Jock stood among his stooks, turning them to the Bass Rock to face the golden, drying wind. This time it was Euphemia who came to him.

'The teachers are saying I can take my Leaving Certificate, Jock. I'd like to do that if you could afford it. I'd like to follow Jessie to Moray House and be a teacher.'

Jock examined the dryness of the corn, rubbing the yellow ears through his dusty fingers.

'Aye, Phemie,' he said. 'Be a teacher, right enough. A grand occupation. Jessie's very near there.'

Agnes the youngest worked away inside at her books. On the four squares of window she saw the wheel of the seasons roll by, over the croft. Over and over.

Then it was her turn to speak to Jock.

There were not so many stooks that year. The sky was an unbroken blue; the sun had wanted to burn the corn, not ripen it.

'But we'll get you to the College of Education, Agnes,' Jock said, his hand on the youngest's shoulder. 'Jessie's teaching in Stonehaven, and Phemie's just a year to go in Embro. It's only right you shall have your turn.'

They all had their turn. They all came back to the East Neuk to teach. Jessie went up country, to Dunino, to teach in the little schoolroom there. The other two stayed among the gulls and the drifters. Euphemia joined the staff of Cellardyke Primary School, and Agnes went to Crail.

All three were accounted very competent teachers of bairns. And all three carried on living at Caiplie, where they looked after their brother. It had taken nine years to get them all through school and college and onto their feet.

Jock was twenty-six.

He went inside the house and looked at the single row of text books up on the high shelf, among the baking tins. They were powdered with flour.

He took down Caeser's *Gallic Wars* and sat down at the table. The window was four blue squares, framing his bent head. The four panes turned purple, black, grey, white, then egg-shell blue. Seasons whirred by. Years.

A red wave passed over Europe, as Jock's teacher had predicted.

So the skies changed with the seasons, and so did the surrounding farmland. But the patch of land at Caiplie did not alter much after that. Jock soon stopped farming it. The sisters had their income anyway and told him there was no longer any need for him to push dirt from one place to another and back again. There were better ways to make a living. Couldn't he try some of them?

Jock browsed among his books, bought in some scrap metal, fed a few hens.

A second red wave went round the world.

He drifted down the years to middle age, old age.

By that time the middens had multiplied like molehills. The scrapheaps rusted and flaked. The croft reverted to ruin.

Over the years Jock's dreaming hulk became known to all the folk on the coast. The bus passed along the sea road from St Andrews to Leven twelve or twenty times a day, depending on how the drivers felt about it. And hardly a day but Jock could be seen, slumped on a silent tractor in the hollow of his field, his forehead deep in a book. The tractor was out of petrol. Or he had just switched off in mid-dreel and switched on to Tacitus instead. It didn't matter. Jock and the tractor sat there together, two tons of rusting energy. Gulls wove whitely about them.

The bus driver slowed down between Crail and Kilrenny.

'That's Jock into Mons Graupius again,' somebody said. 'An awful man for learning is Jock.'

Next day the same folk would see him in the same position. The bus slowed, stopped, the engine idling.

'Has he been there a' nicht?'

There were gales of laughter from the back seat.

Jessie was on that bus, on a half day from Dunino. She got off at Cellardyke, she was mortified, and walked the mile back home, her face on fire.

When she got home she said:

'Jock, have you nothing better to do with your life than shame me in front of a busload of yokels and common seamen?'

The seamen liked Jock.

When they were at the lobsters they came close inshore to Caiplie, and Jock used to clamber out onto the skellies and have a yarn with them. The nattering went on for hours while two fathoms beneath them the creels silently filled up; the cold soldiers of the sea entering the meshes, wearing their Prussian-blue armour.

'Mons Graupius,' Jock said, embarking on the favourite topic of his later years—though he talked on many a subject to any that would listen—'Mons Graupius. The battle that the historians could never properly place.'

Jock could place it though.

Not in the north. That was the mistake all the scholars had made. But with his knowledge of the Gaelic as well as of Latin and Greek, and Ancient History, Jock had pinpointed the exact site of the historic battle, where Agricola hammered the Picts, as being in the Ochil hills of Fife itself, AD 84.

'There's a particular hill there that's like a whale. Very like a whale, you might say. Now this peculiar likeness is vital to my case.'

Then he was off in Gaelic and Greek, and the fishermen were lost. They hauled their creels, and the sea-miracle had happened again, like loaves and fishes. The titbits of cod-heads and conger-eels had gone, and the pots were full of the Prussian army.

'Great stuff, Jock,' the fishermen said. 'You're a lucky man for us. The labsters must like your stories aboot Mons Graupius.'

He told it over and over the years, refining it, modifying, adducing the evidence, maturing it in his skull.

He told it to seagulls and crows.

When the old men took their summer night constitutionals out of Cellardyke, and if it was fine calm weather, they strolled along as far as the Coves. Jock could often be seen on the shoulder of the hill, still as a standing stone, black against the sky's burning gold, his idle scythe propped on a fence stob.

'Come down, Jock,' they shouted.

And he'd start out of his dwaam and climb down to the foreshore among rabbit holes and boulders and tussocks and clumps of whin.

The stories on nights like these would be a long time in the telling, while the still blue tide turned pink and cream, and the stars pricked holes in the sky, and the moon set sail on the firth: a gondolier on glass.

'Mons Graupius will make me famous yet, before I die.'

He said this in his old age.

The patterns of life along the coast changed slowly. But they changed. Like the traditional design in an old shawl, the stitches were pulled out, run down, and the community clad itself in newer garments of work and play and prayer.

The steam drifters thinned out as the Fifies had given way before them, the noisy warlords of the fishing grounds. And even the seine-netters purred themselves into a final sleep. The harbours were visited now by huge clodhopping boats with superstructured hulls. Mostly the harbours were empty: playponds for stone-throwing boys, with no work waiting for them after leaving school.

Only the waves never stopped their comings and goings.

The land-waves rose and fell with infinite inevitability: ploughed, planted, barleyed and stubbled, and ploughed again. And the farmers walked about their quiet decks: decks green with young corn and splashed with the foam of daisies.

Even here there were new sights: blinding swathes of rape-seed, foreign fields laid out in the sun like sheets to dry. The talk for a time was of the Common Market.

The sea-waves never changed, except that they were not so full of fish as they used to be, before the two red waves swept Europe and the world. They sent out few boats; they brought home fewer catches;

and always the catches were smaller. The truth was that the waves were nearly empty.

The steeples continued to point the route to heaven: up through the shredded white net of gulls and into the blue sky, where God lived. But not so many folks crocodiled their way to the kirks on a Sunday. They were inside watching Wogan, The Price is Right, Eastenders.

And then the clever folk arrived. Professors of Sociology and retired Insurance brokers, filling up the abandoned fisher houses after the National Trust had done its work.

The lobsters crept reluctantly into the creels these days. The Prussian Army was thinning out.

It was a Professor of Ancient History from St Andrews who finally put paid to Jock. The professor was doing the Coastal Walk for tourists one fine summer night when Jock flagged him down and took him prisoner.

He marched him into the Coves.

'Look here,' said Jock, directing him to the back of the Chapel Cove, 'do you see these crosses carved into the stone? They were put there by St Adrian and his monks away back in the Dark Ages. Not so dark, eh?'

The professor smiled. His name was Dobsworth.

'They were in all probability scratched there last summer by a couple of tourists, for a lark. Or even by you when you were a nipper. No offence, you know—too young to remember.'

Jock was patient with him. Captive audiences were hard to come by.

'Ah, no, professor. Tell me, look at them closely. Does nothing strike you as odd about them?'

'No.'

'Nothing ever so slightly unusual? Think now.'

'No.'

'Alright then. Here, take my penknife. Now, carve yourself a cross.'

Professor Dobsworth hesitated.

'Go on,' said Jock.

'Very well, I'll do it over here, so as not to desecrate your sanctuary, you understand.'

The professor moved aside a little and carved a tiny cross without fuss.

'There you are,' he said.

'Thank you, professor,' said Jock. 'But don't you see the difference between your cross and the others? Why did you carve it in that particular position?'

'What other way should I do it? I really don't see what you're getting at. Unless—'

Suddenly Dobsworth saw it.

'Of course. The other crosses are all carved on their sides—most unusual, I agree. Nobody would think of carving them from that angle.'

'But somebody did.'

Jock was triumphant.

'Even you, professor, seeing the evidence in front of you, you still followed your contemporary human instincts, and carved yours the right way up.'

A bee buzzed in Dobsworth's brain. It couldn't find the right flower. But for Jock's benefit he put on an easy smile.

'Naturally, naturally,' he said. 'Whereas of course the Dark Age peoples, who were responsible for these crosses, they carved them on their sides because . . .'

He extended an open palm towards Jock in a gesture of polite submission. He was apparently allowing him the luxury of completing the obvious inference.

'Because that way they are meant to represent Christ actually carrying his cross to Calvary. That's why the crosses are all on their sides. I know right well you were stringing me along there, professor. You didn't need me to explain all that to you, and I've seen it for years since I was a boy. But how many other folk know it, eh?'

'Ah, precisely.'

Dobsworth took out his card.

'We gentlemen of learning must stick together—Jock, did you say? And tell me, Jock, what other things have you seen and thought about since you were brought up here?'

That was how it started.

The professor began taking regular walks down by Caiplie. It was no longer Jock's lone megalith that could be seen etched against the summer skies. The two of them were always together in animated conversation: Jock flinging his great arms about, a perambulating windmill; the professor nodding gravely, nodding sagely.

And him quite a young man too.

It just went to show you, folk said proudly, that the Scots could teach the smart-arsed English a thing or two. They ought to point out *that* in the next SNP manifesto.

And there was the high and mighty St Andrews, sitting at the feet of Cellardyke—well, of Caiplie, anyway, and taking notes into the bargain. A busy doctor of learning gathering his academic nectar from an old ploughman on the greyer side of eighty, and content to pass the time of day with him, every day. Not bad for old Jock.

The days dwindled, drifted towards winter. It grew cold for conversation.

The old men drew closer to the sheltering dykes, cutting their crack to a minimum, stamping their boots. The two scholars took to going indoors.

Jock's sisters were delighted to have such a visitor. They polished up their framed certificates, which told the world that they were qualified to deal with Primary Education.

'Tell the professor about Mons Graupius,' they said.

'What's that? You've never mentioned that one, Jock.'

Jock stroked silver stubble. He had been saving it.

'Oh, well, I thought maybe you were more interested in the history of this locality hereabouts. Mons Graupius, that's a different tack altogether. West Fife.'

'No, no, Jock, let's hear it. Anything that concerns the past is fascinating to me. The place doesn't matter. We're two of a kind, you and I.'

Jock explained his theory. Professor Dobsworth listened in silence. His lips and eyes were like stone, but something twitched underneath his temple.

After Jock had finished his spiel, Dobsworth said:

'You know, Jock, with Latin and Greek we are on common ground, you and I. The ground familiar to scholars such as ourselves, you may say.'

The sisters simpered by the sideboard.

'But when you go into Gaelic like that, you rather lose me, I'm afraid. There, mine is merely an academic understanding, I'm, afraid, and not a competent one at that. You were brought up speaking it, along with English, I understand.'

'Mother's milk,' said Jock.

'Quite. You have the advantage of me, you see.'

Jock poured out more tea.

'Do you want me to go over it all again, professor?'

Dobsworth got up.

'No thanks. I won't take more tea, Jock. But I'll tell you what. If you don't mind—my secretary, Miss Barnes. She's terribly keen on just this sort of area, as a sort of spin-off, nothing more, from more important areas of study she's helped with in the past. Perhaps she could come along with me next time and hear you?'

'No reason why not,' Jock said.

'Fine, fine, I'll say goodbye then. Many thanks for the tea, Euphemia. Delicious scones. Agnes, Jessie. Goodbye.'

At the door he paused.

'You wouldn't have any objection to Miss Barnes bringing along her cassette recorder, I don't suppose? And her short-hand note-pad?'

'What for?' asked Jock.

'Oh,—secretaries!'

Professor Dobsworth's dismissive tone and gesture indicated what he thought of them; their infernal tapes and memo jotters; their passion for having things down on record. One simply had to humour them.

It'll keep her amused,' he said. 'keep her out of mischief.'

And so the next night the recording session went ahead. Amid a mountain of scones and jam, and pots of tea. None of which Professor Dobsworth and Secretary Barnes appeared to be hungry enough to sample. In her tweeds and high heels Miss Barnes was not much at home with the sagging armchairs and low-beamed ceilings of Caiplie, where she battled womanfully with pencil and pad.

'Like a cat with worms,' Jock said afterwards to his sisters. 'Her backside was never at peace.'

When they left the professor apologised for their failure to partake of the hospitality that night.

'The talk, you know—so fascinating.'

It was the last talk he ever had with Jock.

The winter term ended, the university closed up, and in the January Professor Dobsworth went on sabbatical.

To write a book.

Jock went back to his *Gallic Wars* and *The Life of Agricola*.

The book appeared in the early summer. It was almost as though it had written itself.

Almost as though somebody had written it *for* the blighter, some of his waggish colleagues sniggered over their Madeira, while the blighter in question sunned himself in California, pulling his salary all the time. They'd heard the rumours. Cunning cove.

That was fair and square, folk argued. Old Jock was a great boy for the talking. But when it came to writing, now that was a different thing altogether. In the end what was Jock but a gossiper? It all just went to show you how it needed a man of proper and finished education actually to sit down and write a book. If Jock had had it in him, why hadn't he done it himself by now? Good grief, he'd had eighty years to see to it. Dobsworth wasn't even forty.

The book had a stirring title—you had to hand it to Dobsworth. *Soldiers, Saints and Sinners.* After that came the sub-title: *Archaeological Evidences of the Romans, Missionaries and Vikings in the Kingdom of Fife from the 1st to the 10th centuries A.D.*

There was an entire chapter on Mons Graupius.

Many of the stories that had been told while the old men puffed their pipes and the lobsters filled the creels were written down for the first time, with illustrations. Most of the lobstermen who had heard them were dead now. If they'd been alive they'd have recognised old Jock's phrases, and recalled summer nights purring home to Crail, loaded to the gunwales.

There was a signing session at a St Andrews bookshop. Locals went up by the score and bought their copies. Not a bad buy at nine pounds ninety-five pence—and a very nice dust jacket, with an artist's impression of the Coves on the front.

During the session Dobsworth sat behind a blue barricade of books that was taken down block by block as his biro flashed and the folk went away examining his swift scrawl.

The photographer from the *East Fife Recorder* appeared. After he'd taken a couple of shots, somebody said:

'Here, isn't that Jock Buckie out there?'

You could hardly miss the man, could you?

'Why not get Jock to come inside?' the bookshop manager suggested. 'You could take him standing next to the professor, shaking hands or something. That would be a scoop, wouldn't it?'

'Better not,' said Dobsworth. 'He's a very shy man in crowds. I'll see Jock myself, in private.'

But nobody saw much of Jock after that.

The standing stone returned to the fields that summer. Only this year nothing could rouse it from its deep containment.

The sisters had to shout louder and longer for him to come in for his tea.

And the day came when he stopped answering altogether.

A cold day it was, but he never seemed to mind the cold. A silent hulk in the long untended grasses of Caiplie, his great back stiff against a dyke. A stone in his hand, and his head bent, examining it.

Finding in it a story that he might never tell.

The Poor Man's King

And so the king came down in winter to the edge of the River of Dreel.

A torrent of black thunders it was, crackling with spate.

The stars shivered on their thrones, waiting to see what he would do. It was not a world in which kings went wandering on the naked spine of winter, and this one alone and unhorsed. How many stars had salted the sky since last a king came to Anster?

He stopped at the fording place, snarling and slapping at his feet. The causey to East Anster was deeply awash. A fast spring tide was ripping up the sands to counter the Dreel's charge, and the meeting of river and sea was a blind white warring. Where the king stood, a thousand water-sprites rattled and foamed in their chains, threatening to break loose.

'Deil confound ye if I am to get weet this nicht!'

The king's curse exploded in a noiseless frost-cloud of breath that was lost among the clash of waters. He was two days out of Falkland and nine miles from St Andrews, still with dry shoon, and without so much as a kenning finger or a narrowed eye laid on him by any of his subjects. They were gannet-sighted and seagull-tongued, the folk of the east coast.

But the guise had worked a treat.

A great cloak fell from his shoulder in a strong brown curve—anonymous as a ploughed field. The hem of the cloak brimmed about his feet and a broad hat tilted its orbit round his head, with one eye tucked under the slant like a star. Yes, he was more like a Wanderer himself than a king; lord of the winds; one of old mother earth's roadsters, for sure. Nobody seeing him would even have whispered it to a stone in the road that the Goodman of Ballengiech, royal James, the Fifth of that name, was making his way across his kingdom.

A secret stitch threading itself through the grey fabric of the land— a single stitch of gold, passing as quickly and as silently as gold does from place to place. Till on that particular night in the calendar the Dreel put a sudden stop to the unconventional royal progress.

His eyes took in the distance to the other side. The thoughts birled

73

beneath the wide hat and another frost-cloud formed on his lips and died on the air.

'Micht as weel be France—or for the maitter o' that, the moon!'

Roaring with winter it was, the Dreel, hardly more than a brattling burn in the summer. But right now it was as though a black artery had been opened in the hills, letting the earth's life-blood run loose. Down it came, gushing and spouting, down past snoring shepherds and stalled cows, clothed with the steam-clouds of their breath and the warm smells of milk and dung; down past the dumb black ploughlands and rime-hung roofs of the cotter folk; ending its mad career by splintering the townstead of Anster into Easter and Wester and spilling itself in froth and fury into the pounding sea.

On the sea side the tide tore into it with a roar, an assault even wilder than the river's unfettered force. The ford itself reeled and seethed. In their drunken crashing and tumbling the interlocked circles of foam broke ranks, swung out dancing into the road, swilling and slurping about the king's legs.

He stepped smartly back. He saw himself in three hours time, hirpling into St Andrews with red feet on fire and winter-legs sodden to bone and thigh. A poor prospect for a man who was only playing at being poor. And maybe even grimmer than that, he thought, studying the commotion. It was fast enough to lose your footing in and go down into Jordan for a second baptism.

"I've been born the aince—I've sair small need to get born aince mair.'

The irony flickered on his tongue like an icy flame. This was not getting him across.

He listened hard.

The night was a seamless robe, winter-pricked. Its billion stars were the small cold portholes to eternity, that black unbeating sea. The blood quivered and tingled in his veins. He looked quickly round about.

A fistful of fisher houses jostled each other down to the shore. There the steady sea-fingers plucked and pulled, plucked and pulled, and the shingle rang and sang—seabells swinging in dark harmony.

But the fisher folk themselves were all in long syne. Their boats were green-hauled, safely beached out of reach of the spray-laced hands of the firth. The king saw the shrouded masts, the hulls sleeping like whales. There was no handy cart, laden with nets, that could have borne him in a blink to the other side. These folk lived with their feet in the water. They wouldn't have thought twice about hurling across an old earthstepper like himself. But now their houses were steeked up tight as winter hay. They were shuttered and bolted and brimming with sleep; they'd be up with the next tide. The lums were stacked blackly against blossomings of stars. He looked hopefully for a spark or two, a release of little red syllables perhaps from the busy conversation going on in the grate, somewhere under the dark roof. And the cold king could all but hear the tongues of flame gossiping among wedges of peat, and the folk cracking stories round the fire.

That was a pastoral myth, he thought. Nobles hunted and fought, burgesses bought and sold, kirkmen prayed on their knees—and the poor folk just worked and slept; nothing more.

Gloomily he hunkered down. The brawling in the road was inexorable; it would not be commanded. Even Canute had failed to stop the moon-pull on the sea. Such, according to that old story, was the breath of kings.

Down on the beach now the breakers were bellowing like bulls; wilder waves swept up the wet sands. The tide was fairly keeping up its tirade. Gathering up fields of sea-wrack, driftwood, boulders, bones, it surged in under the stars. The crossing boiled like a cauldron.

James frowned, fumed. He could feel the frost forming round his beard; an icy brightness.

A tinkle of laughter burst like breaking glass from a shuttered house further downstream. The Wheatsheaf Inn was built on the boundary of St Nicholas kirkyard on the west bank of the Dreel. Sentinelled by tombstones and waves, it took the sea's stress in winter and held back the darker tide of eternity all the year round. It rode out many a storm of its own every other night—and right now an ale-storm was brewing up in there, behind battened hatches.

The king licked the fiery frost from his beard. A mulled ale would work the world's wonders now on his bewintered belly. A second flagon would work its way down to his feet, taking them through the churning flood without a care for all those frozen footsteps needed to get him to the West Port of St Andrews.

But after the third flagon, he reflected, I wouldn't want to leave at all—and he pondered the notion of biding there all all night. In his head though, he saw the eager, questing eyes fixing on him over a circle of frothing rims, heard the sharp, speiring tongues of the east coasters, unlocked by ale. That would not suit his purpose, to let word get through the West Port by morning that the king was on his way. and get through it would, like a whisper of wind up the water. He clung tightly to the all-concealing cloak, and he continued to sit there, brooding over the chaos of waters.

'Hast thu thocht o' biggan a boat, Maister Noah?'

The voice broke warmly on his shoulder, but the girl wasn't even looking at him. Her eyes were already measuring out the best route for the crossing. She kicked off her wooden shoon, tossed them into the wickerwork scull she carried on her thigh—a gleaming purple wetness of mussels filled it to the brim—and stepped barefooted into the river.

'Bide there!' commanded James, rising to his full height. 'Tak me owre, wilt thu?'

The girl turned, her basket resting on the one hip, her free hand on the other. She tilted her face at him. A fine figurehead she'd make for a fair vessel, the king thought. She seemed not to notice the ice-cold clamour that was going on round her ankles.

'I canna tak in what I'm hearan,' she lilted above the din. 'Here was I thinkan you micht have offered to bear a poor lass's burden for her. But no fear o' that, gentle sir, thu wants me instead to tak it up ane hunder fold. Awa wi' thu!'

James pointed at the dripping rim of his cloak.

'Certain it is, then, that my hosen and shoon, aye, and maybe my breeks forbye, are like to be fair drookit in the Dreel—and what's on my back and legs is all my warldly goods, let me tell thu.'

'God bless thy bonny stockans, man, then thu hast owre muckle!'

The fisher lass sang defiance at him and the young king under the cloak was stirred to a kind of flushed surrender. But that was but courtliness. He wanted to be the master of this fair craft, whose words tumbled out of her like the sea's blue wine.

'Cannot thu see there's some folks have even less on their backs than hast thu, to pleiter through the watter wi'?'

There was a crust of salt on the voice. He drank down her speaking greedily.

'And so a sicht less than thu to fret aboot, as poor's thu sayst thu art!'

She kicked a footfull of frothing droplets at him, showing him her naked feet and unstockinged legs.

'Then what has thu in the warld to lose, lass?' countered the king. 'Tak me owre and thu shalt have my benison.'

The girl had waded deeper into the broil and the cold roaring was by this time past her knees.

'Thy benison's small use to me, man. And I canna see for why a lass like me should shouther a sturdy roadster like thasel—and all to keep thy auld duds from the weet. Just wha dost thu think I be?'

'Aye, lass, and just wha dost thu think that I be?'

The girl turned slowly in the water. The voice was now a young man's voice. It rang like a gong between the stars and the white surge. Never before had she heard such an accent of authority.

The man's teeth sparkled out of his beard.

'Nine miles near hand to gan this nicht, my lass, and it will be wi' bitter banes and sodden soles except thu gets me up thy back.'

His tones were softer now, but were unlike those of the old man of the road.

'And thu kenst what they say in these pairts—if thy feet's cauld, the rest o' thu's cauld.'

Still she made no move. River and sea lathered her bare legs. The star-strung sky dripped its rime. The king waited.

'Return, return, O Shulamite!' he intoned wooingly.

The girl came laughing to greet him then through the hissing wilderness.

'So,' she said, staring into the shadows of his face—the hat was like a targe on his head—'thu 'rt the Goodman o' Ballengiech himsel, art thu so?'

The laughter flickered about her lips. James removed the shielding hat, and she saw the rusty hair of the man she had sometime heard tell of as the king of the realm.

'Or art thu by ony chance The Red Fox?'

'That's twa titles by whilk some folk cry me,' he said. 'And afore this nicht's oot thu michtst call be by ane ither. Wilt thu tak me owre nou?'

The fisher girl laid down her basket at the king's feet.

'Weel, since thu wantst owre to East Anster, I'll tak thee, man. But if thine airt had lain from easter to waster, I wouldna have taen thu supposan thu hadst been ilka ane o' all the Stuarts rowed up thegither!'

James laughed loud and long.

'And what the deil's the difference, lass, atween easter and waster, except thu 'rt on the sea?'

'Bide here ane day or twa, an thu wouldna be speiran a daft thing like yon!'

She flung back her field of fair hair. Already the king wanted to grow wild flowers in it. Here was neither courtship nor rhetoric. And who indeed would learn to be servile before the sea? I might bide a night in this place after all, was the silent thought of the Red Fox.

Aloud he said, 'Weel, I'll no mak question o' thy quaint ways, bonny lass. Just tak me owre and I'll be fine pleased.'

The girl started kilting up her skirts, tucking them into her girdle. James looked at her long cold white thighs. Later that night he would bring warmth to them.

'Is't as deep as thon, dost thu think?

'The bairns are for aye playan at the ford. Ilka chuckie stane has been cast oot to sea lang syne. It's nocht but a mush o' mud, the bed o' yon burn.'

James twirled his cloak at it.

'Thon's some burn!'

'Aye, all things are waur in the winter, that's for certain. And wi thy wecht on me I'd be sure to gan doun deep.'

She turned her back on him and held out her arms.

'Climb aboard, my lord—and pray I dinna capsize.'

And she carried the cloaked king into the welter of water. The flood soon boiled up again over her knees, the white tongues of foam licking her thighs like white fire. James felt her sinews strain with her sinking and striving through the sucking mud as she struggled to keep her footing. He hoisted himself higher up her back, wrapping his legs round her hip-bones.

'Hing on, man!'

'Dinna thu fret—I'm gaun up the craw's nest!'

The flurries of water flew about them. She was wet to the waist and splashed from girdle to face by the time they had reached the other side. Lumps of froth spattered her hair.

'Thu canst step ashore nou, maister!' she shouted at him in laughs and gasps. 'Albeit thu didst near hand cowp the boat!'

James slid down and she placed her hands on her flanks, arching herself back to relieve the strain.

'And what do folk cry this fair vessel I have just taen passage on?'

'Phoebe Holland, at thy service, sir.'

And I'll take your helm in hand, fair Phoebe, he told himself, looking at her wet loins and her bright flushed face.

'What's thy fare, fisher lass? Thu shalt have a king's thanks.'

The girl shook her head at him.

'No siller, my lord. To have taen the king himsel oot o' Wast Anster is fee enough for me.'

'But thu has kilted up thy skirts for the king's sake, Phoebe, and the king hath pledged thee his benison.'

'No wi' siller, my gracious lord.'

James whipped off his cloak and threw it about her.

'Very weel, O Phoebe fair. Then thu 'lt let me fetch thee thon scull o' mussels from across the Dreel. For as thu 'lt bring to mind, thu has left them in West Anster.'

And without another word he was floundering through the Dreel. He was back with the basket in less than a minute, soaked and shivering by her side.

'What in God's good name did tak possession o' thee, man? After I
had taen thee owre as dry 's thu started oot on the road!'

Her eyes were wide with wonder. The king's eyes crinkled.

'Ane favour deserves ane ither, they say. I was in thy debt, fair
Phoebe—nou thu art in mine. So it may be thu 'll have ane fire,
whaur I can get myself warm aince mair, and dry for the nicht?'

He pulled his cloak tighter about her and crowned her with his hat.
She gave him a slow smile.

'The fire has been low a lang time, sir, and I'm richt cauld mysel.
But I'll warrant we can steir the embers and warm oorsels something
weel.'

The king shouldered the scull.

'Lead thu the road then, Phoebe lass—and the king will look after
thy bait.'

And royal James followed the fisher girl down to the shore, where
the sea sang loudly on the east sands.

'Whaur's the grate?'

They stood blindly behind the cottage door that had so suddenly
shut out the stars. The room was a total eclipse.

Then the familiar world started to come back to James through the
tips of his senses: that silent roaring of air when it is encompassed by
roof-beams and walls; the whiff of scoured flagstones; bed linen,
bannocks and broth; the salt smells of the sea, the peat smells of the
earth; a wave of remembered warmth.

She led him to the grate. Except for her cold hand in his, she was a
shadowless whisper by his side. She had not yet been formed out of
the darkness.

Then he heard her blowing, and kneeled down beside her on the
stone hearth. Like the birth of myth, the earliest points of light winked
and went out and glowed into life again, tiny red stars from millions
of years long syne, swimming into ken. He saw her bending face laved
in the palest flush of the first dawn; her lips pouted at the bars like a
budding rose.

On one of the panelled ceilings at Falkland palace there was a
painting of the dawn wind. She was shown as a goddess, with
blowing lips just like those of the fisher lass. Spring flowers trailed
from her mouth, and her breath chased a forest of fading stars from
the sky. Her hair was the foam of the sea, her billowing dress the
daisy-flecked fields and sheep-studded folds.

He had seen such a face, too, in the corner of an old map. Rosy-

cheeked, blowing out ships into the world to meet its wonders—
mermaids and slumbering continents and whales.

'Phoebe,' he whispered.

Her ear was a sounding shell.

She did not take away her lips from the gathering redness: she blew
and blew till the grate was a cluster of stars. He twisted his hands
through her long trailing hair, lifting away its fiery points from the
glowing hearthstone.

'Thu has used thy lovely mouth enough, Phoebe Holland. Nou let
me try mine.'

His cold lips felt the warmth of hers. Two shadows trysted silently
on the walls.

The first flame suddenly burst in the grate. The shadows leapt and
danced like water.

'Oh, haste ye, dinna us waste ony time nou!'

She quickly bent again and laid on some kindling and a handful of
black nuggets.

'Whaur dost thu get coals in these pairts?'

'They be from the beach,' she answered. 'The sea's a quick
provider—aye, and it's quick to tak awa.'

At first the driftwood sparked and the sea-coal whistled and
squeaked and spat. The old sounds of forgotten forests, pressed by
milleniums beneath the rolling fathoms of firth. Red-hot bees fizzed
out about their legs, making the king jump and yell out.

'Wheesht! she breathed. 'There are neebors will hear thee—I shall
be affrontit!'

But before long the room was a bright quivering bay of light. As
one, they shed their clothes in a cold clump on the floor, a tangled
togetherness that started to produce steam. And king and commoner
stood dressed in the same golden flames, attended by shadows. There
was a wordless language of lips, hands, eyes, hair.

And for a long time after that they were king and fisher girl no
more, but only a man and a woman under one anonymous blanket,
underneath the shutters. Two tides meeting in the silent throbbings of
the fire.

Outside the stars slipped and tilted; the waves crashed up the east
sands, nearer the black cottage with its heart on fire. Closer and
closer, till the tarred walls were lashed with white splinters of sea.

Over at St Nicholas The Wheatsheaf Inn lurched through its
nightlong tempest of ale. A hurricane of oaths was raging at full force.
There was a crashing of tankards and heads. In the belly of the
kirkyard the dead slept on into the eternal ebb of time.

The man and the woman lay still now. Two sleeping statues

sculpted by a single hand, they had come together on a wild tide of their own making. Huddled between the white beatings of the sea on the one side and the red beatings of the fire on the other, they lay in the harbour of one another's arms, till the stars drained to the west, the shingle-sucking tide withdrew into the firth, and the fire was a white drift in the grate.

Two heads whispered in the stilled shadows of the hour-before-dawn; two breaths embraced; two tongues shed their secrets.

'Tell thu a truth to me, Phoebe,' said one of the heads. 'What's the difference atween East and Wast Anster?'

Two laughters together, muted and curtained still with the heaviness of sleep.

A seagull skimmed low over the grey wet sands. During the night the sea had slipped quietly away. The bird rose, skirling, in wide white spirallings, then banked sharply and settled on the cottage lum. There it tore the quiet hour to shreds. The stars were bright fish quivering in the dawn network: lacings of light and dark.

The tangled pool of hair lying beside the king rippled and stirred. A drowsy giggle came out of it.

'Och, they're full o' notions aboot themsels, the fancy folk o' Anster Waster, and weel enough do they ken that the East Anster folk have cracked jougs for heads. But I'm no so cracked in the head mysel as no to ken that the Wasters think themsels a station aboon us poor fishers east the Dreel.'

'But forwhy, Phoebe?'

'For they're a stane's cast nearer Embro, or Falkland for the maitter o' that. So they are just that bit closer a king than a cou, and that's the burden o't!'

'Weel weel,' laughed the king, 'wars in my kingdom—and I never kent!'

'No wars, man, no wars—yet we keep to our ain side o' the bed. We maun wed and dee on either side o' the Dreel, that's all. Twa kirks, twa kirkyards, aye, and wha kens—maybe twa eternities.'

They lay silent for a time after that. Then James spoke again.

'And hasna thu wed yet on the East side, Phoebe—thu that's come closer to thy king nor even the proud folk wast the Dreel?'

The gull left the lum and flew off wailing into the yellow lanes of light streaking the skyline.

Haiee, haiee, haiee, it cried.

The dawn net was in shreds. The cold blue morning was pouring through.

'I was wed aince, sir, a twelvemonth syne.'

The king raised himself on one elbow. He stroked the rivulets of yellow hair running across the bolster. The blood-red blades of early sunlight striped his nakcd skin. Underneatli his hands the girl's eyes stayedshut.

'And whaur's thy bonny young man nou, Phoebe?'

Haiee, haiee . . . the cry came over the firth, an echo from another time.

Silence.

He needed no answer now. But soon she talked a bit about the sayings of the old folk, that the spirits of drowned fishermen turned into gulls. Then their liberated voices could be heard crying from shore to shore, calling on their loved ones to follow.

'Thu's a richt young widow, Phoebe. Hou old was thy man?'

'He had twenty years on his back, no mair.'

'The same age as mysel,' James murmured to himself. How much too bonny was this Phoebe Holland to be the bride of gulls, and wedded to sea-sorrows and dirges of death.

Haiee, haiee, haiee . . .

Then he told her, to banish that empty wailing from her ears, of the many times he'd turned his back on the greybeards of Falkland. How they wagged their sage, counselling heads when he told them he was off again.

And forwhy, they'd speir? And what for this time?

To strike up kinship with the road, he'd say. For the road has no friends, and the folk of the road have only the road itself, and one another for a short time. Aye, and that's short enough. God kens.

So he followed his feet, stopping when the fancy took him to linger by firth and field; to grind a pickle oats between the millstones of his unringed hands; or lift a flounder out of the sallows of the sea.

Above all else, he said, just to sit down and take a crack with his own good Scots folk, and see how they lived. All those folk who tend the fields and sea with tiller and plough, who have nobody to look into their lives but God, while they fare across the surface of this earth. Blue furrows or brown furrows, salt clods or clay, what's the difference? They all get ploughed under themselves one day, by coulter or keel, the ordinary folk. And no man cares.

What good is a king except he cares?

So he went out to pay court to Lord and Lady Poverty. And they called him The Poor Man's King.

'Thu couldna hope for a better title,' she said.

'What dost thu hope for, Phoebe?' he asked.

Her eyes were empty as rock pools.

'Nothing, I suppose. Nothing that's on earth, or in the blue sea oot yonder. I'll just pick my mussels and dee.'

A shadow slipped into the bed and lay between them.

'Dinna thu speak like yon,' James muttered darkly.

'Oh, and what canst thu hope for thysel, thu that's a king, and hast the realm at thy feet?'

James opened the shutter a crack and saw the sea glintering away out past the sands. He looked at the horizon a long time.

'The kingdom's no at my feet,' he said. 'It's stuck fast in my thrapple.'

The wind from the far sea lifted his hair and he wrinkled his nose.

At last he said, 'But what I hope for maist o' all things in this warld, is ane son.'

'Ane son for ane heir.'

'No. Ane son o' mine, to call mine ain, that is for all.'

'What dost thu mean?'

'I never kent my father. Flodden was no just his dounfall, Phoebe, it was the field on the whilk all my broils and battles just began.'

She looked into his face, pale with morning. She tried to read the meaning of all the troubles that were written there. James closed the shutters and smiled.

'Never mind that nou, Phoebe, the sun's weel up and I maun gan. Let us see if I can depairt and no shame thee.'

At the door he pulled the hat low over his brow, swirled the great cloak like a field of furrows about him, and put his hand on hers over the latch.

'God save thee, Phoebe Holland, fair fisher lass.'

A meeting of lips under the lintel.

'Pray the Lord thu 'lt get thy son, dear king.'

He threw open the door. The ruffling currents of air caught his cloak and smothered her in it. Holding her for the last time, he pressed his hand into hers.

'And if ever thu shouldst get a son thysel, fisher Phoebe, spend this on him, for me.'

Then he was out among the gulls and the quick winds of morning.

A minute after that he was just a hat and a cloak striding away from the sea, over the fields to St Andrews.

Nine years later he was dead.

The Poor Man's King became the scourge of the Scottish nobles, who did not forgive his vindictiveness over them.

Two years before he died, the tide of history brought him in a pearl: his first son. And the same tide took him out again. One year after that, another tide came and went with the second boy.

The shadows lengthened over his mind.

After Solway Moss he stepped inside himself and put up the shutters.

On his death-bed, still a young man, he heard of the birth of Mary, the Queen of Scots to be. His sorrowing words are known to history.

'It cam wi' ane lass, and it will pass wi' ane lass,' he said from his cracked heart.

He turned his face to the wall.

And, when she heard that he was no more, a fisher woman wept for him in East Anster. For only she knew that he did have a son; one that lived and was never known to history.

But he was known well enough in Anster.

James Holland grew up to be a good fisherman. The herring dripped from his nets.

When seventeen winters had passed since the highest Stuart in the realm crossed over the Dreel, his mother gave him the gold to buy his own boat. Where and how she came by it, though, was the talk of the town on both sides of the Dreel, for she never had wed out of her widowhood, and got by with baiting and mending, other folk's nets and lines.

They christened the boat *The Fisher King*. That was Phoebe's naming of it.

James Holland had such good fortune with the vessel that he became famous in the East Neuk, and a substantial man forbye.

The folk there called him King James.

Phoebe Holland always laughed at the bye-name and said she could tell a story about that.

She never properly did.

Until old age took her, and inclined her to chatter a bit into her sunken wreck of a chin.

By that time James Holland had followed the way his name pointed and was a big name in the Low Countries, where even the skippers of the Dutch herring busses hailed him as King James.

He seemed to like it. Phoebe had been a proud one in her youth, and that was doubtless where he got it from, his vanity.

For years his mother sat under a soot-stained roof, mumbling something about carrying a king across the Dreel. Untrimmed, the wick drowned in the bowl of fish-oil that sputtered and stank. The ruby heart in the grate ceased its beatings and crumbled to a rusty pile of dust. Spittings of rain flew down the lum, churning it to a slow black mush.

A cat looked through the open door, twitching its tail in a blue oblong of sky.

'Aye,' she said to it—for there was nobody else to listen to her now—'and for nine months after that, I cairried ane ither king across the Dreel, back and forrit for three seasons, I cairried the king across the watter.'

The cat turned away in disgust—there were no pickings to be had here—and glowered at the gulls, foraging on the wrack.

'And thu 'art the image o' the king himsel, wha never kent father nor son.'

For a second the old woman's eyes were two shawled candles in her white shrunken skull.

A smile lingered like a strange perfume on the withered rose of her mouth.

The candle flames brightened briefly and went out.

As You Came From The Holy Land

When he stepped off the boat he put his hand into his belt and brought out a piece of Byzantine silver.

The fisherman called Jan looked at it.

'It shines like one of my herring,' he said, 'but what use is that to me? At least I can eat a dead fish.'

The soldier smiled.

'You Hollanders have your feet flat on the ground, for men who spend so much of their lives waltzing about on the waves. Here, take this instead.'

He delved into his tunic, rumpling the white Maltese Cross on his surcoat, and handed over a glittering yellow coin.

Now Jan grinned.

'That's what I call talking.'

He held it up in the sky, flashing eyes and teeth at it.

'It's like the moon, my friend, but without the blemishes. Thank you.'

His passenger watched as he thumbed it like corn.

'Strange, isn't it?' he said. 'Gold is even greater than Latin. It's a language everybody understands, even the ignorant, from here to Jerusalem.'

He took back the Byzantine crown.

'Still, the silver I offered you was good payment for such a short passage.'

Jan nodded.

'True, sir knight, the North Sea is not so wide. But it is deep enough. A single fathom will suffice to drown you in. And it is a web of storms.'

He seemed to debate with himself for a moment.

'The gold will also buy you a horse.'

The knight gazed at the great Dutch herring buss, a migrant castle waiting on the waves, ready to move off again. Though he smiled himself, his eyes were as destitute as the water.

'I saw only cold bellies in your hold, fisherman. Anything remotely four-footed seemed to me to be well salted down.'

Jan laughed.

'Yes, I live by the herring, but not by eating them, not if I can help it.'

He made a sweeping arc with his arm.

'There are farms all along this coast. Mention my name at any one of them. Van Hooght. And you'll be given a good horse. Tell the farmer I'll settle up with him on the next trip. I'm bound for Leith by tonight's tide.'

He dug an oar into the shingle and the keel danced lightly on the quivering tide. The boat ploughed a single furrow all the way back to the mother vessel, the oars fluting, scattering silver spores into the wake.

'Which way to Kilconquhar lands?' shouted the soldier.

'Ride west-south-west,' came the attenuated voice from the boat. 'The castle's not ten miles from here.'

The knight turned his back on the sea. Over the black boglands he could make out bright squares of cultivation: stubble, stooks of hay, a quill of smoke scribing whitely on the sky.

'They don't eat many herring up at Kilconquhar these days!'

The voice was by now so skeletal he thought at first it was a seabird's reedy crying. He turned an ear to the east.

'Not since Adam of Kilconquhar went off to the crusades!'

Had the words not signified something to the soldier he would not have been able to piece out what the fisherman was saying.

He smiled to himself with cold lips.

Adam of Kilconquhar was dead.

'And so I've come to make her a widow with my words,' he told the farmer at Crail. 'She that's been widowed these two years and not knowing it.'

After his sea-journey he mounted the wave of brown muscle with the relief of familiarity and set its ears west-south-west. The herring buss in the firth was rigged now with high cries of laughter in which the breath of ale blew strongly.

'Only Dutchmen would drink the health of a gold piece,' the soldier muttered.

But as he rode up the coast to Kilconquhar, the far shouts brought back other sounds, clamouring to be heard; sounds he had tried to exclude from his thoughts. And he saw again that terrible heraldry emblazoned on the protective shield the brain put up in vain.

Adam of Kilconquhar on the shattered ramparts of Krak des Chevaliers, disappearing under blocks of masonry that horses would not shift.

A bloodless face stared out at him from the rubble. The eyes sought a focus, rolled round the empty Syrian sky; the ears no longer heard the whooping of the Muslims massed on the plains beneath.

The white face opened its lips to speak. And a red well bubbled up over the bleached beard.

'Robert.'

He heard his own name spoken as though under the sea. He placed his ear close to the broken mouth, but all that he could hear was the sound of that red sea dragging boulders across its dying shore. He sat up again, shaking his head.

'Adam, I can't make you out. Can you hear me?'

A giant hailstone, sizzling hot, whistled past his ears and the wall behind him shivered and ceased to be. He coughed frantically in the acrid backwash of dust. When he opened his streaming eyes he saw that Adam of Kilconquhar's eyes were fixed on eternity.

There was little time to consider what he might have been seeing. Another rock from Muhammad's sling screamed its way into the ramparts. Adam of Kilconquhar went over the edge, with an avalanche of stones for his cairn.

But that was not the end of it. War has its own wizardries.

Pinned between two cracked megaliths, one ironclad arm of his friend still remained, torn off at the shoulder, and beribboned with red shreds of sinews that hung in festoons. Even under the armour he felt his own skin go to gooseflesh. The attitude was unmistakable: it was pointing due west, its forefinger rigid as a blade.

'Yes, friend, I see I must have no option but to follow your sign and carry the tidings—if I ever get out of here alive.'

A leering face thrust itself like a gargoyle over the holed battlements and he hurled his axe, halving it like an apple.

'There you are, Saracen, that will widen your grin for you!'

Two days later the Castle of the Knights fell to the Muslims.

'And tell me, sir knight, are the streets of the Holy City really laid with gold?'

A leprous beggar sat by the wayside, a pathetic patch of rags, huddled over a putrid herring. The fish was already a metropolis of maggots. He contemplated the snow blisters, where once a face had been.

'Can't you tell the difference between the old and the new Jerusalem, friend?' asked the soldier.

'I don't well understand that, knight.'

Lazarus repeated his question.

And why, thought the soldier, why destroy this poor creature's vision of riches?

Yet again the words came at him, more a plea than a demand.

'Are they paved with gold then, as people say?'

'That they are, my friend—and walled with pearl too.'

A smile lit the white face: the sun in the winter remembering the spring. He saw again the drained face of Adam, the red well, and that grisly pointer.

'Can you spare a piece of that holy gold, sir?'

The leper's half jocular request tugged him out of his reverie. He drew the silver that the Dutch skipper had refused and tossed it into the beggarman's lap.

'Here, try a piece of Byzantium!'

The pile of rags fluttered with joy. Before it could find a tongue the soldier had spurred on his way.

No. Jerusalem the Golden was a fantasy.

One of his ancestors had taken part in its capture, in the First Crusade, and all he could remember were streets strewn with bowels and brains and doorsteps awash with blood. His stories had been passed down from mouth to mouth, a pitcher brimming scarlet. He saw drains choked with arms, legs, heads. Not an ounce of gold. The stories of crusaders riding up to their horses' bridles in blood were merely an exaggeration. But that the Jews were massacred by the Christian knights in their own city was unfortunately true.

Now it was in Saracen hands.

But stories of God's golden city and a land flowing with milk and honey had put reins and helms into the hands of the first volunteers. Two hundred years ago such stories had steered ships and horses eastwards to wrest the Sepulchre of Christ from the infidels. They simply mortgaged their lands, deserted their families, and left. After all, Christ himself had spelt it out clearly. Whoever does the will of my Father in Heaven is my brother and my sister and my family.

Two centuries later the stories still cast their spell, as they had done over him.

Stories spun out of the gold of imagination.

He had heard them from his great-grandfather, who had fought in the Third Crusade, with Richard.

Of how forgiveness of sins continued to be granted to all who travelled to the holy land as soldiers of Christ. Of how Richard the Lionhearted had come down with fever, and Saladin had graciously sent him jewelled caskets containing peaches and pears, and snow from Mount Hermon to dowse the furnaces in his head. And when he saw Richard's horse fall in battle, the same Saladin, with great magnificence, had sent him a groom and two fresh horses, and so had lost the battle himself.

Of how fortunes lay like spawn spilt across the east. With one hand a man could simply bend down and scoop up a hundred times more than he'd spent to buy his passage out.

And of the deep carmine carpets, crimson hangings and damask tapestries—forests of civilisation; the tables inlaid with ivory from the tusks of Hannibal's elephants; new fruits called lemons and melons and apricots—grown from bird-borne seeds, birds that had flow past Eden five thousand years ago, when the world was first created; new spices, ginger and cloves, to whet men's craving for the wine of love; new colours, lilac and indigo; and muslins and satins that whispered strange desires to those who wore them—perfumed ladies veiled to the very eyes.

And music to unlock their bodices and knees . . .

'Some good, my gentle master, for Jesu Christ's sake!'

Another beggar stood in the bracken. A bent thing with one arm extended like a knotted stick from its rags. So bent, he couldn't tell whether it was man or woman.

'Two beggars in the same quarter of the hour,' the soldier said. 'How is this? I thought that bread was in every mouth in the time of Alexander.'

The voice that came out of the rags was of equally indeterminate sex, a candle long gone down to a guttering whisper.

'Adam of Kilconquhar sold many farms, my master, and made many a beggar for Christ's sake. Do you hear tell of him out there?'

'God hears tell of him.'

The soldier took out another silver piece and spun it at the begging creature, who caught it expertly and froze it in the air.

A hunchback holding a star.

'Your name, good master, that I may mention it in my prayers?'

The knight touched his horse's flanks and sawed at the reins to get past.

'Pray for the soul of Robert tonight!' he shouted over his shoulder.

Aye, the soul of Robert stands in sore need of patching. It too has been in the wars since I left my own lands for holier ground.

He came over the rise and Kilconquhar loch flashed like a buckler beneath his feet.

The reality, in truth, had been different from the dream.

In the idealism of his youth he had taken monastic vows and followed the Benedictine Rule of poverty, chastity and obedience. He took the road through Asia Minor to join the Knights Hospitallers, and to care for sick pilgrims on the route to the Promised Land.

God knows, it was easy to fall sick on the way to God's own acres. The sun beat down on their helmets, grilling their dancing brains. Insects and bees maddened them inside the mailcoats, where blisters festered and spread like lichens on gravestones. Many of his comrades threw off their armour on the trail. A thousand breastplates caught the sun between Aleppo and Tripoli and bounced it back to Spain. Ruined horses crumpled under their riders, desiccated mountains of flesh that never rose again. The Syrian sun and the burning birds of prey fought between them to see which would strip the dead beasts first. Two hours of black putrefaction, then an eternity of white cages through which the hot winds blew, their doors gaping open. Dissension, distance and disease, all took their toll, and the Turkish guerillas picked off man after man, making a mockery of chivalry.

When he came to Krak des Chevaliers, he found that the crusaders had changed their character since the days when his ancestors had carried Jesus on their lances. Prisoners earning remission, debtors escaping their creditors, bounty hunters, dark, obsessive spirits, and troublesome younger sons, sent out to do some good in the world and give their fathers peace on their pillows. Beneath the Maltese Crosses buzzed an inferno of sins.

Then the power of the Muslims came to a head, and the crusaders were simply ringed in to make the best of it. Acre was under constant threat. Antioch had fallen. It was with a feeling of relief that he saw the soldiers of another god come to crack the great carapace. And at the burst heart of the battle, a dead man's hand pointed the way home.

So he set his face to the west. Anatolia, Italy, Germany, Holland. A ten month slog . . .

'Look out there, sir knight!'

The hunting party had found him at the edge of the loch. The horse was drinking among the reeds, its rider a drooping statue, contemplating his own dejection.

'Do you wish help and hospitality, sir?'

He stirred and passed his hand over his forehead. The sun was dancing on the water. He'd seen these false waves a thousand times before, in the mirages of the desert.

'He's a Hospitaller, my lady,' cried one of the grooms who had accosted him. 'Not long back by the look of him.'

The lady in charge of the chase cantered along the bank. She studied him curiously.

'I doubt that all of him is back yet,' she said quietly.

Her voice made him look up. With the light in his eyes it was hard to make out her face, but he knew that she was pretty. He saw only a woman clothed with the sun.

He reached for his voice.

'May I inquire your name, lady?'

'That may depend on you, sir, according to the news you bring me.'

He pulled at the reins, taking the horse out of the water and facing her on the bank.

'My news is that Adam of Kilconquhar has paid the soldier's price.'

Now he could see how tall and slender she was, even as she sat on her horse. He gazed at her for a long time in silence. No-one else moved or spoke, according to courtesy.

'And how do you find me, sir knight, now that you have taken your fill?'

'I beg your pardon, lady. You are a lofty and a lovely tower, in which a man might lie captive many a year without complaint.'

She smiled.

'I see that you have had the time to study poetry in the east, sir. Anything else?'

'The tower in question has a gracious window, my lady.'

And not heavily curtained, he thought, like the dark windows of the east.

She read his thoughts.

'And,' she added, 'you are perhaps wondering why this window is not already misted with the rain of tears?'

The soldier admitted that some such thought was in his head.

Then she said:

'Before I came to Kilconquhar lands I was Countess of Carrick. Now I am plain Marjorie, it seems. How long were you abroad?'

'Nearly three years.'

'Adam of Kilconquhar left here nearly six years ago. Perhaps he found the veiled windows of Palestine more interesting than the more open aspect you see before you now?'

The knight watched a heron winging its way out of the wood to the far side of the loch. It settled itself like a scholar to read between the ripples. The lady's eyes twinkled.

'Well, you have your loyalties, sir. But much hardship has been in Kilconquhar lands since he left.'

'I know. I saw some of it on the way here.'

'Now I have fewer tears left to spend than shillings, sir. And that's precious few. If Adam is dead then lady Eve must find another rib.'

The soldier looked hard at her. The sun fingered her hair. He admired her clear spirit.

'And where will you start, my lady?'

She nudged her horse forward and laid hold of his bridle.

'I shall start with you, sir. You are my prisoner and must return with me to my castle. What have you to say?'

'Before such a lady,' he answered, 'I have no wish but to submit. I place myself at your mercy.'

'A quick submission. Then I shall grant you the gift of mercy. Now follow me, sir, and tell me how you like my chains, for I have a mind now to enclose you in the high tower you speak of .'

The knight unbuckled his scabbard and belt.

'In that case I surrender my sword into your safe keeping, Lady Marjorie,' he said.

'I believe that is the custom, sir. And in addition you must agree to be led in triumph through my gates.'

She removed the long sash she wore as a girdle and tied it round his waist.

'Lead on then, lovely Marjorie.'

And in that fashion, the courtesy talk now over, he was led a prisoner of love through the castle gates.

She took him to her room and washed him down in old wine.

'A forgotten cask,' she said, 'that's past drinking. And Adam is past drinking it now, in any case. And it's good for old wounds.'

They drank the dregs between them.

And in one hour between her white breasts he completely forgot his youthful vow of chastity.

Together they rose and stood on the castle ramparts to watch the moon come over the firth. He saw Jan Van Hooght's herring buss, etched quietly for a moment on the moon's red shield, a sleepy whale drifting down to Leith.

It was then that he forgot his vow of obedience to the code.

Two days later the countess and the crusader stood in front of a priest.

'Marjorie, Countess of Carrick, and Robert de Brus, Lord of Annandale, I pronounce that you are wedded in the eyes of our Lord Christ Jesus. And may your loins and your lands prosper together.'

It was then that he forgot his vow of poverty.

Soon they had their first son.

'What shall we call him?' asked the awed father, looking down at the white, stricken vessel in the bed, and the strange cargo she carried now in her arms.

She smiled him a tired smile.

'What else should we call him but Robert, my lord? It is your own name.'

'Yes. Robert de Brus, young lord of Annandale.'

'And to think we might never have met,' she murmured.

He stroked her hair, a tangle of dull sunlight scattered across the pillow.

'It's most like we would never have met,' he said, 'but for a dead man's hand.'

He smiled at her, and looked kindly at the little baby boy, pondering as he did so the crooked paths of destiny.

The Saga of the Green Island

The great ice-sheet came down from the Southern Highlands, crossed the Tay and the Ochil hills, and so passed outwards to the European continent, moving easterly.

The island was a white castle on a white snow plain that made the whole globe glitter in space. Its crenellations twinkled under the stars.

Creatures of tusk and tooth padded across the German Ocean, swathed in furs.

There were polar bears on the firth

A billion tides rolled under the ice. The stars shifted slightly, in star time. Some constellations floated off, scattering stardust, and went out, like dandelion clocks.

The ice began to melt.

The snow castle threw off its white surplice and put on a garment of green. Centuries went over the land.

Millennia.

The surrounding sea showed no change.

Time's hand grew busy, though, on the green dress, embroidering it with masses of sea pinks, campion, milkwort, wormwood; stitching in sorrel, clover, celandines.

Tides of buttercups and daisies drifted in with the long lone summers; nettles scattered their sweet dust over the silence; thistles spiked the blue air.

The dragonfly hung, electric, in pre-history.

A great web of birds arrived, shuttling over the island; the cliffs clanged with their noise. Herring-gulls, blackbacks, guillemots, shags. Long before the Roman Eagle the cormorant extended its wings on the wind; the gannets bombed the offshore waters; the puffins sat like pirates on the stacks.

Among these airborne armies the butterflies and moths fluttered noiselessly: An aimless side-show to the great pageant of migration; snails tunnelled humbly through spillings of stonecrop; seals barked among the bladderwrack and kelp that swayed about the island.

A new child was born one day to a mainland Pict, anonymous in a broch on the shore.

Another was born in the Roman providence of Judaea, splitting time.

And in time the Roman Eagle did pass by the island, borne by oar and hoof and a thousand marching feet.

Still not a foot of man had bent the island grasses. But a soft, many-footed thunder was heard by the mice and voles. It was the sound of rabbits' feet. Soon the island was pocked with burrows: a honeycomb of sweet flesh and fur.

It was ready for the first men.

It was a woman who came first.

In those days King Loth ruled in the Lothians, on the southern mainland. He had a daughter called Thenaw who was a famous beauty in her time, and a great songstress. Chieftains rode the border hills bareback to come and hear her sing.

Her mouth was a red harp.

There was a prince called Ewan who fell under the spell of her music.

But soon Thenaw herself fell under a spell. It was the baby of Bethlehem who held her in thrall. She listened to the story of his star and took to praying instead of singing.

Her fingers on the clarsach had made the still air ripple like the sea. They were clasped now in a white tight silence.

The red thread of her mouth grew thin and pale and ceased its plangent quivering.

That did not please Ewan. One day when the folk were out hunting, he took her by force. When she grew round-bellied Ewan pointed out to her father what he had done. King Loth told Thenaw, 'You must marry this prince.'

'He has dishonoured me,' Thenaw said. 'I will have nothing to do with him, or with any man. I am the bride of Christ.'

When they heard that the priests put chains on her. They found it an easy matter to persuade King Loth that she was a danger to the ways of the tribe. She was hauled up high to the top of Traprain Law to be hurled into eternity, she and her unborn baby.

That at least was the plan.

Somehow she survived it, and the baby too. She cried a miracle. She had descended unhurt, she argued, on the wings of Christ. The priests took a different view. They said she was clearly a witch.

Those proud warmakers took her then, stripped her with their iron hands, and placed her in a coracle. This was done at Aberlessie. From there she was taken down to the firth to the Green Island and cast adrift on the bare, open sea.

The white crests took her.

'Go and ask your god if he is as good with the waves as he is at subduing the hearts of our women,' they sneered. 'Go and walk on the water if you can—over to Palestine.'

All the way to the island she was followed by a long shoal of fish. It sped after her like a comet as she was carried east of the island, her child coffined inside her.

At that point a soft wind blossomed and crooned her back to the island.

The coracle reached the southern ness, where there was a scrap of beach. She walked naked against the sands, carrying in front of her the great prow of her belly: a holy figurehead. With difficulty she clambered over the skerries to a small cave, where she found a well of clear water springing through the chalice of the rock. Because she rested there and drank there, the cave and the spring became known as the Lady's Bed and the Lady's Well.

They called the beach the Maiden's Hair.

Then she made her way back to the coracle and curled herself into a sleep. The tide carried her off again, whispering her back up the firth to a place near Culross, where a saint called St Serf took her ashore and succoured her in childbirth.

That son of hers was called Kentigern.

As for the glittering escort of fish, they stayed and settled round the island, its attendant spirits.

At nights the waters flashed with their cold fire.

Harangued by seabirds, tattooed by rabbits' feet, the island was a green and pleasant place. In time it would be famous for its harvests of fish.

Still it stayed as it was, untrodden by the foot of man.

Eventually the hunters arrived with traps and snares; fishermen with spears of bone, polished elm, iron. They spoliated the island and its shores, as men do, till there was very little left in the way of fin or fur; just the occasional flicker. Great holes appeared in the once close-knit net of gulls. The gannets moved off to the Bass Rock.

Then the hunters moved off too, as hunters do, to ravage another place. And the rabbits and fish swarmed once more, as though these men had never been. The cliffs whitened with the chalky droppings of birds.

Not many boats went up and down the firth in those days.
Things did not stay like that for long, however.
The saints were on the move.

In curraghs and coracles they came at first, drifting where God's
winds would take them. Only animal hide and a little tar between
them and the pitching sea. Many of them were skewered on the teeth
of rocks. Most went straight down to the ocean bed and stayed there,
prostrate.

And a long cold prayer that was.

Some were washed up on deserted beaches, and in time their bones
were ground up with the mother-of-pearl winkles and scallops and
cowries, to make the white, ribbed shell-sand whiter still: blinding
snowdrifts of sandbars and startling miles of shore.

One of these saints sighted the Green Island in his passage
northwards, but voyaged on. The cloud of life surrounding it made it
too attractive a prospect for him: he was looking for the remotest
retreat he could find, where the world presented its worst, most
inhospitable frown.

He found Skellig Michael, falling westwards and southwards again.
Others found the Faroes. Iceland. Spitzbergen. As far north as a man
could go. There they kneeled down, content until God should see fit to
wake them out of their slow, frozen vigil.

There was one saint who did not turn his back on the island. Bent-
backed scholars have sometimes called him Ethernan.

The island remembers him as Adrian.

St Adrian was not a hermit. He brought with him many men, he
and his friend St Monanus. They came at first among the mainland
Picts, God's seafarers, mysterious in their white robes. The Picts
grumbled and murmured but did nothing to begin with.

The saints landed on the island's sheltered western coastline, where
the flat rocks received their wet, shining footprints.

'I name these rocks the Alterstones,' said Adrian.

He expelled the evil demons from the island, crossed it in Christ's
name, and made it a place of prayer. To feed the young church they
brought with them some cows and sheep, two goats. They sowed an
armful or two of grain.

'In the celestial fields we shall neither sow nor reap,' Adrian said.
'Even here, look at the gathering of fish and flesh. This place is the
nearest we shall come to the Garden of Eden.'

But Monanus grew restless. He was a recluse by nature.

One moonlit night in summer the firth shivered with fish. A
fisherman passed by and anchored off the island. He had come to

catch herring. Monanus watched him standing in his small boat, his net in hand, bobbing on the swell.

He shouted to him.

'Are you catching many tonight, fisherman?'

'They'll be catching me if I'm not careful,' came the reply. 'There's so many of them!'

'The stars are like fish,' Monanus said. 'Just look at them all up there.'

'Ah,' said the man in the boat. 'I saw a school of fish like that once. If you'd dipped your nets in you'd have sunk the boat. That was a long time ago.'

He stood, a dark statue against the glimmering waves, his hands and face silvered.

'Aye, you'd have torn your nets to shreds in a second, that you would.'

Monanus answered him.

'God's nets have no holes, my friend. One day they will catch every star in the sky and make it sing in heaven.'

The fisherman laughed and started pulling in his nets.

'You lose me with that kind of talk, holy father. To my mind fish are fish, and stars are stars. That is enough for a man like me.'

The saint decided to persist with him a little.

'The story is told of how God sent a whole shoal of stars down from heaven to protect the blessed Thenaw when she was set naked on the sea. They turned into fish and followed her here, right down the firth to this island.'

The man's nets shrugged with herring, fragmenting the moonlight.

'I don't believe that,' he said simply.

'Yes,' said Monanus, as if he hadn't heard him, 'that shoal of stars became fish and wrapped itself round our island in a belt. Heavenly bounty. They are the very same fish as you are catching now, the very same, take my word for it. The Milky Way you see up there is only a reflection of them, that's all.

The fisherman took up his anchor and headed the boat's nose away from the island.

Monanus shouted after him.

'Between a star and a fish, my friend, there is no essential difference.'

'Madness.'

The parting shaft came faintly from the boat.

'It is not madness, brother,' said a voice in the shadows.

Adrian had been listening to the conversation. He put his hand on the other's shoulder.

'It is not madness and well I know it. But to most men, mysticism is indistinguishable from madness.'

Then he said: 'Much as I love you, brother, it is my opinion that you are unfitted for this communal existence of ours. Go, and discover your truths in a cell of your own.'

So Monanus crossed west to the mainland and came to a place called Inverey, where the burn met the tide. There he found a very small cave, wetted by spray, thunderous with sea-noises.

'This is where I choose to live and die,' he said.

And so he stayed there, collecting his thoughts. He taught all who visited him about the stars.

'The day will come,' he said, 'when men will throw up their own stars into space, and strive to be as gods. Such stars will be the sharks of the night. They will travel in disguise among the celestial shoals. But God's legions will prevail against them. In the end they will be torn from the sky.'

Few heard him. He lived with his visions. Spears with sunbright tips whistling out of the east. A dark rain falling on the firth.

He died himself from the weapon the saints feared most: the Viking axe. That was when the Picts finally leagued with the Danes to rid them of their holy confessors. Monanus was martyred in his cell at Inverey. Adrian himself went from cave to cave along the coast. But he fell on his island retreat along with most of his followers. They ran from the Alterstones all the way downwards to the southern ness. The Maiden's Hair was dabbled with blood.

When the Danes had gone home the survivors crept out of the fields and forests on the mainland and rowed heavily back to their island. It was a red shambles. Adrian was laid in a stone coffin, with a round niche specially cut to receive his head: a nimbus of stone. They laid him in the Saints' Graveyard, close to the sea.

Soon Adrian was a story on men's lips; nothing more. Then a memory.

Then a name.

In time hardly even a name.

A record, over which quill-wielding clerks squabbled in ink.

One winter a storm struck the island.

A south-easter.

The waves, raging warmen, white-haired unregenerates, came pounding up the rocks and sands like the Vikings of old. They tore into the Saints' Graveyard, avid for desecration. When they left they took with them the stone coffin containing the remains of the great saint. Unjointed by centuries, these were quickly scattered over the floor of the firth.

The same storm, such was its force, dragged the coffin north-westerly. It was washed up at Anstruther, tumbling off the tide, battered and lidless, but still with that quiet circle cut into the head, where stone dreams had been made.

The age of saints had passed.

There arose in Scotland a great builder of churches: a king called David. He built a chapel for the martyred St Monanus.

He was that king who gave the island into the keeping of the black-cowled Cluniacs.

A tiny monastery was built on the island for these monks from the south. It was little more than a stone cross at the island's heart: a recumbent Christ. The nave was his body, the transepts his arms, the studded doors his nailed feet, the chancel his wounded head. In the chancel stood a statue of the murdered St Monan, his own head crowned with wounds from the Norse axes.

Now bells were heard coming from the island, at matins and vespers, when the sea bled redly, east and west. On black starless nights, the sea and the sky invisible, the glow from the monastery merged with the unearthly music that spoke of the four last things: Death, Resurrection, Judgement, and the hope of Heaven.

The island hung in space like a little world vibrant with praise.

Sea voyagers heard the music in the darkness and glimpsed the light, and the helmsman coursing up and down the North Sea turned safely to starboard, to port.

'Thy word is a lamp unto my feet and a light unto my path,' chanted the brothers.

The keels sped softly through the night waters.

One year a Norseman called Swein Aslef came down with a gang of followers in a longboat.

That was in Abbot Baldwin's time.

He told the abbot that he was really an ambassador from Earl Ronald in Shetland. The monks and the so-called statesmen sat down to dinner together.

'This is an excellent dish,' said Swein. 'What is it?'

'I am flattered it is to your liking, my lord,' Baldwin said, 'but it is nothing more than rabbit and a little fish.'

'Ah, but the serving is delicious,' Swein said. 'Tell me how it is done.'

Baldwin laughed. He was surprised that Earl Ronald's ambassador should take such an interest in the preparation of fish and rabbit stews.

'If you really want to know,' he replied, 'I shall tell you. The rabbit is served with bay leaves and the fish is sprinkled with warmed fennel seeds. These are fennel leaves that have been used to dress the fish, and the other leaves are dandelions.'

'I also taste marjoram,' Swein said.

'Quite right,' beamed the abbot. 'Fancy a great man like yourself having such a knowledge of the kitchen. Perhaps you should have been a monk.'

Swein laughed.

'Except that I should find it difficult to live on water, excellent though this particular vintage tastes.'

'That's very true,' Baldwin admitted.

He pulled a rueful face.

'When we were at Reading I used to enjoy a cup of beer. These days we make do with Adam's ale from the Lady's Well. A very old vintage.

Swein finished his draught.

'At least there won't be thick heads in the morning,' he said.

Some of his men chuckled.

'Such a civilised man,' said Baldwin to the night brother as he prepared for sleep. 'Let this incident be recorded in the scriptorium tomorrow. They are not all barbarians in the north.'

That night the Vikings rose from their pallets and ransacked the monastery. The brothers waited in a black huddle to be sacrificed on the altar.

But after they had tied up the few treasures in a blanket, Swein told his men to put away their swords. He turned to the monks.

'On account of your excellent rabbit and fish fare, good brothers, you will be pleased to hear that we do not intend to do away with you.'

He threw the blanket over his shoulder and it clanged on his back.

'I can pick up baubles like these anywhere,' he said. 'But Baldwin's recipe is the greatest treasure I take from here before matins. I know a woman called Ingrid who will be expert in this dish before long. Now goodbye, holy men—and God be in your kitchen!'

The boat was anchored off the Alterstones. Once they were all aboard, Swein shouted up to the little band:

'Be careful—if I should happen to call again I might expect a different recipe. Vary your dishes, good brothers—and remain alive!'

There was a rough burst of laughter from the deck.

The monks looked at Swein, standing tall and strong at the prow, his hand on the dragonshead.

'He wasn't bad, as Norsemen go,' mused Baldwin.

'Maybe you should have been a Viking,' said one of the brothers. Baldwin smiled.

The firth lay quiet, like a pink, dripping rose.

Soon the longboat was the size of a wasp.

But when Swein Aslef sailed up the firth to Edinburgh and told King David what he had done, the king did not find it amusing.

'Baldwin will have to be recompensed for his losses,' David said, 'and for damages.'

'I'll offer him a good Norwegian dish by way of compensation,' said Swein.

'What is it?' the king asked him.

'Raw fish,' Swein replied, his eyes crinkling. 'I'm a great believer in the exchange of cultures.'

'It seems to me you have the best of the bargain there,' the king said.

But in due course an amicable arrangement was arrived at.

One night a dark music was heard issuing from the island.

The monks were singing masses for the repose of King David's soul.

Kings came and went after that, as they had always done. Bannockburn, Sauchieburn, Flodden, Solway Moss.

The age of monasteries passed.

The sea continued to beat upon the island. Time broke up in particles on its shores. Some heard the song of eternity in its stringent beatings. For others it was monotonous and without meaning.

The age of sea-kings passed.

Always the fish and the rabbits stocked the island. And the island continued to collect its toll of storm-driven wrecks, even after a beacon lighthouse was erected there, as a star for seamen.

Not all seamen steered by the light of the world.

But in time even the age of the godfearing crews passed by. The day came when the lighthouse worked by science and not by art. The fish were caught in the same way. Long gone the days when the fishermen paid their tithes to the monks, and went against wind and tide with only faith in their hands. Casting their nets in the name of the Lord.

The shoals began to drift away from the island. One by one the stars went out in the bright zodiac of fish.

Then a farmer came to the island, under the moon.

He carried with him a single rabbit in a sack. In its blood it carried a merciless disease. It mingled with its fellows, this leper from the mainland.

For a time the entire population of rabbits sat quite still, as if trying to puzzle it out, this thing that had gone wrong.

The crows descended.

Eyeless, the rabbits fell over and died. The sound of thudding feet was never heard again in the burrows. The many-chambered heart of the island ceased pulsating.

No, said the clever folk, it didn't happen like that. The disease was rife on the mainland. A gull must have carried over an infected flea, and that was how it had spread. There was no other way it could possibly have happened. Why would a man contaminate an island? Men had more important matters to attend to. They were busy exterminating seals, seabirds, whales, trees. And such like menaces.

Now the island was a fishless, fleshless desert.

The Oil Age dawned.

It was brief, as most ages were, in those last days.

The drilling in the North Sea had scarcely started when it stopped. Great rigs floated on the firth at first like lighted sea-cities, passing in the night. Then the huge steel structures rusted and gloomed: skeletons drifting derelict like the plague ships of old.

Men hailed the Nuclear Age.

The drilling began again. Not around the island now, but on it, in it, and through it. Deep down they drilled, into the main mass of the island, deep enough to contain the waste, the poison. It had all been proved by experts, said the politicians. The island's geology made it an admirable dumping ground. No leakages could ever happen. This was a different affair from rabbits.

So the great canisters went down, lowered like coffins, deeper, much deeper than the bones of the saints.

And the graves were covered up.

The birds left the island.

The nettles filled up the old floors, where the brothers had knelt, chanting their psalms.

For years the island lay like a tomb. The sea moaned round it, a dead mass. Echoing in the ruins.

Agnus Dei qui tollis peccata mundi: dona eis requiem.

The saints slept on.

Agnus Dei qui tollis peccata mundi: dona eis requiem sempiternam.

Then came a single terrible day.

Libera me Domine de morte aeterna in die illa tremenda.
And after that day of burning, a long bitter sleep.
Men called it the Nuclear Winter.
The ice-sheet returned, clamping the island in its white fist. Overhead wheeled the spent shells of St Moiran's false stars.
Cold snowflakes coursing the dead spaces.

Beachcomber

Old Mansie stayed on his own among the things he took from the sea.

The cottage he lived in was nested high on the Randerston cliffs, from where he could watch through his binoculars how the mouth of the tide spoke to the shore. The quietest word between wave and sand had him reaching for his glasses and pulling on his boots. Once down among the rocks he would walk for miles along the murmuring lip of the water, following the lines of foam, the curving whispers of surf. Down there he always found out the secretest happenings of the sea. If he didn't he'd go out among the skellies to the waterline, up the skirts of the firth as far as a man could go.

His house brimmed with the tiny irrelevancies of tide: those tokens of time's indifference. Flotsam and failure, sown on the waves, were his daily bread; his frail fortunes founded on other folks' wreckages and loss.

Broken fishboxes were the meanest of the sea's offerings. But he quickly nailed them and mended them with his neat hands, converting detritus into an impregnable round of domestic shapes: an open cupboard fixed to one wall; a bookcase by the fire; a tea-table, a log-box, a row of kitchen units; a throne of an armchair fitted with a lifebelt for a seat and a cushion in the centre; and a spare bed padded with foam rubber. Some of his furnishings he painted white, others he planed and varnished. The house had the look of a ship that had come ashore. On windy days when the reek flew from the lum, Mansie wouldn't have been at all surprised to see it chugging back into the waves.

It had been four bare walls when he first moved in. But the tides had been friends to him. More so than his own boy, he sometimes used to say, for over these past two years he'd not seen much of Kevin and his wife in Cramond, Edinburgh. He'd stayed with them ten years near hand, since he'd become a widower—till they'd wanted him to go to the old folks' home in Marchmont, once their family had put on height.

'If only they'd all been boys, dad,' Kevin had said. 'Jason and Julian can still sleep in the same room, and they're under ten still. But Samantha's the problem—coming up for thirteen now, you know. She's got to have a room of her own . . .'

So they showed him the brochures from the Eventide Home.

'Money is no problem, dad, no problem at all.'

No, not with a solicitor for a son, and one who had his own practice too. Though God knows how he ever graduated, Mansie thought to himself.

'And Marchmont is just a bus run from Cramond.'

'But I canna get a sight o' the sea from up there,' Mansie insisted.

'Dad, you fished it for sixty years since you were ten, and you've sat at that window there every day in the last decade and looked at nothing else. Haven't you seen enough of it?'

'Come on Mansie,' said Jane. 'Take a 41 bus from Marchmont and you can see your precious water every weekend with us. The kids are getting under your feet and I'm not home much these days to see to your eating. You'll get three full meals a day at the Eventide Haven.'

Mansie was taken up to Marchmont to look at the place.

'That's not a home,' he said, when he came back. 'It's a bloody waxworks, a museum. Do you know what they're like? They're like cod lying, up there, that's what they're like. I've seen more expression on a flounder than on any o' that lot.'

'At least give the place a try, dad.'

'More life in my old bloody walking stick, I tell you.'

'Well then, you're just what they're needing, dad—some salt about the place.'

'The Eventide Haven,' Mansie snorted. 'I'll tell you what, the only haven I'm going to is the one I came from.'

And without more fuss Mansie gathered up his years and went back to the East Neuk, to the old cold salmon bothy near the beach. He lit the fire, polished the dust from the windows, and watched the sun warm the walls.

The tide shook the shingle.

'Should've come back years ago,' Mansie said.

A seagull landed on his chimney and he went outside, nodded to it, and listened to the sea scouring the stones.

'Should never have left it in the first place.'

He settled his cap on his head, agreeing with himself.

When you reach my years, Mansie told himself, the first thing you look for is heat.

That was easy. The sea, a kind king, gathered his winter fuel for him, depositing it below his doorstep every morning. It was odd how you rarely saw timber afloat on the tide, yet it came in with each water, as secretly as dew on the grass, and the shoreline was fringed with kindling and large sized logs for the night burning. The driftwood whistled and sparked in the grate and Mansie cracked away in turn.

'Nothing like a bit o' conversation from a fire.'

He remembered the clinical silence of Kevin and Jane's gas central heating system.

'Auld Reekie,' he said into his beard, bent forward slightly into the glow. 'Auld Reekie, aye.'

The flames were his quiet companions now, lapping his lum.

'Nowhere to look if you haven't got a grate. And nowhere to put your bloody feet.'

When a massive spar of pitch pine came crashing past on the breakers, he didn't mind getting his legs wet to haul it to shore before it charged on down the firth. Then he lashed it to his shoulder and sweated up the road like a plough-horse into the wind. He sawed it into ingots which he stacked by the fireside. A drowned forest with salt in its veins where the sap had run dry: the cortege of winds and the wreaths of waves had brought it to Mansie's door.

When a man falls, Mansie thought, he's just no use at all. Silently the tongues of flame agreed with him.

'Like these corpses up in the Eventide Haven,' he said aloud.

But a tree now—that had some use. And it was wonderful where they all came from.

'The cedars o' Lebanon,' he murmured, smelling the sweet scents squeezed out of the wood by the fast-working fingers of flame, busy in his chimney.

'Aye, aye, the cedars o' Lebanon, right enough.'

And he went outside for a minute and watched the sparks sprouting from his roof: a scattering of bright seeds to fertilise a cold forgotten corner of the earth with their golden burning, and bring back the birds, some time in a primaeval future.

There were some chunks of wood though, Mansie couldn't bring himself to burn: the waves had put too much work into them. Tireless old journeyman, the sea tossed a tree from coast to coast, scrubbing it to a skeleton, and the artist waves went to work with sculpting fingers that were free from the egos of self and system. At last it was washed up on a foreign shore, eloquent of the sea: a whorled dancer twisted with tides, an Indian naiad naked as bone, an everlasting moment of pure movement and form.

A bit of tree just like that stood in Mansie's kitchen, wave-whitened and wave-worn. He couldn't give it to the red fingers in his chimney—what the blue fingers of the sea had taken so long to perfect. He used it instead for hanging up his kitchenware. The naiad reached out for the mystery of things—and found cups and ladles, toasting-fork, potato-masher, carver, colander, sieve.

Mostly the things in Mansie's house were useless in themselves. But strewn about his walls and floor, they added up to something: an anthology of stories for which they provided ends and beginnings, or something in between: scraps of sea-narrative that could be scanned for a lifetime without ever yielding up the essence of the tale.

An old-fashioned wooden leg such as seamen wore. At one time for certain a man had been steadied by it, before it was unbuckled by currents colder than bone, and the leg kicked upwards again and took the tide.

An ancient glass float from one of the old trawler nets. They hadn't been in use for forty years. This one must have drifted decades in and out of tides before the waves washed it into Mansie's hands.

The carved lid of a sea-chest with the initials B. B. dug out of the inner side. Whose initials were these that read like something out of *Treasure Island*? It didn't matter. Bones in a hammock now, the owner, swung by seabed shuttles, or dreamless in the earth.

A tattering of sail with some faded words painted on it: *The Lord be your defence Until* . . .

And glass stoppers and paperweight pebbles and crabs' shells; sea-urchins, pink and purple pearls from the mussel-beds, misshapen mostly; and a hybrid of bones from the armoury of an old time hero—scimitars and sabres and crescent moons.

On the table over by the window was a great turtle shell, upturned, polished, gleaming. The turtle had been caught in a lobsterman's lines near Crail, and drowned. Now its shell was bright with apples and nuts: a sea-dish full of the fruits of the earth.

So Mansie lived in this way.

When he was not out walking, he sat at his high window, watching the waves as they shrugged the sea's detritus from one to another and onto the sands. Sometimes, down on the shore, a salt wave wept in him when he considered the unwantedness of things, the dumb drift of the beach. A piece of cracked crockery, reminding him of those sad aunts who sat alone among their teacups; a legless doll, a rubber boot, a rusted pram; the joyless jetsam of people's lives. And how people themselves were cast off in the end—worn back to the bone, to white anonymity; hidden in the last black tide of earth, a fathom under the sweet green grass and their droplets of daisies and buttercup crests.

Yes, it was sad. Better at least to be washed every day by the cleansing water and hear sea-bells in your skull, than to be a deaf undreaming clod. Ah, but what did the fate of your bones really matter?

And Mansie sat down on a rock and grew heavy at the sheer size of the sea from down here and the mystery of the horizon. Till a passing fisherman hailed him from his boat and threw him a haddock from close inshore.

'Hey Mansie, you'll never make your fortune that way. Fry this up for your tea—you'll feel richer on a full belly!'

Some days he humoured the lobsters from their hidie-holes or teased out the partans; and a roasted crab sang in his dish on a cold winter's night when Sirius was a snowflake on his window pane.

And that was his life.

It's not many more winters I'll be disturbing this shore, Mansie told himself one night when the wind cried out of the south east. It had been a day of deep storms and the sea crackled frostily on the small stones of the beach. The hard weather had come at last in December; the next day was Christmas Eve.

But I suppose it wouldn't be right to wish for a really great find before I die. If that ever happens I'll be Santa Claus yet to these grandbairns o' mine across the water. It's no their fault their folks are what they are.

And he went to bed with the breakers grinding in his ears, wondering what was the richest thing in the ocean. Hope settled like a grain of sand in his old brain, and his dreams began to irritate it, coating it with pearl.

The next morning he knew before he opened his eyes that there was snow. He heard in his ears its feathered silence, telling him that there would be no gleanings from the beach that day. Sure enough, when he went to the window he could see how heavily it had fallen during the night, wedding fields and shore under the same secretive bedsheet, so that they were one.

'I'll soon rumple that, though.'

Mansie sipped the first scalding of tea from the pot. The bubbles blinked at him over the rim.

'Aye, I'll go anyway.'

He banged down the heavy black-lacquered frying pan that he'd excavated from the sands, and cracked an egg into it. It shone inside him. That would do him all day, he decided. He put on his boots and overcoat and left the house. And he walked south and west for many a mile without seeing so much as a dimple on the white shore. His breath came in clouds about him, his legs fell shorter in the snow, the cold hit harder and harder. What else was there to do? He was an old man walking the fringes of a lonely sea.

A Fifeness yawlman saw him from his small boat as he purred away past the Carr reef, and he shook his head, his hand thoughtful on the tiller.

'Aye, Mansie's no long for this earth, I doubt.'

He bobbed and wheeled for a second on the uncertain swell before turning the boat's head back towards the Old Haikes, where he remembered catching herring when kirk steeples were higher and carried the sun.

Mansie toiled on in the other direction, wheezing slightly. At Anster he had to come in off the rocks and walk along Shore Street past the harbour. The doors of the Salutation Arms were open and he paused in the warm current of air. He had the sea in his throat and winter in his bones.

'Come on in Mansie, and wet your whistle.'

It was the voice of Pusk, the man that came down with the fish van once or twice in a month. Mansie couldn't make him out through the noisy blue fug. Two leather-jacketed youths piloted a space machine that flashed its foreign lights and jingle across the pub. A juke box pounded in the corner. Mansie opened his mouth to say something, moved on wordlessly.

At Pittenweem the boats were all in. The fishmarket had been hosed clean; the stones shone like wet sands. It was Christmas Eve, and here too everybody was in the pub. He passed the last houses in the town, where doorsteps were splashed by the sea. Years ago he had stopped here, a young man, and the slippered old wives had sat on the sea wall and poured him cups of tea to make him stay and talk. He'd been a great talker in those days. It was winter now and the windows were shut. Most of the houses were untenanted holiday homes. At some of the doors colossal American cars loomed like tanks.

He returned to the beach, stumbling on boulders that slowed his progress along the anonymous white coast. It was like walking on another planet. The air tasted thin and difficult to breathe. But his eyes continued to read the snow.

West of the Old Kirk at St Monans he stooped to pick up a green bottle, all but its neck basketed with whiteness.

'It'll hold a candle anyway,' Mansie muttered. 'Nearly all plastic rubbish these days.'

A mile further on he rescued a small knob of wood that was wedged between rocks. He liked it for its shape.

'Nice job the water's made o' that one.'

He threw it into his sack along with the bottle.

By the time he reached Ardross the rock pools had frozen hard on the shore. He told himself to try one more mile. At Elie Ness he bent down to look at an old crab encased in its coffin of ice, its claws extended.

'Wonder why it didn't just crawl out, when it felt the cold coming? Ah well, I've come all this way just to look at that.'

It was starting to snow again.

He tightened his cap and scarf, turned north, and faced into the whitening wind. Long before he reached St Monans he could hear the singing from the Brethren Hall down at the pier.

> *What can I give him*
> *Poor as I am?*
> *If I were a shepherd*
> *I would bring a lamb;*
> *If I were a wise man*
> *I would do my part.*
> *Yet what I can I give him—*
> *Give my heart.*

Beautiful words. But the notes were so drearily drawn out across the swirling sea that the message behind the music sounded gray rather than glad. The holy crew inside were making the trip to heaven sound a long slow haul.

Mansie was tired now, really tired. He was breathing in snow and his chest hurt. His legs had turned white—the wind, veering to the east, blowing the blizzard across his path.

In Pittenweem and Anster the singing was going on in the pubs. The streets were deserted. Mansie was a walking snowman. It was dark by the time he approached Fifeness.

But the cold had unclenched a fraction and the shore was softer again under his feet. The snow was still blowing heavily.

He was turning up to the foreshore when his boot struck a hardness. Mansie knew a boulder when he hit it, and this was something else. He bent, felt with his gloves at the thing buried in the snow. Its size was hidden from him but it was bigger than he'd thought. He brushed off the white flakes and scraped at the crust of frost underneath, his fingers feeling the unusual length and shape of it through the fire in his mittens. He pulled hard and sat down on the cold bouldered beach. His eyes crinkled, his snowbeard parted to show his teeth, laughing now among the stars.

'Would you credit it?'

His words cracked in his mouth like whips.

'It's a whale's skull . . . it's the skull o' a bloomin' whale!'

The sea rustled and the stars listened.

Mansie peered at it. His eyes told him it might have been a forty footer. It was as white and unbroken as a piece of new-baked bread. The tides had polished it like a coin. The snowflakes fell glittering on the great brow.

Mansie sat and sat.

'What a find for an east coast beacher like me!'

At last he hauled himself into a standing position with his arms around the skull. The pain in his chest had gone away. And with a glad face he waltzed up the whitened tracks to Randerston.

Later, standing in the red puddles of firelight, dried off after supper, Mansie examined his finds.

The snow had melted from his wine bottle, so that he could see in a blink just what an unusual thing it was, and how old it must be. A flattened green bubble with a ship's decanter base; blown when Botticelli was a boy, for all that anyone could tell. It was cratered with barnacles, and a fistful of limpets had landed on it, making Mansie think of the face of the moon. On the glass itself the waves had been at work through long nautical aeons of sail and steam and oil: Leonardo, Turner, Cezanne. Cutting, engraving, embossing, the many-fingered artist had placed its slow anonymous signature on the work before casting it up at Mansie's blind feet.

Had there been wine in it for the first hundred years as it was laid down at the bottom of the sea, till Neptune drew the cork? Mansie had read of ancient wines dredged up intact from the deeps, where they had reposed undisturbed with the silent wars of crabs and congers fought over them for centuries.

Just imagine that wine in it now. He tilted his head, seeing the fire through the glass.

The bottle was a blazing green star on his lips.

The mermaid's tresses had kept it warm in winter and the summer currents had cooled it in the raging sea dog days. This was a draught such as the drinkers in The Salutation Arms had never quaffed; a far cry from Morris's store at the off-licence, where you bought labelled stuff that was bottled a year or two ago. This was three hundred, maybe five hundred years' old nectar that no man alive could boast of having drunk: his wine-cellar the bottom of the sea for half a millenium; his deepest vintage cared for and studied not by the fleeting hand of a passing vintner, fleshless in a mere seventy years, but by the primordial motions of octopus and eel. To release this stopper was to set free an immortal soul.

Mansie gave the bottle a steeper tilt and held it to his lips with his eyes closed.

And for a long minute his head was loud with the songs the sirens sang, and he knew the name Odysseus used when he hid himself among women.

He brought the bottle slowly down and looked at it. He had drunk the memory of its wine. There was nothing left now, not as much as a green thought.

'But it makes a grand ornament,' he said, setting it down. 'You can't pick up a Christmas present like that except from the bottom of the sea.'

His hand moved to the knob of driftwood.

Yes, it was a nice shape. Mansie poked the fire, threw on a dry log. The flames leapt up the lum. They played on the fist-sized lump of wood, which he navigated with his hands. In the web of shadows he explored its intricacies. Then the log fell and in the new flame he saw what it really was. He was looking at what was left of a dead-eye block from an old sailing ship.

Mansie peered into the dead-eye, saw how the invisible ropes of the sea had wound round it—for two centuries perhaps, the sculpting waves smoothing it into a nearly unrecognisable system of shapes. A brainwork of holes and ridges and curves. He remembered seeing an object not unlike it at the local art gallery during the summer. It was a wood carving done by a Glasgow artist and had a label on it saying two hundred pounds. What Mansie had in his hands had been turned over in the sea's mind, mulled for two hundred years in the mind of water, producing whorls of thought that were beyond value. You just couldn't put a price on that amount of time. A pound a year? It was ludicrous.

He held it hard in the line of his eye, recreating its original appearance. Then his mouth softened and his face relaxed into reverie. He looked away dreamily, holding the dead-eye block loosely in his lap, seeing it with his fingers. His eyes ebbed into the red movements of the fire.

Where he saw.

The red waves of dawn that took the clipper out of port, the tall ship of which the dead-eye was a tiny working part. Trimmed and battened and cargo stowed, she took on her captain, cast off her pilot and tug, and made sail out of the Channel.

The men hauled on the ropes; the ship burst like a rose, a white flowering of sails: headsails, topsails, courses. Mansie saw the bow-wash blossoming into spray, heard the reef-points pattering on the canvas, the blocks creaking and the shrouds dripping and the masts bending with the wind. The ship was a symphony of sounds. All things sang their music to sailors aloft and below, and sailors on the bottom of the sea.

So she drifted on through the quiet nights, over her pennants the silver stars and under her keel the drowned . . .

She reached the quiet anchorage of Spanish seas.

A harbour was a golden harp brimming with strings. The moon struck the harp, plucking strange chords from the quivering lines of salt. The sailors raised their draughts to the golden harpist, saluting song with song. They heard the same melody breaking over the roofs and gables of their far homes, flooding the eaves with heartbreak, where the women lay listening and awake. The dark circles of ale heard the moonlight too and the flagons trembled in every hand, spilling back music into the sea.

There was no going home.

Southwards went the ship, west of the Azores and Madeira and the peaks of Teneriffe, setting a south-south-easterly course deep into the Atlantic; plummeting like a bird well south of the Cape to pick up the Trade Winds and be running the easting down.

They were headed for the China Seas.

But there came those windless green unquiet days when the crew could hear the storm in the silence. The sea stopped its whispering and listened. Thousands of miles away, across the Indian Ocean, the Bay of Bengal, the great Pacific, the winds were blowing off the South American coast, working up the waves on the longest stretch of water in the world; generating a swell seventy sailing days distant.

The ship felt the swell deep in its wooden bones.

There came a darkness that was not of sky. It was the sea that blackened as the wave crests reared and frowned, showing the shadows on their faces. Down in his cabin the skipper saw the mercury falling in the glass. He knew what a great wind was ahead of them that they had to pass through. The ship began to plunge and pitch, entering the swell. He left his dark decanter, deep with port, and the portrait of his wife and children. Before he turned away he brought up the dear ones close to his mouth, imprinting a moist kiss on each pale brow, misting their faces. Only then did he come up on deck with his orders.

He saw the dark shreds of clouds on the horizon, telling him where the wind lay in wait like a tiger, clawing the sky. His lips scarcely moved, but each time he breathed his commands men scurried in a dozen different tacks about the ship. They snugged her down, hurrying aloft to take in the topsails, reefing the courses closely as the wind bared its teeth. Everything that could move was lashed down, doors shut, hatches tarpaulined; the vessel was furled up again like a bud against the invading sea. Only the captain stood motionless, part of the ship.

Then the weather burst across the deck.

The helmsman was destiny at the wheel. All heads were turned to the man on whose skill their lives teetered, and fear of the sea was cold in their groins. But it was his shipmates' faces and not the sea that struck him to stone—the wild whites of their eyes staring at him from winches, tackles, shrouds; beseeching him to make no mistake, as the bows disappeared beneath crashing seas and the stern dipped and dipped into the troughs. The crests were sixty feet above their heads, higher than the masts at times, and carrying hundreds of tons of water—death travelling in the sky like a moving mountain waiting to smash downwards on the deck. The hills of water blocked off the wind; the sails fluttered like a failed heart and went out; she refused to answer the helm. The stern slewed round broadside onto the wave, the green peaks poised for armageddon.

The master closes his eyes. He sees the end: a kirkyard stone commemorating the crew whose bodies were never recovered. The wave passes over the whole ship, filling it all along its length.

The sea takes control . . .

But his worst dream—the one that shook him from sleep sometimes in the quiet harbour of a woman's arms—remained a shadow inside his skull. The helmsman brought her head into the wind and forced her to ride it out on the bucking spine of the sea. All night through he stood lashed to the wheel, while he and the ship staggered like two drunkards locked together, their heads mad among masts and stars— and the constellations were smashed across the sky like broken glass.

She came through it battered and broken, a torn rose adrift on the water. Her bows sought the running surf, booming down the beaches of her desire, as she won home in the end, safe into the sunset-laden port of Mansie's mind, quiet by his fire . . .

'My best three finds of the year,' Mansie decided. 'But this last one's the pick of them all—any year.'

He had dragged the skull over to the hearth, and it lay at his feet, bathed in the fire's redness. He put on more logs, knelt down beside it, laid his hands over it, examined its battleship qualities and size. He couldn't take his eyes away from it.

'What a present for a young lad though, eh?'

He shook his head, cradling the great thing in his pondering arms.

'If I'd just had a present like that now, when I was a lad.'

The stars swarmed past his window panes, a throng of bright winter bees. Mansie never heard their song. He fed deeper and deeper on the infinite blood-red darknesses of the skull, deeper than any man had gone into those untravelled depths, into the vanished brain.

The skull grew under his hands.

And again Mansie saw.

How the first seas trembled like a dewdrop on the earth planet's sides as it bulged and glittered in the mornings of space; miles of miraculous life flowering under the blue furrows; gardens of whales growing in the oceans of the world, fountaining into those first summers of time; winters flaking from the whale's sides, the shards of seasons falling in its wake; and aeons pulsing to the beating of its galactic heart. This was Andromeda fallen from the sky, coursing faster than light—this was the whale of all the world.

The whale came down to the German Ocean.

The first men came and felled trees in the water, wielding the horns of deer. With a sigh he thrust them waves away. His mildest murmur landed them kicking and half drowned among the rocks. They had a long way to go before they could conquer the whale of all the world.

He cruised up into Cramond, where the soldiers crossed, and then back down the firth, straining the plankton, lazily following the legions as they marched north. They had a job to do on the green whalebacks of the northern hills. They merely pointed at him with their spears and ignored him. Their wars were fought and won. And a legion marched into the mist, a thing of swords and shields, and the mist closed behind them.

The whale of the world sailed on.

Up the North Sea, passing the red-cloaked Danish fighters who were making for Fifeness. Their bows were a white whisper on the water. The prow was a soundless snarl—it was pointed at the green head-land that thrust out into the sea like a challenge. Fifemen on its muzzle. Waiting. The whale never heeded the clash of foreign tongues and the meeting of strange metals that happened there. (Death sounded the same anywhere) Or the sound of iron on holy bone. Or the ring of the gravedigger's spade, bright on the rocky shore that winter.

No, the whale never heeded them. He was deep in the Davis Straits among bergs and bears and the long polar moons. He was blowing stars from the spout on his head.

That was where the iron first sang in his flesh. The whalemen were after his blood.

Their ships spawned noisily and the water bristled with their brats, suddenly alive on the swell. He shrugged his shoulder, sent out a sea that took the nearest boat ten fathoms down. Some of the men surfaced in seconds but their hearts were cracked and cold. Another boat he slammed with his tail: there was a shrieking of men and timbers parting company. And yet another he came up under and hoisted on his barnacled back, leaping with them into the clouds so that they had a last high view of the mother ship before he drew them with a long slow sucking of salt down into the foundations of the world.

At last he took the harpoons.

The first was a cold smoulder somewhere in his back. He turned away angrily from the irksome thing. The second burned into his belly as he came up for the big dive. He put loops in the iron arrow as he sought the sun, twisting the metal like straw three times round in his mad spiralling.

The lance found out his heart then.

His red blood came thudding into the sea. He took his bitter fill of the sky and turned his eyes to the darkness, hundreds of fathoms below. Trailing the tracking lines and the red ribbons of his own life blackly down to the bottom of existence, yet he swam sixty miles to escape the flensing irons and the hot cauldrons before he completed his plunge, and his fluttering heart failed that should have stopped beating long ago, and his dim eyes went out like stars . . .

The next morning was Christmas morning.

Mansie ate some bread and bacon before he set to work putting a polish on his treasures. When he was satisfied that they looked their best, he took down a tea caddy from a dark shelf. It contained all his money in the world: two hundred pounds in five and one pound notes. He stuffed the paper money into one pocket and took the road to the village.

He stopped outside Alexander's garage. Mick Alexander never closed a single day in the year.

Mansie said: 'I'll give you fifty pounds to drive me to Edinburgh and back in the day.'

Alexander looked at him.

'The boy that does the taxiing is off today,' he said. 'It's Christmas. Come back tomorrow.'

Mansie shook his head.

'Tomorrow's no good. Take me yourself.'

'What about my business, Mansie? I'll lose money by it.'

'Fifty pounds? Will you make that on this day of the year? Everybody's at their firesides and playing with the bairns.'

'Oh, I don't know . . . Make it a hundred to be on the safe side.'

Mansie had expected this.

'Seventy-five,' he said.

'Done.'

'And make it your big van—we'll need that.'

Mick drove him back to Randerston and waited while he brought the things out of the house. His eyes rounded when he saw the great white bone, but he kept his tongue ready for the journey. He'd be telling all his customers in the new year that Mansie had finally cracked. And what could folk expect, with him living all on his own down there with nothing but seagulls to speak to, and wandering the beach from one end of the year to the next?

They were over the Christmas excitement at Cramond when Mansie arrived in his hired van, telling Mick to go up to the Castle for the view and be back for him in an hour or so.

'Dad—what in God's name's going on? And what the hell's that?'

'Christmas, I suppose, and presents. Are you asking me in for a minute?'

Between them they carried the skull through to the living-room, where the loudness of the television was keeping domestic life well in the background. Terry Wogan simpered at one of his own jokes. He was wearing a Santa Claus outfit but no beard.

'Mansie.'

Jane's mouth lost its shape. The children stared.

'What's all this?'

Mansie opened his carrier bag and held out the wine-bottle to Samantha.

'This one's for you, I'd say. It'll decorate your dressing table now that you're fair the young lady.'

Samantha took the gift with her fingertips and looked at her mother. Mansie nodded approvingly.

'That's taken you by surprise now, hasn't it? What's that you're wearing—ear muffs?'

'That's a personal stereo, dad,' Kevin said.

'It's my main Christmas present,' said the girl.

Mansie took the dead-eye over to Julian, where he lay on the floor with his own prize possession. His grandfather asked him what it was, and was told that it was a transformer.

'Does it have a name, this transformer?'

'Optimus Prime.'

'Oh, something out of Star Wars, eh?'

'No grandad, that was years ago.'

Mansie looked at the bit of red and black plastic in the boy's hands. First it was a car, then with a couple of twists it was some kind of robot.

'All the boys in my class have got one.'

'And what does it do?' asked Mansie.

'Nothing—it's Optimus Prime. What does that do?' the boy asked, staring doubtfully at the dead-eye as Mansie put it into his hands.

'Lots of things,' Mansie said.

There was a bar of silence as Julian compared the two presents, one in each hand.

'Nobody else in your class will have one of these.'

Mansie pointed then to the great skull at his feet.

'Well Jason, this is yours, as you're the oldest. Some size, isn't he?'

The older boy reluctantly left his new home computer and looked at the unignorable whiteness on the beautifully sanded floor.

'That beats a typewriter into a cocked hat, doesn't it? Or a television.'

Patiently Jason explained to his grandfather just what it was. Mansie listened softly.

'I'll be able to do a computer construction of a whale any time I want,' he said loftily. 'What do you think of that?'

Kevin laughed.

'More packed away in that little space, dad, than your whale could ever have imagined in its head.'

He winked at his son.

'It's not size that counts any more, is it? Small is beautiful, in modern technology.'

'Computers,' Mansie said.

'If you'd had one of these in your boat forty years ago, you'd have been a rich man by now, dad.'

Mansie's hand involuntarily rustled the paper money in his pocket.

'This must have cost you a bomb,' Jane said. 'Fancy you coming through like that without telling us. We could have picked you up.'

They all looked at the strange gifts from the sea.

'And we've got Kevin's partner and his wife coming for dinner.'

'Aye, I'll be gone in an hour.'

'You'll do no such thing, you'll stay here and have Christmas dinner with us.'

'No, no—my taxi will be back soon.'

'Have a beer anyway, dad, while you're waiting.'

'Yes, and I'd better be getting into my kitchen,' Jane said. 'Clear up all these things now, kids, I want this place tidy in an hour.'

Mansie stared into his beer.

'I think he's gone gaga,' Jane said over lunch, after Mansie had left; and everybody laughed.

'Bit loopy, is he?' asked the partner's wife.

'Over the top,' Kevin agreed. 'More wine, Bob? At least that's not over the hill yet—Chambertin '76. What a year for wine, eh?'

Samantha chucked the wine-bottle with the empties into the bin. She went up to her own room after dinner and held converse with the mirror. She was seeing a boy tonight, in his Sixth Year at the Edinburgh Academy, though her parents did not know that. The boy would take her to Paddy McGee's discotheque in Rose Street. She lifted her long hair like a mermaid's and twisted it round her mouth, smiling back at her reflected charms.

Julian kicked the dead-eye into the corner in a fury.

'Stupid old git!' he hissed between his teeth. 'He could've bought me Twistwin to go with Optimus. It's only £29.95 at Asda. And I saw his pockets bulging with fivers!'

Jason was out showing the whale's skull to his friends. His mother had said he would have to keep it in the garden shed.

'Don't want to keep it anywhere,' was his retort.

'Let's bung it in and harpoon the bugger,' somebody sniggered.

'Brill!'

They staggered down to the water's edge. Four pairs of hands heaved.

'Thar she blows! . . . Oh, nuts—it's bloody sunk!'

They used their driftwood harpoons as swords instead, cracking at each other all along the beach. Jason went in for tea and afterwards took his computer up to his room, where he tried to make a diagram of a whale, jabbing buttons. He lost interest and started a numbers game instead.

By that time Mansie had his fire on and was basking in the blaze.

The shadows were red dancers surrounding him.

'Gold, frankincense and myrrh,' he murmured into the flames.

No-one answered him. The dancers trembled and linked hands round the old man.

Four hours later the embers were a tired rose. Mansie shook his head. His eyes were stones.

'Pearls before swine,' he said. 'Pearls before bloody swine.'

He went to his bed in the corner, and lay looking up at the ceiling, cancerous with black mould.

'Too damp this place is getting . . . I'll bleach that ceiling in the morning.'

During the night the tide turned.

A shadow passed through the sleeping Mansie, like a dark flan of wind sweeping the water.

The stars leaned down with white faces, whispering through his window.

And over at Cramond the currents took the whale's skull, carrying it in slow motion across the Firth of Forth, towards Mansie's outstretched hand.

Hell Fire

A minute from the notorious records of the Beggar's Benison Club, Anstruther, Saturday 28th June 1746

The Most Ancient and Puissant Order of the Beggar's Benison and Merryland, Anstruther, At Castle Dreel in the Year of the Order 1746, and in the Aera of Our Lord 1746, Saturday 28th, vi month.

Proposed by the Laird of Thirdpart that Bethune of Balcarres be forthwith stricken from the Register of Members, on account of his abominations of the foregoing Saturday night, which conduct being deemed riotous and contrary to decorum, is like to bring down opprobrium on the good names, honours and titles of the gentlemen of this Club.

Seconded by Sir Charles Erskine and put to the voting.

Those in favour: The Laird of Thirdpart; Sir Charles Erskine; The Reverend Angus MacNab.

Those against: Bethune, Earl of Balcarres; Sir David Anstruther; Earl of Balcaskie; Robert Lumsdaine; Robert Pringle; Alexr. Blair; Earl of Abercrombie; Earl of Innergellie; Earl of Grangemuir; James Dow; David Rodger; William Ayton; Lord Newark; Thomas Oliphant; Thomas Erskine; Andrew Johnstone; James Grahame; James Moncrief; Thomas Nairn; Earl of Kelly; John Couper; Alexr. Miles; Charles Wightmnn; Dnnial Aithvnlivnd, Bluliup Duvld Luw; jóhii MacNaughton.

Three in favour, twenty-nine against, the President declared the motion not carried.

Nothwithstanding, the Earl of Balcarres made petition that a full minute be noted down by the recorder as to the assemblage of Saturday 21st June, so that no tenebrous insinuations be left in Club Records for Posterity or present Society to guess at, he requiring an absolute clearness upon that particular point.

Accordingly this minute continueth.

The Saturday precursive, it being Midsummer's Eve, much drink was taken by all thirty-two members present, and all of us exceeding

123

merry. Altogether we brought in that night thirteen hogsheads, two tuns of port, six cases of claret, nine casks of cider, numerous bowls of punch and some kegs of small beer.

The Earl of Abercrombie presented to the Club a handsome quarto edition, bound in buckram, of the celebrated Mr Defoe's *Moll Flanders*, and a reading from several of these amorous Adventures was delivered in brave style by Lord Newark. Thereafter the Reverend MacNab gave us a short but salacious selection from the *Song of Solomon*, Bishop David Low of Pittenweem translated some of Ovid's *Ars Amores*, and James Dow recited portions of Dunbar's narrative of *The Tua Meriit Wemen and the Wedo*, which he had by rote.

Subsequent upon this, the porter rolled in a great barrel of cognac, newly come ashore from France. This unexpected visitor having jigged his passage over on the billows by an una*ccustomed* route, with peradventure some helping hand from a good Scots fiddler or two playing a light-headed reel, and he moreover being exhausted by reason of waltzing his way around the skirts of certain Excise Officers, it was thought good to let him rest until the Royal Toast at the hindmost part of the evening.

John MacNaughton, Recorder, and Collector of Customs at Anster, present at this conclave, recalled that he had sent two Officers to watch at Kingsbarns, well removed from the point at which he had good Information the French émigré intended to disembark. This met with approval and occasioned some Jollity.

Next, as the centre-piece of the evening's entertainment, were brought on two sylph-like specimens of the fair sex, night-walking wenches, who diverted all present by dancing the length of the great table round which the company sat. From diverse ends of the board these fillies pranced their way to a mutual caper in the centre, and so passed along, each facing pair of gentlemen lavishing upon their legs and thighs certain Salutes and Civilities thought proper amongst our Confederacy of Males.

To gratify our amorous appetites the more, these lassies were exhorted to oblige us by disrobing before continuing with their frolic, the entire table being cleared of all Inebriant Obstacles to their Rites of Passage.

They would not, however, concur to this proposition without more moneys.

'I propone,' says young Innergellie, 'that for every shilling or more per man pitched upon the table, each alternate wench remove an article of her attire.'

This uproariously seconded, voted, and carried, in one universal Hurrah that stood in the stead of a formal motion.

'And,' puts in the Earl of Balcaskie, in a sudden Flush of Genius, 'the greater the coin, the greater the garment!'

Another Enthusiastic huzzah.

'And damn me if I do not cast the first florin!'

In a general Hush, Balcaskie spun his opening piece onto the board. Before it had rattled itself to a Cessation, off came a shoe. This brought forth a mighty masculine Roaring, as of many waters, and from that point on, each man present advanced the King's head in greater or lesser Mintages, according to the inflated condition of his Purse, whether Generative or Pecuniary.

The cunning minxes must have had some prescience of the like Pro-ceedings, however, for not a man amongst us but marvelled at the multiplications of Habiliments that were tossed over our heads and onto the floor. Skirts came off for Sovereigns, Stockings for Shillings, and many a Pound Scots was paid over to strip them down to the last and conclusory Petticoat. Not to mention Bodices and Stomachers and all manner of Lace.

After Epochs of Expectation we at last had the pair of them dancing Bare Buff, superior to our enraptured Eyes. By this time their toes were fairly twinkling across the litter of Cash that lay scattered the length of the table like a veritable Milky Way. And in and out of the Shining Constellations we had thrown at them, these two whizzed as a pair of Comets with Fiery Tails. Chastity had never darkened the luminosity of their Resplendent Orbs.

This ended with much applause, after which each man diced for the taking one of the Twosome upstairs, Grangemuir securing the one wench, and the last cast of the die coming down to Bethune and Thirdpart for Conquest of the remaining Jade. The throw went to Bethune, greatly to Thirdpart's vexation.

Then our two especial Votaries of Cupid, Grangemuir and Bethune, went off to have bestowed upon them such Pleasant Coquetries as the Possession of Fair Vessels En*tails*, the Customs Officer present allowing them full Powers and Privileges of *Ingress*, *Egress* and *Regress*, from and to all the *Harbours*, *Creeks*, *Havens* and Commodious *Inlets* upon the *Coasts* of their extensive *Territories*, at their pleasure, and that without payment of Toll, Custom, or any other Taxes or Imposition whatsoever.

The remainder of the Company resorted once more to the Bottle. Thus the arms of Bacchus must be sought by those who have fallen from the arms of Venus. And all men alike go from there to seek the arms of Morpheus.

But what hath night do with sleep, as the Poet has said? Instead we pottled lustily, vowing to shun all Bellies that are like to Swell. Pipes then Smoked.

Thirdpart's loss, however, of his Female Haven, occasioned him much mortification, he having seen many a one of his Sovereigns go spinning about the flashing feet of the two Coquettes. The gathering assessed the merits and demerits of these two handsome Hussies, discoursing learnedly upon their Parts and Graces, and allowed them both to be Passing Fair; such debates being an agreeable part of our established Fraternity upon its Nocturnal Assemblies. For as the Serpent took Eve out of her Nakedness and clothed her with Sin, so do we still Strive to bring that same Eve back out of her Robes and Petticoats, and into the State of Nature reserved for the Solace of Mankind.

Notwithstanding Thirdpart swore much during this debate, saying vocably that these wenches were as coarse a Brace of Stinking Cod's Tail as he had ever seen cast away to the beggars. And when the fortunate two came down from their Lovebeds, he quoted as much to Bethune concerning *His* trollop.

Noted that Bethune bestirred not a hair of his head at Thirdpart's Sourness.

Pipes once more, and another reading, this time from one of our Great Favourites, the unpublished MSS of Mr Cleland, whose Spicy *Memoirs of a Woman of Pleasure* is known to us all as *Fanny Hill*.

At this stage an Universal Wooziness signalled the going down of our Intoxicant Star.

In conclusion therefore, the Royal Toast, to be followed by a Nominated Toast. It falling to Thirdpart to propose the toast, and he being a pronounced Whig and eager to discountenance Bethune, who had late come down from Culloden, bereft of his only Son upon Drummossie Moor, Thirdpart says:

'Gentlemen, I beg you to be upstanding One and All, and drink the Health of His Majesty the King.'

The cup was drunk off.

'And,' adds Thirdpart, 'the health of the King's Best Soldier!'

'Who is it that you mean?' asks Bethune, with a look like Nightfall blackening his Brows.

'Gentlemen of the Beggar's Benison,' says Thirdpart, 'I propose the Health of His Royal Highness the Duke of Cumberland.'

Opportunity taken here to place on Record that this was ever from its Inception a Society of Males knit together not by a spirit of Faction but by a love of Society itself, especially the Society of the Gentle Sex. Also it was for aye the Observance of the Club that no Gentleman refuse another's Pledge.

Albeit that Thirdpart had erred in thus surrogating to himself the Second Toast, Bethune stood with the rest of us and drank off the glass. In consequence of which, he, dark in the face, rose up and proposed a third toast.

'Gentlemen,' says he, 'I ask you to drink the health of David Sibbald.'

The two cups having been drunk off, Thirdpart made demur. The Opinion of the Body howbeit was strong that the Free Toast should by rights be accorded to a Second Party, and that Bethune's Bowl be drunk.

'To David Sibbald, gentlemen,' says Bethune.

'And who the devil may be David Sibbald?' Thirdpart makes demand.

'Just drink the toast, Sir,' says Bethune.

'It is the Etiquette of this Club to know something of the Person Pledged,' says Thirdpart.

On that point he made appeal to the President, who moved that David Sibbald be identified.

'Very well, Sir,' says Bethune. 'David Sibbald is a butcher of Colinsburgh, and a damned good butcher he is too! He takes fine care for me of all my Slaughtering, and is right at home in the Society of Beasts!'

'A common butcher!' says Thirdpart. 'No, Sir, I'll not lift my glass to such a one, never. I'll drink to general damnation first, but to the health of a butcher, no sir!'

Then says Bethune:

'And I say that drink his health you will, Sir. For I've drunk your Butcher, and by God you'll drink mine, Sir, or I'll thrust the toast down your thrapple, glass and all, aye, and put you through the window!'

Thereupon Thirdpart flung the contents of his glass full in the face of Bethune, saying that there was the toast in his own Jacobite thrapple, let him swallow what part of it he would.

Bethune, wiping his face with a napkin, gave it as his Opinion that what Thirdpart required was a more generous Supply of Drink for his toast. He tore off the top from the new barrel of cognac and took Thirdpart by the throat, forcing him down into the liquor, like the old Duke of Clarence into the butt of Malmsey. Drawing him out by the hair, he shouts in his Lug:

'Now, Sir, did you drink your grog?'

All to be heard from Thirdpart were several Chokings and Splutterings, and so Bethune shouts again:

'Well, down you go, Sir, for a longer look, just to be certain. And if I don't hear you drink my butcher deep whiles you're down there, then I'd best hear you say it loud and clear when you emerge, or down you'll go for a third part, Thirdpart!'

He was well into his second Soaking, and all begun to think Thirdpart in some danger of a brandefied Asphyxiation, when at last he fluttered his hands in tender of Submission.

Bethune hauled him out once more by the hair.

'Aye, Sir,' says he, 'your Phiz is a brave bloated Purple, not unlike to the grand Duke of Cumberland's face that's so little different from his poxy Arse! But there's enough of Comparisons. Just let us hear the toast now, loudly if you please: I drink your Butcher as you have drunk Mine.'

'I drink your Butcher . . .'

'As you have drunk Mine!'

'As you have drunk Mine!'

Bethune then professed himself near satisfied.

'But,' says he, 'that was a long Tipple, and you must have made a Sop of your Brains. So doubtless now you'll stand in sore need of sobering!'

With these words he haled Thirdpart to the Casement and hurled him straight through the Panes by the Seat of his Trousers. We rushed as One to the gaping hole made by Thirdpart's considerable Bulk, and looked out in Amazement, expecting to see him Dead. The laird had indeed gone down twenty feet to where the Dreel meets the sea. By good Fortune, however, the Ocean was on a full tide, and a goodly Depth of water both Salt and Fresh combined to break Thirdpart's fall and cool his Temper.

This is not the Club of Duellists in which none be initiated who has not killed his Man. Nonetheless we deem that no Censure be borne by either Party.

Except that as Thirdpart's person broke the window, and Bethune's hand propelled him through the same, the cost of making it Good be divided between Jacobite and Whig as follows:

Bethune (Jacobite): three parts of thirty-two of the total Cost.

Thirdpart (Whig): twenty-nine parts of thirty-two of total Cost.

According to the vote.

Done at the Beggar's Benison Chambers at Anstruther on the aforesaid date.

Witness I the Recorder.

John MacNaughton.

Stone, Wave and Star

(*A meditation on the history and legends of the East Fife sea-caves. Based on a piece first written for a reading in St Fillan's Cave, Pittenweem, 27th July, 1983*).

Prelude

Enter the cave, sang the storyteller.

Here the darkness casts no shadows and there is no light to tell you any lies.

Enter the cave.

Stepping out of the sly shelter of window and wall; the gable that glides like a ghost into the ground before it has known the merest millenium; the wasting world of the red roof, weathering into ruin faster than the crumpling graveyards of the sea.

Enter the cave, the rock of ages, sang the poet.

Leaving behind you the slipperiness of the present moment, which has ceased to exist even before the echoes of these words have died on the walls. Syllables that shine briefly like spray, to be sucked away by what surrounds us now—centuries of silence and stone.

Enter the cave.

Abandoning the absurdities of calendars and clocks, and the insidious sun that tricks you into telling time. Shut up your eyes and ears and send the calculating brain to sleep. For even the stars, whose whispering tick is longer than the sun's, are blotted out by the black hole of the cave.

Enter the cave, wooed the voice of the storyteller. Light years flicker behind the translucent curtainings of your closed lids. Aeons beat against your eyeballs; an incredible sea.

This hole in the rock is where you started and where you will end. From sun to exploding sun; from the first stone flung by a Neanderthal hand, to the last nuclear spear hurled by the warmongering monsters of tomorrow: savages in white coats.

129

Enter the cave now.

Time has slipped loose from eternity's dark hand, and for a twinkling of aeons it will dance among the stars.

It is the first day.

(1) *The Song of Creation*

White-hot, new-born, spawned by a star, the world ran like a pearl; solidifying as it slowed and spun.

The ocean coated it, a drop of cooling dew.

Mountains melted like shadows against skylines that plunged and rose.

The pearl hardened then, and the earth-planet's brand new dewdrop bulged to the moon-pull, turning the first tide.

The sea-bed settled; the cell-less sea sang in its green chains its early morning song.

The German Ocean moved south.

On the shores of Fife a bead of water, shaken from the firth, splashed against stone. The cliff lost a single sandstone grain that fell at once to the earth. But not like corn did it fall; there was no growing in it.

Now waterdrops have worried away a forehead, high up on the rock face. And now the sea is edging closer, century by slow century, the wild horses thrusting their white foaming tongues at the land, licking and spitting.

And, drop by grain, on the grey rock face, a whispering mouth appears under the beetling brow. A billion years before the first stones of Troy, the cave has begun.

It holds converse with the sea.

It is eight thousand years since the first primitive houses of wattle and mud and hide sheltered the early Stone Age settlers of Scotland from the winds and spray of the Firth of Forth and the cold North Sea. Tourists come today, admiring the douce dwellings of the now substantial fishing townships. But the axe-bearing, tundra-trekking tourists of that distant age must have gazed with greedy eyes on what were then the noblest mansions in Fife: the east coast 'steddis', or caves, from one of which the village of Pittenweem takes its name.

Go back in your head.

Go back to a day when the clouds are streaming in tattered black battalions up the firth. The raw north-easterlies are girning round the gable end and howling down the lum. There is a whining in the wainscot and a weariness in the old walls.

Outside there is a cold clinging rain.

It reaches down with trickling fingers through flesh and field, to wet the very skeleton, living and dead. Into the house of skin, into the house of clay, drips the many-fingered hand. Cold bones of the dead grow colder still. Gray daggers of air flay the ribs, a ruthless butchery. And the wind sucks the marrow from your spine.

On such a day you can see what the sea-caves meant to the earth's early peoples. Yet very few such caves are to be found, pocking the Fife coast. They must have been fought over like fortresses by early man.

What was he like—the first man to step into this hole in the rock? A poor, shambling creature, no doubt, of little intelligence. But he must have known thoughts and feelings, even imagination and insight of a sort.

Is it possible to enter into these faculties; to fasten hold on that forlorn life of his, even for a few fleeting seconds?

Listen; listen hard. And you will hear him thinking.

(2) *The Song of the First Man*

We came to this place out of the wide loneliness.

North, east and west we had nowhere to go. In the north the great forests filled up one morning with snow. Not a berrry was left unburied; the trees stood rooted in death. We turned our backs on them, fared southwards, fierce tribes guarding the hill-gates of the west, every step we took. The east bristled with waves—the invisible nostril of the fish was safe from our hooks of bone, beneath the churning firth.

Without fish, or berry, or the beast on the hill, a tribe soon dies, struck down by the bitter flints of winter.

The white winds were wasting us when we fell on this sudden shelter.

Only a she and her young were inside. A she without a he-friend. They clung to the comfortable darkness at the back of the cave. We dragged them out under the sky and laid the flints gladly to their throats. There was a hot hurricane of blood from the she; a weak weeping from the little one. A glinting of gore in the snow.

We opened their heads with our axes then, tasted the boilings of their brains. A sweet meal was inside the skull of the little one. Sweeter than marrow sucked from the bone, than honey scooped from the nest.

The white winds parted, showed us the home and haven we had made ours: a stone hole in the world, for the sleeping and sheltering of a small tribe; horns of the deer on the high hill; the cold flicker of fins in the fallow flood.

Blood from the field-beast makes a warm wounding: freezing is the blood from the beast of the sea. Both make a glad fire in a wintry belly.

A red screaming goes on in the mouth of the dying field-beast. In the mouth of the sea-beast blood is cold and silent as a winter sunset. Who tore the voice from the beast of the sea? Can the fishes hear death, quivering under the water?

The shells of the shore carry the coldest of comforts into a hungry mouth. But they cannot run—those creatures of the shells—from the pursuing points of stone and bone. Like bitter berries the black whelks grow on the rocks. Every tide is an autumn. Time is short.

What is this life?

An unfolding of circles.

Beginning with a dark coil of sleep, deep inside the cave of the she-one's belly. A circle broken by birth.

I uncoiled—and entered the circle of being.

Life is milk from the blood-red ring on the she-one's breast; it is light from the golden hole in the sky's roof; it is belonging to the tight circle of backs around the fire. To be shut out from any one of these circles means hunger, cold, exile: a certain end to living.

The hearthstone beats like a heart from blackness to redness and so back again, tonight, tomorrow, and so on and round.

The stars are flung like cold corn by the whirling hand of the north star, the scatterer. The quernstone spins the golden grain into a circle of bread. It is beaten out and broken into four.

There are four quarters also in the coloured wheel of the year: there is a green stirring; a yellow wakefulness; a brown drowsiness; a white sleep of death.

The mead-drink dances like the sun, caught in the stone circle of the stone cup.

Mating is the circle of four arms, unbroken for a briefness of the night. In the golden core of it there is sometimes a moment when that circle seems eternal. But always it ends.

And there is a cruel circle of pain, in which a man is often trapped, like the beast in the ring of hunters. Invisible spears lodged in back, breast and bones. Unseen axes in the skull. Who sends them—and why?

Once I flung a stone into the stillness of the tide. It was under a calmness of stars.

I watched the circles expanding endlessly, spawning stars of water.

For an instant time shattered, and I saw something beyond the tips of my fingers. I saw countless circles rippling outwards past the outermost stars. Where did it all end? There was a wild spinning in my skull. Supposing it never ended. Besides a joy there was a fear in that thought.

But there is one worse thought even than that.

If there were no outermost circle at all, no ultimate boundary. Only never-ending nothingness . . .

Yet, as the last agony curls me up in the corner of the cave-home, I expel that thought like a dead child. They will bury me with my legs drawn up to my chest and my chin touching my knees, like the baby waiting to be born.

Thus death completes the endless circle.

O darkness deliver me.

Swift and bitter indeed must have been the lives of the first Fifers.

A brief breath around the bone.

Cold, hunger, arthritis; the hunter in his twelve years' prime, gored by the foaming boar; the infant turning back again to the door of darkness. Old age at twenty, senile decreptitude at thirty.

Did they see any meaning in the early dawns and the late sunsets? Did they envisage anything at all beyond the confines of womb and tomb? It is impossible to say just how far the frail fancy of the poet may reflect their thinkings. They lived and they perished—that is all we can be sure of.

But for centuries now trodden underfoot they were our founding fathers. The sparks from their ashes still blow on the wind. And these poor people are worth our remembering, in the height of our pride, before we forget for too long who and what we really are.

For what advantage is there in living longer in a world without imagination? And perhaps the terrors of barbarism and ignorance are less frightening than the terrors of boredom and intellectual enlightenment.

They crucified a carpenter in a more enlightened age than that of the Stone Age world. A man of peace. And in a hole in the rock they laid his body like broken bread, sprinkled with the black wine of his wounds.

When his followers came into the cave of death they found the bread of life had risen, in the white-hot temperature of the Resurrection. The tomb of Christ had become the womb of God: a greater beginning than was announced to Mary.

That bread was broken again across the world; the golden grains of God sown by centuries of faith. The years turned over like fields, watered by the red rain of the martyrs. The harvest was the church, its congregation the entire peoples of the world: a new and blinding theology.

The early church was a honeycomb of caves, and the whole earth hummed.

Into the dark clammy cells there crept the sweetness of Christ, made accessible to the spiritual palates of men by the busy monks.

And the monks sang like gold-bearing bees in these bleak hives. They were content to lose themselves to contemplation in the crowded anonymity of their early communes.

There too the hermits hymned out their chaste solitary lives.

Listen again.

Listen to the words of one of these: St Fillan, the hermit of the cave, who arrived on these shores thirteen hundred years ago. He lived out his life in, and left his name to, what is now the oldest house in Pittenweem: the God-formed, sea-made masonry of St Fillan's Cave, perhaps the earliest church in the east of Fife.

A kirk without transepts or nave or choir. A kirk without flying buttresses, vaulted arches, soaring stained-glass windows and aspiring steeple. Just a hole in the belly of mother earth; no more. God's handiwork; as dark as Mary's womb and the sepulchre of Jesus.

Until St Fillan found Light within it, and wrote the Word.

Listen; let us hear. The walls of the old cave are whispering with his words.

(3) The Song of St Fillan

By the grace of God I came from Ireland to this little nook of fishing folk in the east of these islands, and in the year of our Lord six hundred and seventy-nine. And through the grace of our blessed Lord and Saviour, Jesus Christ, I thank God that I fare better than I deserve on the face of this wicked earth.

This cave is my dwelling.

Out of the rock have I made my church and chapel, my bed and board, my work and contemplation, my Martha and Mary. And also my grave among men. For I must tell you that I am alive only unto God, and from the tip of my toe to the crown of my head I am the sole brother of the living Christ, and am dead unto the world.

Until Jesus Christ wake me.

What then, you will ask, is my life? Listen and I will tell you.

The sound of the sea both night and day; the steady beating of waves scouring my ears unto shells, until they are emptied of all vain hearing. An end of frivolous chatter and long, pointless stories at last.

Murmuring miles of blue tide tapping at my door: no more shallow travelling on my part over the brittle crust of this earth, beneath which Hell bubbles like a pot. No more waiting in idleness for the knock of a stranger and his worthless words of news. Such and such a city has fallen; so and so was king of a certain country and has died, somewhere across the sea. What is all that to me?

Sometimes indeed the sea turns white, and there is an angry pounding on my doorsill; a noise that would make the guilty tremble.

That sound carries no fear into my fortified soul, no tidings of a troubled world. The waves are God's angels in their stern summoning, their hair blown wild by all the winds of heaven. And the white surf running about my praying knees—these are fingers from the great ocean of truth outside my door; sent to remind me that this universe is no mere warring of blind elements but a mighty concourse of all God's parts and graces.

Ebb-tide, flood-tide, the world wavers and wanes, while I stay alone in my little chapel-cave, always waxing to the fullness of God's forgiving grace; always the bows of my little bark of faith headed into that tideless sea that drifts towards eternity.

No other soul aboard with me to haul the sails, to share the lonely desolation of the sea. For alone I came into this world, alone must I go from it, when the world is finally lost, that so many fools would falsely win. And so it seems fitting to me that alone I should sojourn as here I stand, naked between two beyonds.

And yet, though I am alone, I am never solitary on this earth, for God is in everything that I do, and it is no small thing to keep body and soul together.

An hour of gathering limpets from the rocks, or bending over the blue musselbeds for bait.

An hour or two of fishing, morning and evening, when the firth mirrors the sky and the fish are on the move.

An hour of gathering strawberries; herbs and honey in the golden summertime; hips and haws in autumn; hazelnuts, chestnuts, brambleberries, bogberries, sweet red apples; and, for penance, the green mantling waterweed of the hermit's well, that washes away sin from cloudy eyes.

An hour of eating at my meagre meal: a seabird's egg, a boiled crab, a beaker of cold water.

An hour of prayer, of singing psalms, of meditation on the life eternal, and on keeping sacred God's temple, the body, and the conscience clear; as clear as the pure water of the well-spring in the front of my little church.

Time soon goes by.

And at the end of the day, a stony hour of sleep on my brief bed, a cold lying down upon rock.

Ah, but mine is not like the repose of that doomed seed upon flinty ground, thrown down never to rise again. Rather when I stretch myself to rest, I think of that other blessed body that was laid low in the darkness of the sepulchre, only to be raised up high among angels and stars.

So, should the morning come in vain for me, the sea beating and the seagulls crying in dead ears, I shall arise in glory, leaving behind me that poor, abused brother of mine, my body—like a penitent's white shift, cast off, for men to burn or bury or do with what they will. For in truth, the flesh was a fashion in wearing that I never truly took to; one that was handed down to me from Adam long ago, and which I shall willingly throw aside.

In fact St Fillan's mortal remains were treated with some care.

The day had not yet come when a few splinters of saintly bone would be worth more than a string of choicest pearls. But even in these dawning days of the church, well before the men of a craftier age came to appreciate the commercial power of relics, St Fillan's left arm was removed and enshrined in silver. This was because the arm boasted a miraculous hand.

What is the story?

Let the holy saint speak again in telling of it.

(4) *St Fillan's Song of the Miraculous Hand*

It was twelve days to Epiphany and I suffered badly from cold.

The stars were bright with expectation of the Christmas Festival. In shimmering companies they stood over the firth, waiting, like me, for the great advent. How could a man ever be lonely in such a crowd?

But there was no moon to wash the back of my little church-cave with her bleak beams, and so provide me with the celestial light whereby I might continue the task of writing. My lamp of fish-oil had guttered to a grotesque and greasy stench at the end of the third verse of St John, and I had no tallow left. I had not felt the tug of a fish on my line for many days, under the wintry wave.

And I had so wanted to complete my transcription of the Holy Gospels, for Christ's sake on His birthday. Truly some fiend of hell had been in that ink from the first letter to the last I had copied, and with the lack of light the work was difficult enough.

I started to transcribe, with my eye almost touching the manuscript.

In ipso vita erat, et vita erat lux hominum: et lux in tenebris lucet, et tenebrae eam non comprehenderunt.

It was no use. The chill chinks of stars were not enough. My feet had grown to stone, the fingers of my writing hand were clamped into a claw by the fierce frost that had even found its way into the church that night.

A frost so cruel I feared the very roof of my cave would split under its white fists.

Wrapping myself about with both my sheepskin coverings, I rose from my hewn table and went to the cave mouth. The stars swept the sky (how unfriendly they suddenly seemed!) a savage spume of eternity breaking on the very edges of space. I needed a greater light than they greater even than the sun and moon at that moment.

I cried loud out of the darkness.

'O for the Light of the World! *Erat lux vera, quae illuminat omnem hominem venientem in hunc mundum.*'

The brute sea continued its long slow sucking and sighing. My sea of truth was a white welter bursting on the black rocks of the shore. How barbaric was the whole universe which at that pinpoint in the temporal scheme of things I appeared to inhabit entirely alone! How feeble the house of flesh in which my frail soul trembled, like a palsied old widow in her hut of straw!

Where was my dear Lord?

Sadly I turned away from that scene of primaeval chaos. I would lie down on my mattress of dried seaweed throughout the long winter's night and await the coming of another brief day.

A touch on my shoulder turned me round in my slow tread.

A stranger in the night, his head framed by stars, Orion crowning his temples. Sirius was a winter lamp at his side.

I put out my hand to welcome him—for the entrance to my church-cave is ever the arch of welcome to the tired wayfarer—and he took my cold hand in his.

O brothers and sisters of mine, how can I tell you that it was indeed the Light of the World who stood at my humble door? And who would believe me?

The touch of his hand was like fire, and as the blood returned to my frozen fingers I cried out in great pain. Was I to receive the stigmata, I wondered?

But no. As he withdrew his hand I could see the red wound in the centre of his palm and on his wrist. Looking into my own hand, I saw what looked like a wound, but which spilled no blood. What was it?

A tiny heart-shaped ruby, shining in the chalice of my hand. A ruby that ran with rich red light. I raised my arm. The unearthly radiance splashed across the walls and lit up the entire cave, the blood of God streaming across the roof and down to the floor.

Bedazzled by this miracle, it seemed a long time until I raised my eyes again to the door. The stars still straddled the sea; the waves boiled white among the rocks. The benighted stranger was gone.

But the touch of his hand never left me.

I took up my pen and ink, the manuscript now illumined by the hand of God in mine. And all night long I carried on the work of copying out the Fourth Gospel in the red-roomed scriptorium of my cave.

As the morning shadows crept in at the door and the sunlight watered the walls, the blood-red light of the world drained from my fingers, dripping into daylight, and the ruby in the middle of my palm faded and disappeared.

By then however the work of transcription was over.

Sunt autem et alia multa, quae fecit Iesus: quae si scribantur per singula, nec ipsum arbitror mundum capere posse eos, qui scribendi sunt, libros. Amen.

And as an afterthought, I added in the margin:

'And there is no end, dear reader, to the things which Jesus continues to do in this world, and in the next.'

I was ready for Christmas Day.

But ever afterwards, when the evening shadows lengthened, creeping like familiar ghosts into the cave, the heavenly heart in my hand started to throb, an exquisite pain, and the light from that richest of all rubies irradiated the darkest recesses of my rocky abode. And as soon as the sun shook night from the earth and the shadows retreated into the sea, the ruby once more diminished and disappeared.

And so it continued. The heart beat from evening to evening. And day unto day uttered speech. And night unto night shewed knowledge.

Naturally things cannot always have turned out so well for our Fife anchorites, fast bound in their cold east-coast caves.

Listen. Let the tide of the present time ebb from your head. And it will not be hard to hear this lonely Dark Age lament.

(5) *The Song of the Weary Hermit*

Bent-backed and withered in the bitterness of these boisterous winds, I did not think bad weather to have found me out here in such a useless old age.

It is long ago since I gave up the five things I have loved most: a girl; a glass of wine; a great talking over the drink; many candles and much music at the evening meal; and rising at nextday noon from a feather quilt.

But the five things I have most dreaded I little thought to have come between me and the hope of heaven: a fire in the lungs; a mist in the eyes and ears; a wolf in the bowels; a sickness in the soul; and, worst of all, boredom with myself.

Nettle-broth is now the staple diet of one who longs for ambrosia with the angels. And longing, my friend, is the one thing that never wears out.

The wind wears out the pine-tree with its grey harping. But I would give a year of heaven for the clang of a clarsach string.

The seagull and gannet are graceful in their gliding. But I saw many gulls between Brega and the Sound of Barra, and many gannets between the Pentland Firth and the German Sea. And I would give an angel's wings to be gladdened by a dancing girl, barbaric with eastern pearl.

The sea is running cold and high on the sands: my own poor sands are low, and the last few grains are stuck fast in the brittle glass.

Ever shriller and colder the wind, ever lower the sun, shorter its journeying, feebler its wick, longer the watches of the night.

Once I took pleasure in spelling the stars: holy candles held by a hundred thousand angels. And God's tasks were never too long in the completing. Now I wish the night wind would dowse them into darkness, snuff out their destinies and the seeing from my wakefulness.

Once too there were the chessboard's slow ponderings, when the hours fell like roses and my patience wore stronger than oak. Now I watch the snow fall on the shore, filling the sleepless night, and I try to discern patterns and meanings in that, to while away the time. For in my youth I was known to be something of a poet.

Snow.

A white trimming on the green-furred trees; a white dress on the winter jasmine, golden-faced girl of my sea-facing garden.

Snowflakes.

White bees bringing honey from heaven, cold nectar of the saints; fine foam on a mighty mug of ale; the fleeces of the finest flock in Christendom.

Snow.

Pure-cold plumage of the swan, swansdown ruffled by swan's last song; bitter-cold shroud on the greensward grove, last sheeting for the frail, sinful flesh . . .

Ah, my friend, the flesh, the flesh! fodder, foul fodder for the worm that feedeth so sweetly on sinful man. How fast in gravesgrasping shall my flesh lie then, until I return in spirit to my eternal Lord! And O, how long must I yet endure till then, O Lord? O Christ, my Saviour, between our fates so long, between our fates how long!

So deprivation and desolation led to divisions in the soul of the recluse, and to all kinds of desperate delusions. Some won through their own personal purgatories to the celestial gates; some went back into the world, unable to resist the promptings of the flesh and the devil.

Others walked straight into the waves until nothing was left of them but a line of footprints on the sand, to be taken out by the next tide.

It took many more tides of history to remove the last remaining evidences of their sea-smitten lives from the holy caves so many had inhabited before them. Yet the years took out the signs of their existence as surely as the sea washed away the footprints in the sand.

In time only a few crosses were left, scratched into the stonework among the shadows.

And so they came and went, Benedictine monk and Augustinian canon, to enter into the inheritance paved for them by St Fillan and his followers in those natural chapels chiselled out by tide and time.

But eleven centuries ago, when the Northmen devastated Ireland, a saint called Adrian came to Eastern Scotia with six thousand six hundred and six companions and confessors, including among them the white-robed St Monan, who chose to lead his life in a tiny cave two lonely miles west of Pittenweem, at Inverey.

Adrian took to the Coves at Caiplie, leaving the May Island as his place of retreat, and in the year 832 AD, as told by scribes, worked many wonders among the Pictish tribes of Fife.

These are the rags of history—a few threadbare sentences out of which imagination has to weave its own cloth of gold.

Under the sudden yoke of the Scots, the Picts plotted with the Danes to attack their conquerors.

The Danish terror landed near St Andrews in the shape of two brothers, King Humber and his brother Hubba, spoiling for slaughter. Constantine, King of Scots, advanced upon Fife and crushed Hubba's company on the banks of the River Leven. Drunk on the brave and brutal dream of victory, he then led his troops in search of brother Humber, finding him fortified near Crail at Fifeness. He attacked rashly and lost the game, falling into the hands of his enemies.

The penalty was the highest.

Storytelling has it that he was dragged into the cave at Fifeness. There the plunging swords sent him quickly out of the year 876 AD and into that dateless dimension somewhere beneath the bluebell and the bee, where many a buried bone lies slumbering

The cave became known in Fife as The Devil's Cave.

Humber promptly ordered a general massacre

And that was the mad massacre of saints in which so many of the six thousand holy men poured out their blood on the Fife shores.

In one of the Caiplie Coves, on a night of storms, you can still hear the sound of one of Adrian's monks as he relives his time of terror.

Listen.

(6) *The Monk's Song*

Wild the winds tonight, tearing the waves' white hair. Tonight I fear no sudden foray by the firth. No wild warriors of Denmark, coursing the German Ocean.

Bitter the winter tonight, no stars' cold torches on the sea. Tonight no chant arises from our small monastic cell. No holy plume of words reaching God's ears, smokeless among the stars.

> *A furore Normanorum libera nos Domine.*
> From the wrath of the Norsemen O Lord deliver us.
> *A furore Normanorum libera nos Domine.*

It is nearly nine years since they came to Caiplie. It was on a night such as this, a full and running tide. The swiftness and surprise of the attack are what impressed me most of all—the keels' sudden crunching on shingle, the dragonshead prows biting the air, snarling at the saints.

They were leaping into the water well before the longboats had even grounded—the men I had heard tell of with such terror but never until now seen with my own eyes.

How could I ever forget them? Their beards were thonged with spray and their lips with the froth of their own fury. A hundred crimson cloaks rippled and billowed like clouds of blood sailing across a winter sunset. And their berserk battle-cries were worse than the loud bursting of the sea.

We were as sheep before wolves.

Snatching up the Holy Eucharist, I ran to the small mortuary cove where the bodies of the brothers gone before us mouldered into bone (their open putrefaction allowing us the benefit of studying what we really are).

I crept in among the corpses and lay down as one of them. There was little in that stench and spectacle of old death to terrify me that I had not long grown accustomed to. A frozen fish-eye; a socket black as a starless night; a gaping jaw; an upturned crab of a hand, clutching at nothing. What was there in all that except the decomposition of rubbish now discarded by the immortal soul?

Yet as I lay there, fear turned me as white and stiff as my cold companions of the charnel-houses. Fear not of death, but of dying itself—in a painful and brutal manner at the hands of those pagan barbarians. So stark with horror was I indeed that my fear truly saved my life. For one of the Vikings charged straight into the mortuary, his torch flaring. In the light of the lurid flames we stared straight into one another's eyes. But it was dead eyes he saw in mine, and so passed on and spared me.

For a time perhaps I verily was dead and no mere actor. The slaughter on the sands came to me through the cobwebbed sockets of my skull, the spaces where my ears had hung centuries ago. I witnessed the carnage as if across a desert gulf that separated me from my chosen companions. And I had in front of me the whole history of the world in which to itemize the terrible details of their end.

Brother Aldhelm ran down at once to meet the men of terror, and to plead with them in Christ's name.

He sank to his knees before the leader, holding up to him the holy cross. A sword-blade whirled once. The hand holding the cross was swept away. The cross clanged among the rocks twenty paces off but the hand did not let go.

Aldhelm bowed his bald head to inspect his bleeding stump. In an instant that milky pate of his was crowned with a dripping rose. It was with a look of surprise on his face, finding himself wearing such a ridiculous flower on his head, that Aldhelm put up the fingers of his other hand to feel the wet red petals that were already kissing his bloodless lips. He shook them, shuddering, from his mouth, and died.

The company scattered then. Javelins flew, swords flashed, axes fell.

Some ran into the Chapel Cove and fell against the altar, to be pinned there by spears. Some ran into the sea and drowned. Or were butchered there, like gentle seals slashed by killer whales. For a very short time there was the meeting of wound and wind and wave. And the shore was swept by blood.

The blessed Adrian himself escaped through the back of the Coves, and he made his way on horseback over the fields with the leavings of the brothers.

Ah, but the invaders were relentless.

For days they hounded them, killing them on moors and beaches. Hell burned in their hearts. Our chapel-caves were desecrated, our treasures taken, the holy golden chalices spoliated, melted down into rings and bracelets. To make circles of fire on the wrists and fingers of the warlike women of Denmark.

Even this was not sufficient to make them desist.

On Holy Thursday the mild-mouthed St Monan was murdered in his cave at Inverey. And the blessed Adrian was martyred on the May, where Monan's lips of love had been the first to preach the gospel. And all the monks of the May died like cattle in that murderous attack, the splashing dew of the sword-wounds still cold on their corpses as they lay unburied after many days.

There was a great gorging of seabirds on that island. A red shambles littered its rocks and beaches for weeks afterwards. Some say its sands were never white again.

Tread thoughtfully all you who visit these shores in time to come. For many a saint and monk lie martyred on this little mile of land.

Battle-axes and javelins cannot conquer the religious impulse in man. And although the monks never came again to Caiplie in such numbers, gradually the holy men crept back to their caves, drawn by their fascination for those wave-battered, sea-torn fissures in the rock, where somehow they found God.

Long after the Viking incursions, at the end of the twelfth century, a religious recluse inhabited the cave at Randerston, a mile north-west of Constantine's Cave.

He had been a follower of Peter Abelard's, and like his old master, came to know the cravings of the flesh.

Listen again.

His struggle goes on.

Sit alone in that cave on a windy night and you will hear passion in the waves.

(7) *The Ascetic's Song*

I sat alone in my cave-cell, at one with seagull and seed and star.

My whole concern was to enter the Kingdom of Heaven.

The folk of that coast left me to myself. They went to a church on a hill, in a long, straggling line. They worshipped God in a flock.

I said to myself, 'There are many paths to God: there is the path of the dream, the path of good works in the world, and the path of communal worship. I have chosen the path of withdrawal, and of solitary contemplation.'

And so I lived alone, intent upon Paradise.

But one day God saw fit to put temptation in my path.

There was a fisherman's daughter who gathered limpets on the shore for her father's lines.

Every day she passed my cave-cell walking eastwards with her empty basket; every day she passed westwards again with her basket full, and received my blessing before going home.

When times were hard she gave me some of the limpets from her basket. In return I prayed for her soul and sang psalms for her at midnight.

Then her father took to beating her if her basket were not full, and I forbade her to give me any more.

Ah, but brothers and sisters of mine, *Spiritus quidem promptus est, caro autem infirma*. The spirit indeed is willing, but the flesh is weak.

There came a cruel winter. The fish deserted the firth.

The limpet-gatherer again gave me from her basket. Home she

walked into the setting sun, and I made the sign of the cross at her back and settled down to my meal.

A limpet is a bitter dish in winter when one has not eaten for five days.

Next day the girl held out her basket to me. There among the limpets was a crust of bread and a shining fish. A little bar of silver treasured from her father's nets. I knew that the fish were scarce and that the girl must be beaten for it, but I could not help myself. I fell upon it greedily. The girl smiled, watching me eat.

After she had gone I closed my eyes, meditating upon Heaven and upon the Life Eternal. Under my veiled lids however, I saw not the blessed Mary, Queen of Heaven, but the little limpet-gatherer of the shore. I prayed earnestly for salvation.

But when spring rustled the fields and sea, the girl came oftener than the tides to my lonely cell.

The fish had returned to the firth, and now her basket always contained some tempting morsel of haddock or herring, or succulent cod. Sometimes a large crab for the roasting, or the delicate white meat of the lobster. These she cooked for me with her own hands. I sat by her and watched her preparations, thinking how much lovelier she was becoming every day.

Soon I was thinking more about the limpet-gatherer than about the gathering of Christ's saints at the end of the world.

By the summer's end I was looking oftener westwards in the direction of the fisher houses, than eastwards towards the Holy City.

The sea murmured gravely at my feet.

One day she held out her basket, and there on the pile of limpets was a sweet red apple from the apple-trees of the wood. It shone like a new planet among the starfish and bitter shells.

I shook my head

'I only want to be your friend,' she said.

'And I wish only to befriend my Lord,' I replied. 'You must go away from here now and never return.'

She put out her hand in appeal. The dust of the harvest was sweet on her arm.

'Go!' I shouted, clasping my two hands to my head.

I heard her loud harsh sobs among the seagulls all the way along the shore.

Her grief was filling the firth.

Only when the seabirds' cries were unmingled with her own did I remove my hands from my face. My fingers were wet.

That night I left my cave-cell and went down to the wet sands that were so full of stars.

I fell to my knees. How beautiful the stars seemed to be, thus reflected! But when I dug deeply into the sand, I scooped up never a star, but only a clodful of dull sodden grains. How easy is it thus to reach after an illusion and so fall into mortal sin, and disillusion.

And I remembered Abelard, my master, and I looked up at the stars of the sky.

And I said, I will go softly all my days in the bitterness of my soul.

I took another fistful of sand, and another and another. And I moulded and moulded, like a child playing on the shore, until I had made myself the little limpet-gatherer for my wife. Her breasts burgeoned slowly beneath the rising moon and I covered them with empty limpet-shells.

Then—O sweet Jesus—I made myself a little son out of the same star-strewn sands that had given birth to his mother. A son cradled in his mother's arm, baptized with my own scalding tears.

It was all night long I knelt beside them on the wet shore. Myself and my own little family. Steeped in white moonlight, and with stars shining under our feet and wheeling over our heads. And God's eternal sea thundering in our ears.

Till the tide came in before dawn and swept them both from my arms.

Thus with Christ's help I resisted the temptation to fall into error. I stood up with great pain in the pale morning and walked slowly back to my empty cell.

The limpet-gatherer never came back.

I chanted many a midnight orison to do penance for my mortal cravings. And ate many a cold limpet in the bitter winters that fell then.

In my ninetieth year God sent a shining angel into my cell.

'I am sent to tell you,' the angel said, 'that you have earned the greatest gift of all.'

'And what is that?' I asked.

It seemed not unusual to me that an angel should be standing in my cave.

'The Kingdom of Heaven, of course,' replied the angel, a little surprised.

'Maybe I no longer want it,' I said.

What anchorites may have won or lost eternity in these caves, who can say?

The time came when the devotees of the Church of Rome left them for grander premises. After that Protestant and Covenanter hid there when questions of spiritual conscience could take a man to the stake, and when political conscience could mean a short step to the gallows. For hunted Jacobites laid themselves down in these same shelters where so many had lived and died.

After the Cave Age, after the age of castle and cathedral and manor house, came the rise of the red, pantiled roofs, weatherbeaten by the Fife skies. Stone Age settler and sainted hermit, monk and marauder, fugitives from political and religious oppression—they have all passed through these caves like the figures in a dream.

Where are they now?

In that great silence which follows that question, it hardly seems credible that the caves were every really used at all.

For a time it seemed unlikely that they would ever be used again. St Monan's Cave will never again see the light of day. In the enlightened year of our Lord nineteen hundred and eighty four, the North East Fife District Council, in their great wisdom, built over it a solid concrete patio for the benefit of summer strollers. A far cry from the mentality of monks.

But one cave—the small mortuary cave at Caiplie—was occupied in modern times for thirteen years. The inhabitant was a local recluse by the name of James Gilligan. He stayed there until he was too weak and old to see to his own needs, and they came and took him away.

His is another story, to be told for itself, at another time.

We began with the first man.

What of the last? For the caves will surely be inhabited one last time before the world quite ends.

To hear the voices of the past in an ancient place is not hard. To catch a pre-echo of the future is less easy—almost impossible.

But the imagination of the storyteller is always there.

(8) *The Song of the Last Man*

So this is how the world ends—just where it began. From the magic of the first primordial spark to the last flake of ash falling into the sea. And the earth a cold cinder in space.

A million years from the marshes to the moon. Then the final madness—and mass suicide.

What did we throw up in the process? The wheel, the sail, the plough, the plane. Buildings, books, ideas. A sense of beauty. A sense of God.

There were some great times too, when we hit the high spots. Mesopotamia, Athens, Jerusalem, Rome. The twelfth century, the sixteenth century. Renaissance, Revolution, The Church. And a handful of geniuses—Socrates, Shakespeare, Bach. For a time we even had a feeling of permanence, of belonging; what it takes to make a civilisation, and to hold on to it.

What went wrong?

All kinds of errors, but what does it matter? I'm not keeping the books. Nobody is now.

In the end what happened was, we lost touch; that's all. Lost touch with the creator. Thought we were an imperishable species, thought we were unique. Thought we could make it on our own.

So we started putting ourselves first.

Not like in the old days, when men saw themselves as stewards of the earth, caretaking it for a while before passing it on to the next man. Stewards of their own bodies too, that was the theological theory, anyway. At least it gave them humility.

Unlike us. Not strong on humility, not strong on selflessness or caring. We became idle and vain. So busy getting and spending we let our leaders run mad. We handed over the traces to a race of lunatics who thought in abstractions and forgot about people.

So they rigged up the earth like a booby trap. They drilled the holes, slotted in the charges, told us it was all in the name of peace. Told us nothing could go wrong. Then they waited for it to happen.

Scotland was wired for extinction from the very first day.

That was three days ago.

I was in here at the time, by a kind of miracle. Doubtless miracles have happened in here before now. St Fillan's Cave the locals call it. Used to call it. There aren't any locals left. It'll be a miracle if I'm still alive in three days, though. I feel sick already. My hair is sifting into a neat little pile between my knees.

As I sit here like a rabbit, not moving. I saw one with myxie once. That's what I feel like.

I wondered what really happened out there.

All I remember is, the firth flashed like a mirror, and from St Monans to Kilrenny the five steeples of the kirks retracted like the fingers of a hand into the burnt burghs. The fringe of gold on the beggar's mantle. It's not much of a Golden Fringe now.

Strange, I don't remember hearing any screams. I suppose they're really the lucky ones out there. All dead. Safe from flagellation and fornication on graves and whatever comes next for those with time enough left to parody the art of living.

In time people will murder one another for a place in this hole of a cave. A nice little number.

> *Rock of Ages, cleft for me,*
> *Let me hide myself in thee.*
> *While the bombers thunder past,*
> *Shelter me from burn and blast.*
> *And though I know all men are brothers,*
> *Let the fall-out fall on others.*

Sixties poet. I thought it a bit sick at the time. Rather O.T.T. for a man nourished on Chaucer and Milton. Real culture! Well, now I know. The poets have seen all this before in any case. Time of the Black Death. What would they make of it as a war game, I wonder?

> *Ring-a-ring o' neutrons,*
> *A pocketful o' positrons,*
> *A-fission, a-fission,*
> *We all fall down.*

Am I hallucinating?

Drifting into sleep, I thought I saw the periscope of a sub practically on my doorstep. A black dragon surfacing in the firth. Wonder what the prow of a longship looked like a thousand years ago to some poor bastard stuck in here. Not a pretty sight, I reckon. Though even war had its art forms—*was* an art form—instead of being what it now is. Sorry—*was*. Our wars are done my friends.

A pushing of red buttons to make whole countries keel over.

It's raining today. A black black rain of death. Is this the start of the nuclear winter?

O Wind, if winter comes . . .

> *O nuclear wind when wilt thou blow,*
> *That the small rain down can rain?*
> *Christ that my love were in my arms . . .*

Almost over now.

I've managed to curl up in a corner. A circle of sickness and pain.

I feel eight thousand years old.

O God, if you exist, if you're there—

Enter the Cave.

O blessed St Fillan, St Adrian, St Monan, come down and comfort me. See again the world you so rightly renounced. Come down, come down.

Enter the Cave.

There's only darkness here now. I can't hear. I can't see.

O darkness deliver me . . .

The Diary of St Adrian

Author's Note: The Diary of St Adrian began life as a simple East Neuk Nature Log, and may still be read as such if the reader chooses to ignore the italics. As I recorded the events of the natural year however, I was struck by the contrast between the innocent happenings of nature and the mainly grislier man-made events that occurred on the same days in the year. By logging these in, I have recorded a double story: one written by God into his world; the other written by man into the world he has inherited. The natural story is a typical one in the cycle of the East Fife year: the human story is also, I fear, typical of man's behaviour in that larger world. Hence I give no actual years—only days. The following events could, in the essential sense, have occurred in any given century and will happen again, over and over. This is a book of days, not a dictionary of dates.

Why St Adrian in particular? St Adrian, who features elsewhere in this collection of stories, I imagine as a kind of East Neuk Tiresias, the presiding genius of these shores, who sees all things at the same time and sees them steadily and whole, the lesser and the greater. The spawning of a shore crab may be just as important as the birth of a star and the Battle of Actium—and maybe even greater. This is, above all, an East Neuk lesson in perspectives.

C.R.

JANUARY

1st   Solemnity of Mary, the Mother of God. The robin is singing at 2 am. Regulus rises out of the sea at 9 pm—a star of spring. *At the Dardanelles the sea is red with blood. It will be one more week until evacuation is complete.* The first whiteness appears on the south side of the firth—a slight dusting of snow north-east of Pelder.

2nd   The face of spring unborn is on the fields. Already there is a difference on the nights. *Ovid is dead. Ian Brady, the Moors murderer is born. The Japanese have taken Manila.* The whins are sparked with yellow on the west braes, St Monans. *Peter*

151

Sutcliffe, the Yorkshire Ripper, is arrested tonight in Sheffield with the prostitute who was to be his fourteenth victim. Snowfall during the night all along the coast.

3rd   *USA breaks off diplomatic relations with Cuba.* The fieldfares arrive in large numbers after the snow. *Joy Adamson, author and naturalist, making a study of leopards, is stabbed to death by 17-year-old African herdsman Paul Wakwaro Ekai. Lord Haw Haw, William Joyce, is hanged for treason.*

4th   Wood owls sound at Balcaskie, north of St Monans, 12.30 am. *By this time Albert Henry de Salvo, the Boston Strangler, has claimed his thirteenth and last victim, Mary Sullivan, aged nineteen. Britain declares war on Spain in the Seven Years War.*

5th   The whelks come out on the bottoms of the shallow pools, a spring sign. The first soft edge is detectable this morning on the west wind. *Later in the day, in South Armagh, ten Protestants are lined up against a bus and machine-gunned by the South Armagh Republican Action Force.* The sound of spring is unmistakable in the peculiar quietness of the air at sunset, over Kilrenny.

6th   Festival of the Epiphany. First clear seawater this morning, Kilrenny Mill Bay. *The Germans bomb Yarmouth.* The blackbird clacks at sunset, East Green, Cellardyke.

7th   The trees are full of young nettles, Burn Woods, west of St Monans. *Land attack ends at the Dardanelles.*

8th   Crabs spawning, east rocks, St Monans, *during excavation of the Dobrudja in Rumania.* Same afternoon, brittle starfish appear at Bucklands, east of Cellardyke.

9th   Increased birdsong this morning as *Edith Thompson and Frederick Bywaters are hanged for the murder of Percy Thompson.*

10th   First snowdrop is in bud at Dunino. *French troops occupy Ruhr in Germany.*

11th   *The Russians enter Warsaw.* A heron wings its way over Wormiston woods to feed on the shore, 6 am. *Albania declares war on Austria.*

12th   The snowdrops are starting to open at Balcaskie. *In East Africa Mafia Island has surrendered.*

13th   Mistletoe to be seen at Dunino. *President Sylvanus Olympio of Togo has been assassinated.*

14th   Dandelion bursts into flower on the Crail side of Caiplie Coves. *Yarmouth is again bombarded by the Germans*

15th   Very sharp echo from the morning waves, Kingsbarns, betokening frost. *Later in the day Sir Abubakar Balewa, the Nigerian Premier, is assassinated.*

16th   *The battle of Corunna ends in the death of Sir John Moore.* Overnight frost as expected. *Two US military aides are shot and killed by the Rebel Armed Forces Communist Group. Provisional IRA gunmen shoot dead Judge William Doyle as he leaves St Bridget's Church, Belfast.* The small spiders' webs on Kilrenny Common are hung with frost.

17th   Sun in the morning silvering the firth, but not enough strength to clear the frost. *Captain Scott reaches the South Pole, oblivious to* Orion lying due south at 9.45 pm, with Sirius glittering brightly east of Berwick Law.

18th   *The German siege at Leningrad ends.* The Bass Rock still sparkles whitely in sunshine and frost. At 10 pm stars are being born in Orion's sword, out of time.

19th   Baby partan crabs and spawning granny fish appear in the shore pools at Bucklands *as Fuchs reaches the South Pole.*

20th   St Agnes Eve. Dry mud floats on the flood tide at Caiplie. This is the first really warm day. *Adrianople has been occupied by the Russians.*

21st   First faint traces of daylight visible in the western sky after sunset this evening. *Mr Mansur, Premier of Iran, has been assassinated.* Woodcock cluster round Kilrenny Kirk. *A vast crowd watches as Louis XVI is guillotined in the Place de la Revolution.*

22nd   Overnight rain—the clear weather disappears. *Allied Forces establish a beach-head at Antium.*

23rd   Flocks of scaups fly over Boarhills. *Japanese naval offensive begins in the Macassar Straits.* Sleep. Tomorrow begins the time of rest and breaking bud.

24th   Weather unsettled. *Battle of the Dogger Bank.* Balcomie Bay is flecked with purple sandpipers.

25th   Gannets appear in the firth in stormy weather this morning. The weather clears in the afternoon; *the Japanese victorious in Macassar.* There is still plenty of daylight in the sky at 5 pm. *The Russians take Voronezh.*

26th   Massive flocks of oyster-catchers off the Briggs, Balcomie. *Barcelona falls to Franco.*

27th   A beautiful 'heading' in the evening sky—the cloud-streamers all pointing north-west of Kilrenny Kirk. *Germany is bombarding the Suffolk coast.*

28th   Wind during the night from the north-westward, the direction of yesterday's heading. *Burke, the murderer and body-snatcher, is hanged in Edinburgh this morning. Charlemagne is dead.*

29th   First cool spring wind from the eastward. *The Battle of Brienne fought today in the Peninsular War, and the Allies defeated.*

30th   St Basil the Great, St Gregory the Theologian, St John Chrysostom. *Bloody Sunday. Thirteen civilians have been killed by paratroopers in Londonderry in street riots.* Continues windy all day, growing colder. *Gandhi is assassinated.* Six gannets dive off Randerston. *Charles I is executed.* Seagull gives bad weather cry, west rocks, St Monans. *Adolf Hitler becomes Chancellor of Germany.*

31st   Seagulls wailing this morning, Billowness, Anstruther. *Guy Fawkes is executed.* South-east gale in the afternoon, with freezing cold rains continuing past sunset. *Lynda Ann Healy, a student at the University of Washington, disappears tonight from her room. Theodore Bundy, her murderer, will kill more than twenty such victims in the next two years.*

FEBRUARY

1st   St Ignatius. First fulmar flying off Cellardyke, 9.10 a.m. *King Carlos and Crown Prince of Portugal have been assassinated.*

2nd   Candlemas. The Purification of Our Lady. Blackbird sings loudly, Blacklaws, Kilrenny, 4.35 pm. *The Germans surrender in Stalingrad. The Russian dead at the end of World War II will stand at 20 million.* Blackbird continues its song over Blacklaws.

3rd   Spring movement of whelks noticeable this morning, Kilrenny Mill Bay, *unseen by George Pigott, hanged at Manchester for the murder of Florence Galloway.*

4th   Sudden hard frost this morning, the fields bright with rime. *In Yorkshire, later in the day, an IRA bomb goes off on board a bus coach transporting British soldiers and their wives and children. Twenty-five are killed and wounded. One family with two children is totally destroyed in the blast.* Arcturus glitters over the Firth.

5th   Ice in the dirches at Blacklaws, the skylark singing loudly over Renny Hill. *The Americans have captured Kwajalein in the Pacific.*

6th   The small short-spined sea-scorpions start to appear in the sea off Caiplie. *The legal government of Prussia is deposed by Hitler. George VI is dead.*

7th   The snowdrops at Dunino are almost in flower. *In the Peninsular War the Allies are the victors today at the battle of Bar-sur-Aube.* The elder is already in bud, west of Crail

8th   Drier weather today, a little warmer. *The Japanese have invaded Burma. The Russians take Kursk, Mary Stuart is beheaded.*

9th   Woodcocks at Redwells this afternoon. *The Germans occupy Bulgaria.*

10th   Ploughing begun north of Pittenweem, hundreds of gulls in the dreels. *Lord Darnley is assassinated by persons unknown.*

11th   Our Lady of Lourdes. First real spring skies and a calm sea towards the north, *as James Caffyn is hanged at Winchester for the murder of Maria Barber.* 10.30 pm. Rigel and Aldebaran are bright across the water, over Edinburgh.

12th   *The Macon airship disaster,* the blackbird singing clearly over Kilrenny.

13th   Dog's Mercury in blossom south of St Andrews. *Dresden is bombed and badly damaged by British and US air forces. Russia takes Budapest.*

14th   Festival of St Valentine. *During last night Argyll's Regiment massacred the Macdonalds of Glencoe, on whom they were quartered.* The teuchat's call from the fields at sunset, north of Anster. *Earlier in the day Bruno Hauptman is found guilty of kidnapping and murdering the child of Charles Lindbergh.*

15th   Small dangling spiders appear indoors. *The Japanese capture Singapore.*

16th   The first lumpsucker skins come ashore, Kilrenny Mill Bay. *Donald Neilson, the Black Panther, makes his first armed raid. He will kill three sub-postmasters and a young heiress.*

17th   Kilrenny Mill Bay. The whelks have come right out onto the rocks and skellies. *The Lancastrians are victorious at the Battle of St Albans.* The lesser celandines are beginning to appear at Renny Hill. *Meanwhile Provisional IRA terrorists bomb the LeMon restaurant in a Protestant area of Belfast. Thirty are badly injured. Twelve are burned to death.*

18th   Elm blossoms about to burst, St Monans. *The Germans open their submarine blockade of Britain.*

19th   Rooks building early at Wormiston. *The Dardanelles proves bloody.*

20th   The brave wee troopers (the snowdrops) appear in force. *Eden resigns as Foreign Secretary.*

21st   The lark's pre-song notes heard today over Cellardyke in the morning. Shortly afterwards *James I of Scotland is assassinated. Malcolm 'X', leader of the Black Muslims, is also assassinated.*

22nd   Masses of snowdrops now at Dunino, with the daffodils well in bud. *In the Officers' Mess of the 16th Parachute Regiment Headquarters in Aldershot, an IRA bomb has exploded killing and wounding twenty-two persons. Among the dead are three waitresses and a Roman Catholic Army Chaplain.* Bluebell shoots appear in the woods at Wormiston. *The battle of Verdun is under way.*

23rd   The fieldfares and redwings begin to leave us. *Francisco I, Madero, President of Mexico, is assassinated. Also Vice-President Jose Pino Saurez.* First sun sparkle on the firth at noon. *Desire Landru has been guillotined for the murder of ten women.*

24th   Porcelain crabs appear at Caiplie. *Durazzi is taken in the Balkans.* Blackbird sings 2.30 am.

25th   *Elizabeth I excommunicated today.* Crabs spawning west of Pittenweem. *Fighting has begun at Douanmont between the Germans and the British.* Pair of fulmars fly off Cellardyke.

26th   *Napoleon escapes today from Elba.* The first midges appear, Kilrenny Common. *Kermanchah has been taken by the Russians.*

27th   The fieldfares and redwings, it seems, have all gone by for now. *The British are defeated at Majube Hill, ending the First Boer War.*

28th   The eiders coo and gather in large numbers at the Coves this morning. *By now Hitler has abolished all freedom of speech and the press in Germany.* Flowering currant blooms near the Bel Craig, Dunino.

29th   Thornback crabs appear, Caiplie. *Agadir in Morocco has been destroyed by an earthquake.* The aconites are in flower at Dunino.

MARCH

1st   St David's. The skylark sings at Willie Gray's Dyke, east of Cellardyke. Gannets now occupy the Bass in growing numbers. *German troops occupy Bulgaria.* First spring clearness on the south side of the firth. Spica appears in the sky, 9 pm.

2nd   Razorshell comes ashore at the Mill Bay and gannet activity increases off the shore *as Ambassador Noel and other officials are murdered in the basement of the Saudi Arabian Embassy in Khartoum, by Arab terrorists.* Meanwhile the whelks are out in clumps on all the skellies.

3rd   Baby blennie appears in the Mill Bay in beautifully clear water *as Mary Blundy murders her father by arsenic poisoning.*

4th   First ladybird appears on ash branch, Dunino Den. *A bomb explodes in a Belfast restaurant killing two women and wounding 186 others. One woman who has just bought her wedding dress loses both legs, an arm and an eye.* First honeybee on snowdrop, Balcaskie.

5th   Blackbird sings 4.30 am. Drying winds and very rough seas. Herring gulls adrift on the winds in very large numbers. *Stalin is dead. His price: twenty million lives.* The first parachute spiders are now to be seen, and the first small moths. Masses of daisies out at Caiplie. The time of Spring awakening.

6th   Many fields ploughed all along the coast—the clods drying fast in the wind. The spring call of the collared dove heard over Redwells woods, between Crail and St Andrews. *And in West Germany a shot rings out as Klaus Grabowski, child-murderer, is shot dead during his trial by Maria Anne Bachmeir, the mother of one of his victims.*

7th   Shrimps appear in the shore pools at Randerston, past Fifeness. *A policeman in Bathpool Park climbs down a drainage shaft and discovers the naked body of Lesley Whittle, hanging from a wire rope. She has been murdered by Donald Neilson, the Black Panther.* The yellow hammer and chaffinch sing on Kilrenny Common the same afternoon. *The British have again attacked the Dardanelles forts.*

8th   New seaweeds grow at Caiplie. *The Second battle of Aboukir is fought. The IRA bomb the British Army's recruiting office in central London and the Central Court at the Old Bailey.* There is increased birdsong up Kilrenny common. *Hitler begins his persecution of the Jews.*

9th   Green egg packets with worm on the shore between Wormiston and Fifeness. *David Rizzio is stabbed by Darnley's followers. Germany declares war on Portugal.*

10th   First green water of the year appears this morning at Fifeness—NW wind. *The battle of Neuve-Chapelle is being fought.*

11th   *Amiens is taken by the Spanish. Bagdad is captured by the British. German troops enter Austria.* Dozens of dandelions flowering now east of the Coves. *South of Haifu PLO terrorists kill and wound 135 persons.*

12th   St Gregory's. Dog's Mercury and pussy willows appear at Frithfield, near Crail. *Germany annexes Austria.*

13th   Teuchat's call, Caiplie, 11 am. Bull-heads among the rocks. At Dunino the crows and rooks sound loudly in the treetops. *In Russia Alexander II is assassinated.*

14th   The shelducks arrive at Mill Bay *as Tsar Paul of Russia is assassinated.*

15th   Small night-flying moths arrive; *Columbus arrives at San Salvador.*

16th   The spring caw of the crows is loud over Wormiston. *Hitler denounces the Treaty of Versailles.*

17th   St Patrick's. The coltsfoot is in full flower, Smiddy Brae, Kilrenny. Second spring clearness appears on the south side. *John Gacy is born in Chicago. He will murder and sexually assault thirty-three boys.*

18th   All the lesser celandines are now out at the Coves. *Edward the Martyr of England is assassinated.*

19th   A red-breasted Merganser off Kingsbarns. *Murdoch Grant, an itinerant pedlar, is murdered in Assynt.*

20th   Primroses begin to burst, Balcormo Den, north of St Monans. *A car bomb has exploded in a Belfast street. There are 147 civilian casualties. Napoleon returns to Paris.*

21st   Vernal Equinox. First steam rises from the fields. *First Battle of Alexandria.* The daffodils at Dunino are about to open. *A Swissair plane, bound from Zurich to Tel Aviv, explodes and ignites in mid-air killing all on board. A splinter group of the PLO admits responsibility for planting the bomb.* Seaweeds breaking out anew in all the shore pools. *Fighting breaks out again on the Somme.*

22nd   Tadpoles in Burn Woods, St Monans. *The Reich takes Memel by coercion.* Frogs begin to rise here and there.

23rd   *Przemysl has surrendered to the Russians.* Cowslip in bud, Kilrenny.

24th   The green sleet is growing fast on the rocks, west of the Old Kirk, St Monans. *The Battle of Lake Narotch goes on.*

25th   Lady Day. Festival of the Annunciation. The whelks are out in huge clusters on the east rocks, St Monans. *King Feisal of Saudi Arabia is assassinated.*

26th   Very clear water all along the coast. *Adrianople surrenders to the Bulgarians.* Long lanes of green sea off Kingsbarns. The bright star Arcturus shines tonight over the May. Spring is here.

27th   *Earthquake at Anchorage kills 180 people.* The tangles are now exposed at low tide, Billowness.

28th   *England and France declare war against Russia in the Crimea.* A flock of redwings passes north of Anster. *Virginia Woolf commits suicide by walking into the River Ouse.*

29th   Sand martins fly west of Pittenweem. Hares box at Wormiston. *Gustavus III of Sweden is assassinated.*

30th   Lovely thrush sitting in the nest, Kilrenny Common. *Airey Neave, British MP, is murdered by the IRA.*

31st   *The Rebel Armed Forces Communist Group have kidnapped the West German ambassador, Count Karl von Spreti.* The sticklebacks have come in at Bucklands on a big tide.

APRIL

1st   The first primroses flower at the Hermit's Well, west of the Coves, Caiplie. *Hitler begins dictating Mein Kampf to Rudolf Hess.* Vega brightens the firth, 9 pm.

2nd   *Mirabeau is dead, Franco is victorious.* Up and down the coast the birds are gathering their nesting materials. *Nelson, at the Battle of Copenhagen, attacks the Danish fleet. Argentine forces invade the Falkland Islands.*

3rd   First easterly haar comes in off the sea, 6.30 am, but clears in morning heat. First occurrence of water mirage on the Blacklaws road this afternoon. The bluebells are beginning to flower. *The fighting continues on the Somme.*

4th   The nettles come up and the snowdrops are fading fast. The wheatears arrive at Kilrenny. *Dr Martin Luther King is assassinated at Memphis, Tennessee.*

5th   *Napoleon has abdicated.* The birches are flowering at Dunino, the ash leaves starting to open. *The body of Count von Spreti is discovered, murdered by the Rebel Armed Forces Communist Group.*

6th   First real bird's-egg-blue sky today. *The Germans are bombing Belgrade. They invade Yugoslavia and Greece.*

7th   The violets are in flower, Randerston cliffs. *The British take Masulipatam in the Seven Years War. The Chief-Prosecutor of West Germany is murdered by the Baader-Meinhof gang.*

8th   Masses of dandelions, Balkaithly, Dunino. *The Entente Cordiale is signed between England and France.*

9th   Black Monday. *The Black Prince's army suffers terrible losses in a storm. The Germans sieze Copenhagen. Battles at Arras and the Vimy Ridge.* White patchy fog appears again on the easterly winds.

10th   *The Battle of Kohima begins.* Haar continuing. *Belgium and Holland have been invaded by Germany.* The wheatears arrive at Fifeness.

11th   The thickness now gone from the coast, the sea very dark blue, the skyline razor sharp. There is a splendid clearness. *Meanwhile three PLO splinter group terrorists from Lebanon murder eighteen men, women and children in an Israeli housing block.*

12th   A sunny, windless morning along the coast, very quiet. Heard the tide-cry, 1 pm. A breeze up immediately afterwards. *President Tolbert of Liberia has been assassinated. The Germans occupy Belgrade.*

13th   Wood anemones and speedwell are in flower, Dunino. *Russian armies invade Austria and capture Vienna.*

14th   Blackbird singing, 4 am. Two pairs of wheatears arrive at

Fifeness. Very large sea anemones appear at Caiplie. *Abraham Lincoln is assassinated by Wilkes Booth.* Sea-urchins appear at the Coves. *The White Star liner, the Titanic, has sunk after striking an iceberg. During the night 1500 people will die.*

15th   *President Sadat's assassins were executed at dawn this morning.* First bumble bee on the East Green, Cellardyke. First tortoise shell butterfly, Wormiston, 2 pm.

16th   Red dead nettle and heartsease, Wormiston, many ladybirds and insects active. The terns arrive past St Andrews. *The Battle of Culloden is over and Butcher Cumberland is already busy earning his title.* Scores of frogs and toads are spawning in the ditches. Eiders, cormorants, gannets and terns are in the firth. Much bird activity in the North Sea.

17th   Three terns appear off Wormiston *as Warsaw prepares for its ghetto rising.*

18th   Young flounders swim into the Mill Bay, Kilrenny. *Anti-Castro forces invade Cuba from Florida.*

19th   Bats active on the St Monans–Elie road, 9 pm. *Charles Manson and his followers are sentenced to death for mass murder.* Lobster casts shell close inshore, Caiplie. *The Battle of Arras goes on.* Young eels swim past the Coves.

20th   The first faint trace of the sun's afterglow can now be seen in mid-Cassiopeia North—a sure sign of summer on the way. *Adolf Hitler is born at Brannau. His Third Reich will cost thirty million lives.*

21st   Green appearance on hedges and general growing in the fields and ditches. *James Bloomfield Rush was hanged this morning at Norwich for the murders of Messrs Jermy, senior and junior.* The trees are misted with green.

22nd   Dog daisies start to flower between St Monans and Abercrombie. *The Second battle of Ypres begins. The Germans are attacking with poison gas.*

23rd   The sticklebacks appear at the east end of Cellardyke. *The Battle of Imjin River takes place as Shakespeare dies, or is born.*

24th St Mark's Eve. The swallows arrive at Innergellic, Kilrenny. Willow warblers arrive in large numbers on the Common. *The Irish rise in Dublin.*

25th Festival of St Mark the Evangelist. Blackbird sings at 2 am. *The Australian and New Zealand armies are landing at Gallipoli.* The first hedgehogs brave the roads.

26th Sycamore and ash in full flower, Balcaskie. *Landing at Cape Helles in the Dardanelles.*

27th Hedgesparrow's nest north of Anster, containing two eggs. *The Fighting at Lys not yet over.*

28th *Benito Mussolini has been executed by Italian partisans.* A fine dusting of speedwell in Dunino kirkyard today. *A mutiny occurs on HMS Bounty.* Vega comes into prominence in the evening, north-west of Wormiston, the torch-bearer of summer.

29th *Battle of Orleans.* And more frogs awakening at Redwells.

30th St Catherine of Sienna. *Luis M Sanchez Cerro, President of Peru, is assassinated by Abelardo Hurtado de Mendoza. The Crimean War is over. De Gaulle resigns. Hitler is dead. Also five million Jews.* The burn at Kilrenny is full of marsh-marigolds, Forget-me-nots appear in the kirkyard.

MAY

1st First summer dissection of the Bass Rock and the May Island due to heat. *Albert I of Germany is assassinated.* The swallows have arrived at Caiplie. Lumpsucker eggs appear at the Coves, whitethroats at Fifeness.

2nd Starling eggs hatch—fragments by the burnside, Sandy Kirn, St Monans. *Berlin surrenders to the Russians.* Antares comes out of the water.

3rd Archedoris appears at Caiplie. *The German occupation of Greece is complete.*

4th *Battle of Tewksbury.* The shore crabs cast their shells.

5th   A fieldfare at Bucklands, perhaps migrating. *Napoleon dies at St Helena. The German forces surrender in Denmark.*

6th   Willow warblers and wood warblers near Balcaskie. *Lord Cavendish is assassinated by Fenians. Ian Brady and Myra Hindley are found guilty of the Moors Murders, including the torturing to death of a young girl.* At the Sandy Kirn, St Monans, the hawthorn is white with blossoms.

7th   The swallow twitters for the first time this morning, Caiplie. *At the Dardanelles the battle for Krithia goes on.*

8th   Apparition of St Michael the Archangel. Flourish is out on Kilrenny Common. *Elizabethan Act of Supremacy.* Abundance of tadpoles, Burn Woods.

9th   Sea pinks blossom at Fifeness. *Marshall Saxe captures Antwerp.*

10th   The gannets dive off Fifeness. *The Germans invade Belgium.*

11th   Coltsfoot with seed head north of St Monans. *The Baader-Meinhof gang bomb the US Army's Headquarters at Frankfurt, killing one and wounding thirteen and causing one million dollars damage.* Badgers and bats active at night. The pipistrelle bats appear. Sagittarius above St Abbs at midnight. Antares shining east of the Bass.

12th   The sands at Pittenweem littered with jellyfish. *Amsterdam is liberated.*

13th   Sea urchins among the rocks at the Lady's Tower, east of Elie, gannets hitting the water close inshore. *Pope John is hit by five bullets from the gun of would-be assassin Mehmet Ali Agca, the 'Grey Wolf' Turkish terrorist.*

14th   The campion appears on the Kilrenny to Crail road. *The Germans occupy Amsterdam. Henry IV of France is assassinated.*

15th   A huge flock of gannets left the Bass this morning to feed in the North Sea, flying between the May and the shore. *Three Popular Democratic Front terrorists attacked an Israeli school at Maalot and executed sixteen children. Five die later of wounds.* The gannets returned to the Bass Rock in the evening, keeping to the eastward side of the May. *At Ypres the fighting goes on.*

16th First swift appear overhead just outside Cellardyke, 8.05 am. *The British engage the Germans at Festubert.*

17th First lightning this afternoon—no thunder. *Four terrorists of the Turkish Peoples Liberation Army invade the residence of Ephraim Elrom, the Israeli Consul General in Istanbul and demand freedom for every political prisoner in the country.* A sudden explosion of swifts across the fields between St Monans and Pittenweem. *In Dublin Loyalist car bombs explode at the peak of the evening rush hour. Twenty-three die instantly, eleven more later. Two hundred are wounded.*

18th The time of bringing to fruition. Astronomically there is now no night until 21st July. A summer twilight will reign from sunset to sunrise. *Napoleon is now Emperor of the French.*

19th Woodcocks at sunset up on the Common, house and sand martins and lapwing chicks. The first bluebottle buzzes indoors. *The French fleet has been destroyed off Barfleur by Admiral Russell.*

20th Lady Mantle blooms, Kilrenny. *General Venustiano Carranza, President of Mexico is assassinated.* The afterglow is now very plain well after sunset.

21st But now the 'coo cwauk' arrives—the thick cold weather: May mists, strong easterlies and drizzling rains. *The Germans occupy Amiens.*

22nd The cold weather continues, rawer than February. *The Germans are attacking Calais. The Wars of the Roses begin.*

23rd The thickness clears away this aftrnoon and the sun comes out. *Italy declares war on Austria.* Baby mallards are whooing along the shore at Wormiston in the early evening. *The body of Ephraim Elrom is found close to his consulate. he has been shot in the head three times.* There is the first smell of foliage on the damp evening fields. Leo sinking onto Kellie Law in the early nightime, Antares climbing over the southern firth.

24th   The swifts are increasing rapidly. *By now twelve thousand Polish officers have been massacred at Katyn by the Russians.* First thunder to the northward, 2.15 pm.

25th   Octopus in large shore pool west of the Coves. *Franco's planes are bombing Alicante.*

26th   Five shelduck babies this morning at the Hind, Cellardyke. *Edmund the Elder of England is assassinated.* Eider babies at Elie Ness, 3 pm.

27th   *The Germans have taken Calais.* The Bass Rock is a blizzard of birds.

28th   A lovely luminous gloss now on the trees, their leaves liquid green. *The Battle of Goose Green is fought on the Falkland Islands.* The woods at Wormiston and Dunino are misty with bluebells.

29th   At Balkaithly, Dunino, a field full of buttercups—a golden fleet on a green sea. *The Spanish Armada has left Lisbon.* The cows stand full uddered among the flowers. *President Rahman of Bangladesh has been assassinated.*

30th   The crab apple blossoms out, Balcormo Den, north of St Monans. *General Rafael Trujillo, dictator of the Dominican Republic, is assassinated.*

31st   *The Battle of Jutland.* The wild roses and raspberries are in leaf at Frithfield. The thistles are coming up strong. the hum of insects is loud at noon.

JUNE

1st   The Glorious First. The corn still bright green. *Howe is victorious over the French in the open sea off Ushant.* The barley brightens.

2nd   *The Girondists are overthrown.* Sand eels appear at Kingsbarns. *Peter Sutcliffe, the Yorkshire Ripper, is born.*

3rd   The poppy is in bloom, Willie Gray's Dyke. *Dunkirk is evacuated.*

4th   South-west breezes today, very soft. *Abdul Aziz, Sultan of Turkey is assassinated.*

5th   The first wild rose in flower, past Ribbonfield, near Crail. *Senator Robert Kennedy is assassinated at Los Angeles.*

6th   Stone crop brightens the tops of the dykes between Cambo and Kingsbarns. *The Allies invade France.*

7th   Hips and honeysuckle flowers now in the hedgerows between Balcaskie and St Monans, Sandy Kirn. *In the June War Israel has by this time taken control of Old Jerusalem, the Gaza Strip and the Sinai Peninsula.*

8th   *The Black Prince is dead.* The elder flowers begin to come out on the Kilrenny Common. *Richard Coeur de Lion arrives at Acre.*

9th   A grasshopper chirps loudly, west braes, St Monans. A fine morning jabble on the sea. *Later in the day Captain Bligh reaches Timor Island.*

10th   The laminaria is exposed at Fifeness, the tangles steaming at low tide in the morning sun. *The Germans occupy Dieppe. Michael, Prince of Serbia, is assassinated.*

11th   The red clovers bloom. *Columbus arrives at the West Indies.* Altair, the summer star, beautifies the firth. *James III of Scotland is assassinated.*

12th   Assemblies of bluebottles sunning themselves on the sunny sides of the dykes near Cambo. *Wat Tyler's men assemble on Blackheath.*

13th   Bats and owls very active in the early nightime. *The fighting continues at Messines.*

14th   The wheatears appear to have gone from the coast. *There are battles at Marengo and Naseby.* The skellies and rocks are now covered in the green sleet. *Argentine surrenders to the British. German troops enter Paris.*

15th   Haymaking at Wormiston. *Battle at Carberry Hill.* The burns are now down to a trickle, most ditches dry.

16th   *There is rioting in Berlin.* West of St Monans the dog roses burst into full bloom. *Keith Bennett, a twelve year old schoolboy, disappears this evening on his way to see his grandmother in Manchester. He has met Ian Brady and Myra Hindley. His body will never be found.*

17th The elders are in big white blossoms on the Crail to St Andrews road. *The Berlin riots are crushed by Russian tanks.*

18th *The Battle of Waterloo seals Napoleon's destiny.* Barn owl sits on a fence post outside Crail in full daylight, 10 pm. *Russian forces march into Estonia. The German air raids on Britain have begun.*

19th *146 persons are imprisoned in The Black Hole of Calcutta. Only 23 will survive the night.* The wild roses are bursting out everywhere.

20th *William Probert hanged today for murder.* Yellow irises and water cress at Dunino—dragonflies hovering over the burn.

21st Summer Solstice. *The Russians defeat the Hungarians at Pered.* White cap visible on the black-headed gull, Caiplie—the first sign of winter in the midst of summer.

22nd Wild mustard blooms, Balcaskie. Eider babies in the Hind, Cellardyke. The Great Square of Pegasus is rising already—a sure sign of autumn on the way. *Field-Marshall Sir Henry H. Wilson has been assassinated in London.* The Square well up at midnight between the May and the Bass.

23rd Midsummer's Eve. The numbers of shelducks on the coast have visibly declined. *Led by Mirabeau, the Three Estates refuse to separate. Revolution is in the air.* Skuas flying just off Kingsbarns.

24th Midsummer's Day. Nativity of St John the Baptist. *Sadi Carnot, President of France, is assassinated. Bruce fights and wins the Battle of Bannockburn.* Later in the evening a strong scent of the honeysuckle on the Balcaskie to Pittenweem road.

25th *The English attack on the Chinese forts is defeated at Taku at the mouth of the Tien-Tsin-ho.* The skylark sings loudly at Ardross, east of Elie, 8 pm.

26th *Douai surrenders to Marlborough.* Thistledown floats on the afternoon air, St Monans.

27th   *Cairo is recaptured from Napoleon.* Little silver lumps of cloud all
        over the sky all day. Very hot with a shimmer on the firth.
        *Terrorists at Athens airport hijack an Air France plane and force it
        to land at Entebbe, Uganda. Entebbe is stormed by 200 Israeli
        commandos and the terrorists killed. In retaliation the Ugandans
        murder Mrs Dora Bloch, a 73 year old British Israeli grandmother.*
        All along the coast the first golden tinge appears on the grain.

28th   Fields of jellyfish are floating off Elie. *The Archduke Francis
        Ferdinand of Austria-Hungary has been assassinated at Sarajevo.*
        Mergansers and seals in large numbers west of Pittenweem.

29th   St Peter's. Flatfish in St Monans harbour this afternoon—the
        water was very green. *In the Dardanelles the fighting at Anzac is
        not yet over and the sea is red with blood.*

30th   *George Joseph Smith is convicted of the murder of Misses Mundy,
        Burnham and Lofty in the Brides in the Bath case. Ernst Roehm
        and General Schleicher and his wife are assassinated by the Nazis
        and 90 dissentient Nazis are shot.* First noticeable difference in
        the light tonight, following midsummer.

JULY

1st   The Most Precious Blood. *The First Battle of the Somme opens.*
        The leaves start to lose their gloss and are noticeably drier in
        the morning breeze. Capricornus shines faintly over the firth, 9
        pm.

2nd   The willowherb in abundance, Inverie Burn, St Monans.
        General Garfield, President of the USA, is assassinated.

3rd   The Dog Days. Wild strawberries at Redwells. *Constantine I
        defeats Licinius near Adrianople. In the First Crusade Antioch is
        taken.*

4th   Tangles ashore at Anster in a south-east gale. *The Italians are
        invading the Sudan.* Heavy rains.

5th   Meadowsweet fragrant after rain between St Monans and
        Abercrombie. *Tom Mboya of Kenya is assassinated in Nairobi.*

6th   The shelducks are seldom seen now on the shore. *Sir Thomas*

More is beheaded. An oil-rig explodes in the North Sea, killing over 160 men.

7th   First ghost moth fluttering over Frithfield this evening. *Iran prepares to bury her 290 dead after the Americans shoot down an Iranian passenger plane in error.* Capella twinkles low, north of Fifeness.

8th   *The Battle of Poltava. Peter the Great has defeated Charles XII of Sweden.* Bladderwrack and sleet are coming in oftener now on the tides.

9th   The whelks creep back under the stones. No more rock clusters to be seen on the coast. *The King of Thailand is assassinated.*

10th   The afterglow is dimming fast after sunset. *William the Silent is assassinated at Delft.* The face of the sea darkens again at night.

11th   *The Second Battle of Alexandria begins.* The scent of the grain very malty on the night air,

12th   Birdsong declined considerably today. *In the evening Pauline Reade, aged 16, disappears on her way to a dance, the first victim of Ian Brady and Myra Hindley.*

13th   Hard rains again this morning and heavy seas. Huge waves crash over the east rocks, St Monans. *Later in the day Marat is assassinated by Charlotte Corday.*

14th   The ditches are blood-bright with poppies on the Crail road. But already Pegasus is hoisted high out of the firth. Autumn is close. *The Bastille falls to the Paris mob.*

15th   *The Second Battle of the Marne begins. The Franco-Prussian War has also begun as Jerusalem falls in the First Crusade.* The seafields between Wormiston and Crail are flecked with daisies.

16th   *Tsar Nicholas of Russia and his family have been assassinated at Ekaterinburg by the Bolsheviks.* Birds very quiet today. *The first atomic bomb has been detonated.*

17th   *The massacre of the Champ de Mars.* The insect hum increases as the birdsong declines.

18th   Harebells at Fifeness drenched by heavy rains. *Adrianople recaptured by the Turks.*

19th   Hundreds of bees descend on the lime flowers, Dunino. *The Armada arrives off Lizard.*

20th   *King Abdullah of Jordan is assassinated.* Loosestrife along the burnside, St Monans. *A bomb explosion in London kills eleven soldiers and injures 51 civilians and soldiers. Seven cavalry horses are killed.*

21st   *Bloody Friday. The Provisional IRA cause 26 explosions in Belfast. 141 are injured and eleven die, mostly civilian shoppers.* The herons feed quietly on the shore at Wormiston *as Christopher Ewart-Biggs, British Ambassador to the Republic of Ireland, and his secretary, Miss Judith Cooke, are blown up by a land mine shortly after leaving Glencairn.*

22nd   Festival of St Mary Magdalene. Sweet smelling long nettles nearly six feet high on north side of Burn Woods, St Monans. *Coup d'état by General Mohammed Neguib of Egypt.*

23rd   Bindweed appears, Dunino. *Cairo is taken by Napoleon.*

24th   More bindweed flourishes at Cornceres on the Kilrenny to Crail road. *Joachim Kroll, the West German cannibal killer, reveals today in conversations with the West German police, that he has lost count of the number of children he has cooked and eaten.* Later in the evening myriads of little white moths appear on Kilrenny Common.

25th   Festival of St James the Apostle. Torrential downpour on the Common. Elderflower and meadowsweet fragrant in the warm rains. *First Battle of Aboukir is fought.*

26th   Festival of St Anne, Mother of Our lady. Wild roses, dog roses, campion and poppies in nearly all the ditches and hedgerows. *The Armada anchors in Calais Roads and is met by Howard.*

27th   Butterflies and bees invading indoors. *The Korean War ends.* Woodworm beetles flying north of Anster as the gathering time approaches—the time of reaping the reward.

28th   *Robespierre is dead.* Birdsong ceases, the night sky growing much darker. *Austria-Hungary declares war on Serbia.*

29th   Wild gooseberries ripe at Dunino. *Humbert I of Italy is assassinated.*

30th   Burns still in good spate after the rains. *Robert Vest, a ship steward, was hanged today at Durham for the murder of William Wallace, a pilot.*

31st   *Jean L Jaures, the French Socialist leader, has been assassinated.* First evening mist north of Dunino. *The Third Battle of Ypres has begun.*

AUGUST

1st   Thistleseeds blowing across Kilrenny Common in the early morning. *A little later, at 11.48 am, Charles Wightman begins shooting at members of the public from the observation tower of the University of Texas. The sniper will kill 21 people and wound 28 before he is himself killed by three policemen.* More green sleet and bladderwrack comes ashore east of Cellardyke on a south-east wind. *Germany declares war on Russia.*

2nd   Grasshopper warbler is very loud at Grangemuir. *The Polish rising in Warsaw is crushed by the Germans.*

3rd   The shelducks reappear at the Hind, Cellardyke. First distinct coldness on the NE wind. *Germany declares war on France.*

4th   The fields are beginning to whiten. *The Germans violate Belgian neutrality.*

5th   Dedication of Our Lady of the Snow. A change in the wind, with a distinctly autumnal quality today in the sound of the breezes in the grasses and grains. *Warsaw is evacuated by the Russians.*

6th   Festival of the Transfiguration of Our Lord. Very warm rain today, the barley banks at Wormiston beautifully blurred by mists. *An American plane drops an atom bomb on Hiroshima. The children of the ashes are conceived, are born, and are dead.*

7th   Harebells blow on the Billowness. *Florence Maybrick is convicted of the murder of her husband by arsenic.*

8th   Grasshoppers and ladybirds abounding, west braes, St Monans. *The Battle of Britian begins.* A flat calm on the firth. *The Great Train Robbery takes place.*

9th   Cow parsley abundant beneath Kellie Law, meadowsweet filling the air. *An American pilot drops an atomic bomb on Nagasaki.*

10th   Second flowering of the coltsfoot at the Smiddy Brae, Kilrenny. Baby partan crabs appear among the rocks near the Coves. *By tomorrow the Allies will have captured Florence.*

11th   Dragonflies thread the air at noon around the Carnbee loch. *A squad of four Arab terrorists use guns and grenades on passengers in the lounge at Istanbul airport. Four are killed and 130 wounded.*

12th   Poppies still plentiful by the roadsides. *Austro-Russians defeat the Prussians at Kunersdorf. Britain declares war on Austria-Hungary.* The seals whoo out at sea in the early evening off Fifeness.

13th   Sooty shearwaters fly off the Billowness *as East Germany seals off the Berlin border and begins building a wall.*

14th   *The Battle of Dieppe.* Campion and dog-rose still abundant in the hedges. *Japan surrenders unconditionally.*

15th   The Assumption of Our Lady. *The body of Giacomo Matteotti, murdered by Italian Fascists, is found. Mujibar Rahman, President of Bangladesh is assassinated.* Sand martins feed their young at St Monans. *Two Black September Arab terrorists kill and wound 58 passengers at Athens airport.*

16th   *The Battle of Smolensk.* Harvesting begins along the coast. Lovely moonrise over the May in the evening.

17th   *The French capture Almeida from the British.* The Great Square of Pegasus now visible in the early evenings over the stubble fields.

18th   The swifts leave in large numbers today *as Cardinal Wolsey and Francis I sign the Treaty of Amiens.*

19th   *Anglo-Canadian landing at Dieppe.* Low white mists rolling far inland. Trees beyond Kilrenny standing in a milky white bath. *In Hungerford Michael Ryan shoots down sixteen of the town's inhabitants at random.*

20th   *Russian troops invade Czechoslovakia.* The cattle stand quietly shrouded in the early evening mists rising again from the fields. *Germans enter Brussels.*

21st   *The Peninsula War begins with the Battle of Viniero. Trotsky is assassinated in Mexico.* The afterglow is no longer visible. Arcturus lies west of Edinburgh.

22nd   *The Battle of Bosworth Field. Richard III has been crushed: the Tudor Dynasty begins.* Wasps appear in large numbers, Kingsbarns.

23rd   *George Villiers, Duke of Buckingham, is assassinated by John Felton. The Battle of Mons is fought today.* Lapwings are congregating on Anster shore. *Japan declares war on Germany.*

24th   Festival of St Bartholomew. *Massacre of St Bartholomew in Paris.* Thistledown floating by the hundreds on warm breezes across the fields behind Balcaskie. *The fighting continues at Mons.*

25th   Fields harvested and stooked all along the coast. *Rumania declares war on Germany.*

26th   *The Battle of Crecy fought today.* Plenty of redshanks in evidence between Wormiston and Fifeness.

27th   The swifts appear no more. *Lord Mountbatten has been murdered by the IRA.*

28th   Bubble crabs appearing at the Coves. *Italy declares war on Germany. Germany declares war on Rumania.*

29th   Festival of St John the Baptist. *Battle of Mohács.* Sniper at Caiplie Brae.

30th The wheaters return, migrating south. *Turkey declares war on Rumania.*

31st *The Second Battle of the Marne ends today.* The Balcaskie beeches turn yellow. *The Russians capture Bucharest.*

SEPTEMBER

1st The crabs are breeding again. *Soviet troops crossed into Poland at 4 am this morning. Dieppe is liberated, Danzig is the Reich's.* Baby sticklebacks appear, Kilrenny Mill Bay. *Alicante is bombarded by Cartagenan insurgents. Louis XIV is dead.*

2nd *The Battle of Actium. Massacres at the Abbaye Prison, Paris.* The winds begin to incline today to the north-west. *The whole of London is ablaze in a Great Fire.* Fomalhaut now visible over the firth, early evening.

3rd Bluebottles and flies failing—the spider's webs on the common begin to collect their dead. *Britain and France declare war on Germany. The barbed wire will soon collect its own dead.*

4th Hares congregating among the stooks. *Fighting continues on the Somme.*

5th *At 4.30 this morning Black September terrorists broke into the Munich Olympic Village and murdered eleven Israeli athletes.* Hundreds of ladybirds later this morning on the rocks, Cellardyke. *Industrialist Mr Hanns Martin Schleyer has been kidnapped in Cologne by the Baader-Meinhof gang and his three bodyguards murdered by sub-machine-gun fire.* Baby swallow in the nest outside Crail. *William McKinley, President of the USA, has been assassinated.* The brambles begin to ripen and the rose-hips start to appear.

6th *Battle of the Marne.* The robin's autumn song is loud in the air. *Hendrik Verwoerd, the South African Premier, has been assassinated.*

7th Giant bladderwrack coming in off the Hirst, between Crail and Fifeness. *Mehemet Ali Pasha assassinated by Albanians. The Germans launch a mass daylight air attack on London.*

8th   Festival of the Nativity of Our Lady. The leaves on the common start to fall. *Senator Huey Long of Louisiana has been assassinated.*

9th   *The Battle of Flodden Field. King James IV of Scotland is dead.* The swithers come in at Bucklands. *Fighting continues on the Marne.*

10th   *Elizabeth, Empress of Austria, is assassinated.* Shoals of jellyfish purpling the tide, Wormiston. *Mao-Tse-Tung is dead.*

11th   *President Allende of Chile has been assassinated.* The oaks and beeches are shedding their nuts.

12th   *Haile Selassie of Ethiopia has abdicated.* Scything the long grasses on the verges and ditches.

13th   *Battles at Philiphaugh and Merignano.* Three migrating wheatears appear at the Hind. *General Wolfe has captured Quebec.*

14th   Exaltation of the Holy Cross. *The British bombard Dieppe.* Broken dandelion clocks blowing in stiff breezes over the stubble fields, Balcomie. *Peter Stolypin, the Russian Premier is assassinated.*

15th   Seas of milky fogs low over the fields this evening between Kilrenny and Kippo. *Essex has sacked Cadiz.*

16th   First frosty sunset. A great silence on the fields. *Charles Edward Stuart is tonight in occupation of Edinburgh.*

17th   *The Battle of Borodino.* Very heavy dewfall overnight. The fields drenched this morning. *Count Folke Bernadotte, UN mediator, has been assassinated by Israeli terrorists at Jerusalem.* The swallows are now very sparse. *In Paraguay ex-President Somoza of Nicaragua dies in a hail of terrorist bazooka fire and sub-machine-gun bullets. His reign of terror has left fifty thousand Nicaraguans dead and half a million homeless.* Pegasus is now south-east at midnight.

18th   Two wheatears and pied flycatcher at Kingsbarns, 5 pm. *By now Brest-Litovsk has fallen.*

19th   *Battle of Poitiers.* Redwings at Fifeness. *At Brest the German garrison surrenders after a six-week siege.*

20th   *Battle of Valmy.* The western sky now very dark after sunset. *The mob invades the Tuileries.*

21st   *Battle of Prestonpans.* Clear windy skies tonight. Capella bright in the north-east over the Bell Rock.

22nd   Autumn Equinox. Aldebaran is well up by midnight. *British planes bomb the hangars at Dusseldorf.*

23rd   A great coldness in the sea this morning. *Acre is occupied by the British.* The Plough dips low tonight north of Wormiston.

24th   Sharp easterly winds ruffling the water all day *as Columbus sets out on his second voyage.*

25th   First goosy morning. Very shivery. *The Battle of Stamford Bridge. The Battle of Loos begins.* Taurus appears over the Dun, Dunino.

26th   Robin sings, 5.30 am. *Fighting ends at Arnhem.* And sure enough, here come the geese, passing over Innergellie, Kilrenny.

27th   Swallows passing south over Carnbee loch, early evening. *Edward II of England is assassinated.* The evening shadows are thickening. High gales round the roofs tonight.

28th   *The Battle of Marathon.* Sea bellowing down off Wormiston. A roaring in The Briggs. *Warsaw has surrendered to Germany.*

29th   St Michael. *Richard II abdicates.* Skylark sings autumn song over the Castlehill, Cellardyke. *Chamberlain has flown to Munich.*

30th   *Calais is taken by the Canadian First Army.* Crab casts its shell at Caiplie. Tortoise shell butterflies still active inshore. *Chamberlain proclaims peace in our time.*

OCTOBER

1st   By now nearly all the greenness has gone out of the leaves, *and all Poland has fallen to Russia and Germany. The Girondists are tried today. Many will be executed.*

2nd   *The Duke of York captures Almaar. Poland siezes part of Czechoslovakia.* The sound of frost is in the sea again. *Hitler is becoming supreme as Fuhrer.* Aldebaran glows over the waves in the mid-evening.

3rd   Sea horizons very white today and the sky a dark purplish blue. A nip in the air. *Fighting on the Hindenburg Line continues.*

4th   St Francis of Assissi. Hundreds of geese fly south over the firth. *The Germans besiege Antwerp.*

5th   *The mob marches on Versailles.* Shore crabs very sluggish on the rocks at Caiplie. Winter can not be far off.

6th   Ploughing again, gulls following. North-west winds at sunset. *Earlier in the day President Sadat was murdered by Muslim extremists.*

7th   *The Battle of Lepanti.* A day of white sunlight and very strong winds. Sea horses breaking the North Sea. *The German Democratic Republic has been established in the Russian zone.*

8th   Sheets of spray carried in by the winds across Balcomie fields. *Western Poland is annexed by Germany.*

9th   Thousands of leaves are falling now like snowflakes everywhere. We are into fading and the time of ending. *Antwerp has surrendered to the Germans.*

10th   *The Battle of Tours.* And the first real gale of winter from the south-west. *Four South Korean Cabinet Ministers have been assassinated at Rangoon.* Goldfinches appear, Kilrenny. *Germany has occupied Czechoslovakia.*

11th   The birds are gathering in flocks. *William Taylor, soldier, hanged today at Exeter for the murder of his corporal.*

12th   Blackberries shining like coal on the road to Dunino Kirk. *Luther refuses to recant at Augsburg. There is fighting at Passchendaele.*

13th   A magnificent moonrise out of the sea this evening, south of the Bass Rock. *German troops have begun the occupation of Rumania.*

14th   *The Battle of Hastings. Harold II is shot dead with an arrow through the eye.* The robin sings again his autumn song. *The Royal Oak has been sunk in Scapa Flow.*

15th   *Britain declares war on Bulgaria.* And still the ladybirds and tortoise shells are active.

16th   *Liaquat Ali Khan, the Prime Minister of Pakistan, has been assassinated.* Very severe gales and real wintry weather today. *Marie-Antoinette has gone to the guillotine.*

17th   *The Battle of Saratoga.* Looking down from Kippo to Kingsbarns, many hips on the wild rose bushes and haws on the hawthorns in the hedges.

18th   Festival of St Luke the Evangelist. *Andreas Baader shoots himself in the head in his cell, and Gudrun Ensslin hangs herself from her prison bars when West German commandos free a planeload of hostages for their freedom.* The wintry gales continue, the trees nearly stripped. The North Sea is white with horses in the great gale.

19th   *The body of Hans Martin Schleyer has been found in the boot of a car in France. He has been shot in the head and his throat cut.* At Dunino a tree still heavy with elderberries. *Italy declares war on Bulgaria. The First Battle of Ypres begins.*

20th   Still one or two late swallows to be seen, Blacklaws. *Maurice Bishop, Premier of Granada, has been assassinated with three of his ministers.*

21st   *The Franco-Spanish fleet has been destroyed at the Battle of Trafalgar.* The rooks have returned to their roost trees at Wormiston. *The Aberfan coaltip disaster has killed 140 human beings, mainly schoolchildren.*

22nd   The wind eases this morning, trailing threads of gossamer through the air. *President Kennedy alleges that Soviet offensive missile sites are being erected in Cuba.* Gannet's skull wedged between two rocks at low tide near Craw Skellie, Cellardyke. *The Turkish ambassador in Vienna shot dead in his embassy by three men who walk in carrying sub-machine-guns. Crippen is convicted of the murder of his wife.*

23d   *Battle of Alamein opens today.* Wind drops—mist in the afternoon.

24th   *USA begins the naval blockade of Cuba. In Paris two terrorists have ambushed and killed the Turkish envoy and his chauffeur.* That familiar crackling sound in the sea heralds frost. *There is more fighting at Douanmont.* The Twins walk over the firth tonight, a pair of sparklers.

25th   *Battles at Agincourt and Balaklava.* The fields are white with rime all along the coast and right down to the shore. The whiteness is still there at sunset.

26th   Dog whelks lay eggs, Willie Gray's Dyke, east of Cellardyke. *President Park of South Korea has been shot dead by his bodyguard.* First pink glow on cumulus at sunset. Frost bright in the evening sky.

27th   Dippers at Anster. *The Battle of Ypres continues.*

28th   St Simeon. Soft crabs still occurring on the shore, and baby partans. *Kruschev announces that the Soviet Union will dismantle the rocket bases in Cuba and ship them home.*

29th   The fieldfare arrives again at the back of Castlehill, 9.30 am. *Peter Sutcliffe, the Yorkshire Ripper, begins his reign of terror by murdering Wilma McCann. Columbus discovers Cuba.*

30th   *The Darien Scheme expedition arrives.* A huge flock of returning fieldfare arrives at Willie Gray's Dyke.

31st   Vigil of All Saints. *Indira Ghandi, the Indian Premier, is assassinated.* A tortoise shell butterfly still active in Kilrenny kirkyard. More fieldfares have come back today. *By this time also Father Jerzy Popieluszko has been found beaten, tortured and murdered by members of the Polish Secret Police.*

NOVEMBER

1st   All Saints Day. Tortoiseshell at Kilrenny Mill—surely the last. *The French have capitulated at Kassel in the Seven Years War. An earthquake has struck Lisbon. President Ngo Dinh Diem of South Vietnam has been assassinated.*

2nd   All Souls Day. *The Third Battle of Ypres continues.* Already Orion is glittering on the Bass Rock by 11 o'clock. Yet one more tortoiseshell, on the East Green, Cellardyke.

3rd   Heavy easterlies again. *A Prussian victory at Torgau in the Seven Years War.*

4th   Groundswells in the sea. *Acre has been stormed. The Antwerp Citadel has been burned by the Spaniards.* Huge waves pounding on the sands at Kingsbarns—a roaring in The Briggs again. *The poet Wilfred Owen is killed one week before the Armistice.*

5th   A little local dusting of snow, covering Blacklaws and the surrounding fields. *Edgar André, Communist leader, has been beheaded at Hamburg.*

6th   *Britain has declared war on Turkey.* The first ice has formed, top of the harbour wynd, Cellardyke.

7th   *Ernst von Rath, a German diplomat, has been assassinated.* The winds veer again to strong easterlies. Huge hills of seaweed thrown up along the coast, six or seven feet high in some parts.

8th   *Nadir Shah, King of Afghanistan, has been assassinated by a student.* Calm again, the old folks laying some of the storm-gathered tangles on their patches of ground. *Hitler has survived the assassination attempt in the Burgerbräukeller at Munich.*

9th   Windy again. Water wintrily muddy in the shore pools. *Kaiser Wilhelm II has fled.*

10th   A redwing this morning at Bucklands. The skylark singing. *The Battle of Passchendaele ends. Also the Third Battle of Ypres.* Crabs spawning again.

11th   Festival of St Martin. *The Black Panther is captured by the police.* Driving rains today. Great grey battalions of clouds on the march all day, moving north-westwards across the firth. *The Armistice is signed between Germany and the Allies at Compiegne. Ten million are known to have died. Many more known only unto God.*

12th Winds and rain continue. The last leaves are torn today from most trees. *Captain Scott has been found dead by a search party. The Germans occupy Vichy.*

13th Fogs up the coast. *The Scots besiege Alnwick.* The rowans afire above the mist.

14th *The Battle of Ancre is under way.* Some Blackcaps still at Fifeness.

15th *Carlisle surrenders to the Young Pretender.* Many fieldfares returning with winter migrants, Fifeness.

16th The curlews active at Fifeness *as Jack Sheppard, highwayman, is hanged at Tyburn.*

17th Mallards in Balcomie Bay all day. *Josef Kramer, Commandant at Belsen, is sentenced to death for torture and murder of prisoners.* At sunset the mallards fly in over the fields to feed.

18th *First Battle of the Somme ends.* Geese fly overhead in the direction of the Bass Rock.

19th *Wolf Tone commits suicide.* Lapwings and crows active, Wormiston.

20th *US blockade is lifted from Cuba.* The robin sings 8.30 am.

21st *First Battle of Ypres continues.* Hundreds of shags off Kingsbarns.

22nd St Cecilia's. *President John F Kennedy is assassinated at Dallas, Texas.* At Balcaskie the elms and beeches lose their last leaves—the last to go.

23rd Leo rises in the east 1.30 am. Winter before spring yet to come. *The Battle of Warsaw goes on.*

24th *Battle of Solway Moss. The Poles invade Ruthenia.* Rain driven on an east wind all along the coast.

25th St Catherine's. *Anti-Comintern Pact between Germany and Japan.* Winds in the woods. Roaring audible out of Redwells at half a mile distant.

26th *Battle of Beresina.* Wind drops early this morning; rain falls harder.

27th *The French fleet is scuttled at Toulon.* Burn at St Monans roaring in spate.

28th A sudden change in the weather today—dry and quiet with very hard frost. *The Prime Minister of Jordan has been assassinated in Cairo by splinter members of the Black September organisation.*

29th *The French capture Antwerp.* The burns are frozen now. Waterdrops turn to ice on the overhanging grasses, beneath the Bel Craig, Dunino.

30th Baby thornbacks at Bucklands and the Coves. *Oscar Wilde dies miserably.*

DECEMBER

1st Frost at sea level today, the sea pools frozen on the sands, Ardross. *The Marquis de Sade approaches death in a mental asylum outside Paris.* Sirius sparkles over the firth in fine frosty skies, 9 pm.

2nd *Second Battle of Austerlitz.* Flag rushes frosted at Kilconquhar Loch.

3rd *The Battle of Cambrai ends.* Rime glitters on the trees. *R L S is dead.*

4th Marram grasses like icicles on the Ardross sands. A single gannet dives offshore. *In a bar in north Belfast an Ulster Loyalist bomb goes off, murdering thirteen Catholic men and women and two children. Allied planes have destroyed much of Leipzig.*

5th *An Anglo-French force lands at Port Said.* Old beech tree is split this morning with the hard overnight frost.

6th *The Young Pretender enters Derby.* A crab iced solid in rock pool between Pittenweem and St Monans.

7th   A huge congregation of lapwings invade Balcomie. *Pearl Harbour is bombed by Japanese planes. And at the Droppin Well Inn near Londonderry a time bomb kills 16 persons. 66 others are paralysed for life.*

8th   The Immaculate Conception of the Blessed Virgin Mary. *Bucharest has been occupied by the Germans.* The moles have been active at Dunino. Scores of black mounds litter the whitened kirkyard. *Later in the evening Mark Chapman murders John Lennon in a street in Manhattan.*

9th   Red-throated divers fly over Kilconquhar Loch. *Rumania has been crushed by the Austro-German offensive.*

10th   Eiders coo off the Basket Rock, Cellardyke. *Luther burns the Papal Bull of Excommunication.*

11th   The crabs spawn again at Bucklands. *Edward VIII abdicates.* At Dunino only the holly is bright with berries.

12th   Dippers at Durie Den. *Fighting at Verdun not yet finished.*

13th   Festival of St Lucy. *Fenians attempt to blow up Clerkenwell jail.* The cold worsens. The Pleiades hang over the southern side of the firth.

14th   Leeks frozen solid in the earth. *The Admiral Graf Spee is crippled by three British cruisers off the River Plate.*

15th   The robin sings its full song, 1.30 am. *Carlisle submits to Butcher Cumberland.* Corn buntings sing near Caiplie at noon.

16th   *Nelson is victorious at Copenhagen.* The clear weather thickens at last, the skies clouding over.

17th   The cold relaxes today; the skies are filled with coming snow. *A PLO group uses guns and grenades on an American Boeing 707 leaving Rome for Beirut and Tehran. All persons on board are killed.*

18th   Very heavy snow today from north-north-east. *Jacobite rebels are defeated at Clifton Moor.*

19th   Bloodied rabbit tracks in the snow, St Monans kirkyard. *Adolf*

Hitler takes first command of the German Army. The time of winter or sorrowing is upon us: the dark days and the dead of the year, when time stands still.

20th   Still more ice and frost forming. *The Spanish Prime Minister, Admiral Luis Carrero Blanco, is murdered in Madrid by Basque separatists.*

21st   Festival of St Thomas the Apostle. *De Gaulle is elected President of the 5th French Republic.* The fulmars are back early at Randerston.

22nd   The snow falls thicker along the coast, lying at sea level. *Herbert Schoner, policeman is killed when the Baader-Meinhof gang attack the Bavarian Mortgage and Exchange Bank at Kaiserslautern.*

23rd   Winter Solstice. *Seven Japanese war leaders hanged today. Richard Welch, head of the CIA network in Greece, is assassinated by a masked hit squad in Athens.*

24th   Christmas Eve. *David Berkowitz, an unbalanced murderer, makes his first attack on a series of women. He will terrorise New York for the coming year.*

25th   The Nativity of Our Lord. A clear day of blue skies and brilliant sunshine over the snow. *The Japanese take Hong-Kong.*

26th   More ice and frost yet. *The French defeat the Austrians at Mincio.*

27th   The Martyrdom of St Stephen. Ice and frost even more severe. *The Battle for Warsaw is nearly over.*

28th   The Massacre of the Holy Innocents. Masses of cormorants on Wormiston skellies. *The Tay Rail Bridge has collapsed and many have been killed in the disaster.*

29th   Thaw. *St Thomas à Becket, Archbishop of Canterbury, has been assassinated.* Two gannets dive off Randerston.

30th   A sunny silence over the fields—almost like a spring sunset. *The Russians are now victorious at Kotelnikovo.*

31st   New Year's Eve. Snowdrop shoots at Balcaskie are well
        through. *Soviet troops are in full occupation of Afghanistan.*
        Daffodil spears pricking through leaf litter, Dunino.

        All over the world the battles, the murders and the atrocities
        go on.
        Regulus will rise out of the firth at 9 pm tomorrow.

TWO TALES

The Farmer and the Trees
(for Pat Rush)

An Unfinished Symphony
(for Pat McDonald)

The Farmer and the Trees

There was once a farmer who could not bear to see the trees grow.

He lived in a great house that loomed over his sea-flecked farm like a gravestone. The people of the village would whisper to one another that the house was haunted; and on drizzling November nights, when the moon surfaced suddenly like a drowned boat, and the long shadow of the gravestone stole over the fields and darkened the road, the folk would scurry past for the safety of their snug homes.

'It's a bad place, that house,' they said, when they reached their firesides. 'Very badly haunted.'

And the truth of the matter was that the house was indeed haunted. But not by ghosts. Ah, no—it was haunted by greed. The farmer who lived there just could not make enough money to satisfy his restless soul.

That was why he could not bear to watch the trees grow.

Every year they flourished and fell to no financial end that he could grasp and make his own.

Yes, he was eaten up by greed.

His heart was a coin without a face to it. There was no mintage on earth that could place a stamp on his desire. No matter how great the harvests the mountains of grain never rose high enough for him. Even when their tops brushed the beams of his barn, dusting the ancient rafters with the seeds of life, he thought of building bigger barns with taller gables, loftier roofs. In his miser's mind he saw the hills of gold scenting the sky, investing the very foundations of heaven with their earthly fragrance.

Ambrosia among the feet of angels—and not a drop for God.

It was a vision which brought him no happiness because he knew he could never achieve it. Money tormented him like the spectre of one who had won the world and lost his soul; it rattled its yellow chains and groaned. But the farmer saw only the dull glitter and was deaf to the sound of woe.

So it was that as he looked out from his windows each day, he began to envy the trees the freedom and greenness of their lives.

It was different with his fields and folds. They were made to pay (the thought satisfied him) for everything that they took from the sun and soil and the life-giving washings of rain. Spring rolled back the winter's white tablecloth and got to work with busy hands. The poet walked through the farmer's fields, saw the ploughs wounding the earth, and thought of the land giving multiple birth—every blade an innocent journeyman of God. The farmer saw the seeds tumbling into the cold ground, but he never thought of the Lord's children rising on another day. He saw only money breeding for the fall.

The grasses grew and were chewed by the sheep, whose wool stuffed a thousand sacks, leaving them shivering in the clinging rains of early July. Autumn came, and the farmer surveyed the cutting of his cornfields with a grim joy. One day, after the completion of the harvest, he bowed to the sheaves when nobody was looking. They stood round him in a golden circlet; his clasped hands quivered with worship.

'Stacks of money in the bank,' he laughed to himself in a tight little whisper, 'bundles and bundles of five pound notes!'

The poet brooded over the stubble with a sadness smoking in his eyes.

All summer long he had walked through these fields. The barley had sighed and whispered to him the secrets of human kind. He had heard a billion tongues praising God out of the swaying choirs of corn.

It had been a heavy day for him when the combine-harvesters squatted on the rise like giant red beetles ready to roar into action with their grinding jaws. He knew it had to happen, but he regretted the fall of these golden-bearded kings and counsellors of the earth, who had shared their wisdom with him in a language known only to lovers and kindred spirits; and he heard the song of exile in the October winds and left the farmer's fields for his hut in the woods.

The farmer heard nothing of all this, of course, for his ears were in his pockets, where they listened for a single tune. The jingle of coins drowned out the songs of the earth. He heard it one morning and laughed out loud.

'What a profit!' he shrilled, rubbing his hands together in a tense prayer. 'I'm richer than any other body round here!'

Outside the cock crowed twice on the dungheap and he took it as a sign. He went straight out and bought two of everything for that year, including two deep freezes in celebration of the fact that his sheep had grazed so safely; and two expensive motor cars, one for himself and one for his wife.

But as he sat at his window at the close of the year, counting out the contents of his wallet, a last leaf landed wetly on the darkening panes and stuck there like a lost note.

A pang went through him at once and the trees became a deeper trouble to his days after that, and shook him out of his sleep night after night. The waste, the sheer waste of it all began to gnaw at his mind so that the delicate fretwork of the brain trembled.

'It's just stupid,' he muttered into his bowl of broth when his wife was out of the room. 'They don't do anything, they're not made to work for me, nothing at all, they're without a solitary point!'

He rose from the table, his broth untasted, and glared out at the silent trees.

'Just what are they there for is what I'd like to know?'

His wife came back from the kitchen, a sensible pudding of a woman, and told him not to waste his soup.

Waste. He hated it.

After the spring sowing he shot the tiniest sparrow framed in the entire creation. Though its pip of a heart was smaller than the bullet he aimed at it, he shot it as it sang at its supper, and the stolen seed stuck in its little throat as it died. God saw its fall though, and started to number the hairs on the farmer's greying head.

He hurried after the harvesting machines on windy days, anxious to prevent a loaf of bread from being baked out of the breeze-blown barley that landed on the other side of the dyke, where his fellow farmers worked their own fields. He grudged the smallest grains plucked by the invisible thieving fingers of heaven and given to his neighbour.

No Ruth had a place to stand in the hard heart of his alien corn.

It was long after the potato gatherers had gone to bed that his bent body could be seen against the sharp October moons, scrabbling in the dirt with claws for hands, looking for the marbles they had missed or tossed aside as worthless.

The poet came out of his wood to hold his conversations with the moon, and even as it set, slipping like a coin into the earth's purse, he saw the farmer's image etched against it, a sovereign with bowed head and bent knees.

He shook his head.

Like an unhappy ghost, he thought, raking for treasure in the bowels of the earth.

And when the children came at the end of the month to his turnip fields, hoping for a good sized root to hollow out for a Halloween lantern, they ran screaming at the sight of the death's head that sat waiting for them in the dreels, grimacing worse than any false-faced fiend. A yellowed skull with vacant eyes—everything that had been inside it consumed long since by the harsh cruel flame of greed.

'Ha, ha! I was waiting for you!' he gloated after the fleeing backs. 'You needn't think you can come to me—I won't suffer you, you thieving little scum!'

Yes, he made sure that the very last wisp of his wealth was accounted for. Everything that could be salvaged was poured back into his pockets. The dung nourished his tired fields, the wasps landed on his plums at their peril. His hedgerows were starred with campion but the constellations came under the plough. Ditches that had been adrift with daffodils and spilling with vetch were filled in like graves. Poppies and daisies were sprayed out of existence.

Ah, but the trees remained.

It was the trees which finally whipped him into a fury that knew no bounds. Their slow unmoving attitudes, their unspeaking eloquence, their sheer independence from the world of profit and loss—it was sending him stark mad. In his dreams their roots drove deep into his groin, sucked up sustenance from his spine till he felt marrowless and cold. The stealing tendrils reached into his pockets as he slept in his chair, fingered him, twitched out the banknotes. He woke up sweating and clutching the air.

The doctor came over the fields.

But soon he was frenzied with avarice and hate, cancers that were beyond the doctor's cure. From those God-given places that prevented his growing another forkful of potatoes, a fistful of grain, the trees reached out their arms to the sky, took the sun's yellow goblet in their many fingers, and drank the honey of light and life.

The farmer stood at his windows, his fingers clasped tightly. He watched the trees growing drunk daily on sweetness and grace. Every hour of every day they drank freely out of that golden goblet, so abundantly available, till the sun itself was drained into the pale wash of the west, and the austerer stars pricked the sky.

A throng of celibates whose bleak chalices glittered against the black backcloth of eternity.

He had no time for the stars that told time so slowly only the angels heard their whispered chiming, delicate as the foam of the sea. Stars? Hah! they were useless as candles on a cake. They were not hives of energy like the sun, that sent a billion light-bees buzzing over the fields to scatter life abroad.

And the sun was inexhaustible.

'Drink,' it seemed to say, 'oh, drink abundantly!'

Such open-handed generosity maddened the tight-fisted farmer. The trees tippled and took and waved their laughing green fingers— but they gave back nothing in return.

Or so the farmer thought.

He never saw the poems that they wrote upon the sky in time's despite; spring poems of freshness and hope, yet tinged with an indefinable sadness for those who would never see young leaves again.

He never saw the shade they gave to thirsty cattle under the scorching noons of June.

Nor did he think to notice all the nesting-places for the birds. What good were birds anyway, except for stealing corn? and that was no good at all. Their songs meant nothing to him, praising God in a language older than dragon's blood. Like the songs of the earth, he couldn't hear them—his head was filled with the tinkle of trash in a till.

Autumn came. The leaves stained the white windows of heaven with ambers and crimsons and golds, flooding the fields with the colours of medieval manuscripts, so that the days passed like chapels and the evenings like cathedrals.

All that struck no answering psalm out of the farmer's lonely skull. His mind was a byre, his feet were feet of clay—they went to church but brought back no gospel to his stony grounds. The thickness was in his ears, barren shells in which the sea-fog swirled, so that he failed to hear the rain's high requiem as it pattered its sanctus over the dying leaves.

Even when the white winds of winter played their purest song, with ghostly fingers plucking the black harp-strings of December—even then he heard nothing, he saw nothing, he felt nothing.

Nothing but a self-devouring envy that nothing would cure.

Except one thing.

And so it was, at the time of his high spring madnes, that he ordered his men to cut down the woods to the very last tree. Out came the great axes, the huge saws. Their teeth glinted wickedly in the sun as the woodcutters set about their work. They laid siege then to the walls of those ancient castles, the aristocrats of the earth, and the nesting birds flew screeching from their unhatched broods. They left them cracked and cold among the toppled towers and the green crenellations of leaves. The long grasses waved and the winds and weeds wept over them, and a generation of song flooded the ground.

For days and weeks the work went on till the long mornings and afternoons were hot with the hysterical whining of saws, the chewing of axes. And the shrieking of roots as they were evicted from the earth. An earth they had tenanted for generations before the farmer came along and bought up Eden with a walletful of money.

A fat wad over his heart that fluttered as the markets of the world fluctuated and fell.

It was Eden no more.

Ruined choirs and pews hewed asunder, the choristers flown to other kirks, where aspiring green fingers still pointed to the sky and the songs of God were heard again in a foreign land.

That summer there was no shade for the cattle as they thirsted by the parched trough. These days its old stones scarcely felt the cooling touch of water—the farmer was too busy inside his house, counting up the killing he had made on the trees. His tongue lolloped round his jaws as he reckoned it up over and over, wondering if he had missed a note in the telling.

The cattle by the trough craved for a single drop of water. Their pink tongues stroked the bare twinkling slabs, searching for the merest memory of a raindrop retained by the remembering old stones.

And the scorched stones remembered and remembered . . .

But it was not enough to satisfy the panting tongues.

'I'll count again, just to be sure,' the farmer said for the hundredth time, licking his lips.

And he looked quickly under the table, in case his eager breath had sent a banknote drifting out of his ken.

So the cattle thirsted by the trough and farmer at his counting table thirsted even more.

The July rains came and the stone trough brimmed like a silver harp. But the farmer's love of silver could never be satisfied with silver, and his craving for plenty left him with no peace. The trees, he was well aware, would never come again.

He grew pale and waxy. His eyes burned with a single flame.

Autumn was gray and dreary that year. There were no cathedral windows to filter the white fires of eternity for human understanding; no mosaics of leaves to break up heaven into shapes of sense.

The November rains swept their bleak curtains over a sea of mud. At the high windows of the farmhouse a wild face appeared from time to time, staring through the veils of fog.

And in winter the wide unbroken whiteness of his fields went away from him in endless waves. The sheer flatness of those eternal snows terrified the farmer—he had never before seen such an expanse of land. The trees had stood like people, green and grey. Now, in place of the field of folk, there was an arctic strangeness that numbed his soul.

He stayed inside all winter, afraid to step out into that lawless landscape. His men received their orders from behind locked doors and went out in silence to do his bidding. It was not long however till they began to grow nervous of him. And to tell the truth, he was indeed a ghastly sight by now: a pair of lantern jaws lit from above by a solitary flame. They spoke to him, but the spaces where his ears were seemed not to hear; he turned his head to their inquiring faces, but the holes where his eyes had been made them fall back in fear to the door.

Soon they left off working for him altogether and no-one would come in their place. It was an unlucky farm. Left to themselves the cattle dwindled and died.

Spring came round, greening the dark land, but there were no trees to hear its voice and trumpet forth in answering leaves. The farmer never saw the greenness. He had by this time taken to his bed, where he lay in a still whiteness of sheets, only his finger-ends fumbling blindly with the covers, sifting imaginary pieces of paper. His hands were two ghostly crabs on a snowswept shore.

A nurse looked after him now; each day she took away his untasted meals. His fat wife had left him at the turn of the year and gone to live with her sister in another country. She would not stay, she said, with a man that would neither feed his beasts nor himself. The truth was that he had long ceased to enjoy the taste of food. Money had killed his appetite.

And long before the summer came he died.

This was how it happened.

On the hundredth day after he had taken to his bed, he slipped into a coma.

That at least was how it appeared to his hired nurse. But where, oh where does the mind go to when it wanders far afield of those cultivated tracts known to medical science as everyday consciousness?

After his brain had closed on the patterned walls of his room, and the windows had shrunk to a glimmering white square, the farmer's spirit ebbed out of the house and found itself in a huge forest. Here the trees were taller and straighter than any on earth, dwarfing him like green-caped gods, like titans of truth prevailing over ugliness and error and spite.

This was a forest of the mind.

Long shafts of sunlight penetrated it for incalculable miles. A man of innocent and quiet soul might have wandered freely in that forest, and walked unharmed among the long bright lances of the sun. Ah, but they pierced the guilty farmer like the swords of justice, till he ran to and fro in his gathering panic, seeking an avenue of escape. Everywhere he turned, a blade of light burst like a star in his face. The trees massed and multiplied about him, their arms and hands raised in rebuke, and stern conspiratorial whisperings ruffled their leaves—a dark murmuring as secret as a stream.

Blinded and bewildered, he floundered through the forest—a man drowning, fighting for air.

At last, his ears torn by the screechings of insects and birds, he stumbled upon a mossy aisle, at the end of which, in the incredibly far distance, he saw a tiny white speck. Breathing hard, his hand clutching at his heart, he blundered along this path, his legs sinking in the drifted generations of leaves, sometimes taking him up to his knees, so that he thought he would be sucked under. The rifle-fire of hidden brittle twigs made his failing heart leap from its stalk. After an eternity the white speck swam up to meet him.

It was a gate.

His face cracked in something resembling an agonized laugh as he reached out with one pain-filled arm to fasten on it.

Before he could quite reach it, a figure barred his way. A figure blocking out the welcome fields beyond, where embroidered flowers brightened deathlessly, the butterflies danced, and the larks swung and sung by invisible strings.

A figure clad in black from head to foot.

The farmer halted, trembling, like the hare he had shot down so often from that familiar, frightened pose. Then he breathed again, a little pant of relief. The man in black was smiling and he was carrying an axe. He was only a woodcutter after all.

Yes, you're quite right,' said the black woodcutter, with unmoving lips, 'that's all I am, just a cutter down of trees, nothing more distinguished.'

'But how did you read my thoughts?'

The farmer's breath, so briefly recovered started to falter again.

'Oh, I know all there is to know,' came the reply.

The birds had suddenly ceased their singing.

'You see, I've been in the forest since the first seed was spilt, and I've nothing else to do but wait for the trees to grow tall. Mind you, there are a great many trees and only one of me. I'm kept busy enough.'

An old gray sea began to beat against the farmer's brain, and breaking over it was the dim dawn of an understanding. He tried to get by. The stranger held him by the arm.

'There's really no need to struggle, my friend. You can't go through that gate—that's not the way for you. Your time has come and you have another way to go.'

"No, wait—I have years to go yet!'

'Ah, many folk say that. The fact of the matter is that there's many a tree never reaches its full span. Don't ask me why. As for reasons you ought to know more about that than I do. I'm just a cog in a wheel—a dark, secret cog, yes, but there are bigger things than me, believe me, and even I don't know where the wheel is headed for. It just goes round and on.

But let's consider your case.

I understand you were fond of turning trees into timber. Well, I'm at liberty to tell you that one of the old oaks you had cut down has found its way to the undertaker's yard, and out of it has come the grandest coffin in the shop. Not one that just anyone around these parts could afford. No, this one is made specially for you—good solid oak for a man of substance. Look at it this way, if you like: in your last home you'll be surrounded by your own property. That should be a comforting thought for a man like you.

Comfort. You've always enjoyed it, haven't you? And you've been deprived of it this long while. I know your head has lain on a restless pillow, what with your worries and your fantasies and wants. Well then, you'll be pleased to know there's an end coming to all that. There's the comfortablest pillow the earth affords just waiting for you—and you'll lie like a log. Free from all those fevered fancies that troubled you and kept you from your sleep. It's over—your dreams are done.

And you never did like having to put your hand in your pocket, did you? Have no fears on that count; there are no pockets in what you'll be wearing. Nothing to lose, nothing to worry about losing.

Now what was your greatest pride and joy? It was to be seen in your fine big car, wasn't it? And it bore your own personal number plate, did it not—yours and yours alone? Just wait. A large black model is coming to collect you, a polish on it like you never saw in your life. a chauffeur is laid on, and when the bearers carry you out, everybody will be able to see your own personalised number plate, screwed to your box, bearing your dates and your years. Lovely brass handles too, you were so fond of the brass.

And the leaves will be whispering on your grave like the rustling of paper money, and every raindrop will be the chink of silver in your ears.

Only I'm forgetting—you won't be able to hear. Never mind, just listen to this while you still have hearing.

I believe that you were fond of your tipple—only the greatest vintages to grace your table. Let me tell you then that old Selbie the sexton has prepared a vineyard for you in the finest available site: a resting place right beneath the shade of his elderberry trees. And to this vineyard you will be both the labourer and the grape, the giver of all good. But you won't have to bear the heat and dust of the day yourself.

No, this is how it will happen.

As soon as you're installed, the trees will be tapping their toes merrily at the roof of your house when they hear the dance music of the spring. Then they'll go wild. The first tendril will find a keyhole and the others will follow, breaking and entering. They'll take a sample draught and I'm sure they'll approve. Soon they'll be sucking for all they're worth, and you'll be on your way, mouthful by mouthful, up to the open air again: first into the sharp white flowers of summer, so fragrant with life; then into the black mortuary juices of autumn.

The trees will have made you their own.

In the end the sexton will gather the berries and take home the baskets to his wine-making. He's famous for his elder vintages, but your particular year will be a year to remember. His friends who come round in the evenings to drain their glasses at his table will be remembering that vintage for many a year to come, the deepest and darkest vintage ever they drank. The year of the farmer.

You were never in favour of wastage, were you? So perhaps after all the greatest blessing for you will be knowing that you fertilised the earth and let the trees tap you to the marrow, to the very bone, for the benefit of your neighbour; and that in the end, you, who would give nothing, gave all.

And the many-fingered trees will hold you up to the sky like an offering—a hundred thousand goblets of grapes. And the people will come and drink, yes, drink abundantly . . .'

Long before the black voice had finished speaking, the farmer was on his knees among the leaves. His lips babbled inanely, his eyes burned like coals in his skull, fingers scrabbling on the forest floor, crab-white hands out of their element.

Had the nurse not been out at the time to fetch the doctor, she would have seen him apparently awake from his coma and enter a delirium so great that he rose up physically from his knees and fled from the house.

So when she did return, accompanied by the doctor, all that was there for them to see was a blindly swinging door in the wind and a rumpled wilderness of white sheets.

He wandered far over fields and forest, his bare feet bloodied by brambles, his nightshirt muddied and torn. Had it been winter he would have died of exposure on the first night. But it was high summer and he had a long way to go.

Sometimes he was seen by inland folk and taken for a madman and so avoided. For many a mile though he went unnoticed, travelling beneath the Milky Way, his penitent head silvered by slow stars, passing the planets on route to eternity.

At last he arrived at an obscure wood, in the middle of which, weakened by his titanic trek, illness and want of food, he staggered and fell, stretched like a log among the faded bluebells and the dusty buttercups.

He never moved again.

In time the flesh slid from his bones, leaving a lonely whiteness among the weeds that rose and fell with the ebb and flow of the seasons. It was a nakedness that cried out for the dignity and decency of Christian burial.

But burial he could have none, for no-one even knew where he lay. Nor could anyone have much cared.

In the end however the spirit of the wood dealt mercifully with the little pile of rubbish among the weeds, turning it to something more favourable than dust. It lost its startling whiteness and became as green as moss and autumn brown, taking on the colours of nature. The bones knitted, fused in such a way that the fragments lost their human shape and lay like a hollow trunk on the floor of the woods. Toadstools landed on it, spreckled it with their red and white cushions; squirrels nibbled their breakfasts and played there; and contemplative frogs paid it nocturnal visitations under the vast spawn of stars.

And in no time, so forgiving is the soul of the tree, a gradual crust grew over the changed bones until they were indistinguishable from all the fallen trees of the wood.

It was, in the end, a kind of healing bark, an acceptance of kinship. A natural atonement.

A silent benediction.

An Unfinished Symphony

There was once a young man who longed to play the violin.

He lived in a sea-swept village among the farmers and fishermen and builders of boats. There was a church on a hill, a stone cross crusted with lichens and spray: little bitter time-flowers of silver, gold. In winter the waves wetted the gravestones that stood sentinel as the priest sounded the bell—a black-coated cormorant tugging at a frayed old rope. Thus he kept toll of the sins of the people.

The young man feared the sound of the bell, whose echoes gathered eternity into the air, a gray frost over the fields. He preferred instead to hear the music of the sea. Its infinite strings glimmered like a harp. Day-long, night-long, the young man watched and listened as it was played: by wind and rain, by sun and moon, and by the glittering orchestra of stars, resplendent in their evening dress. That was how he came to long for an instrument, to draw music of his own out of the salt clarsach of the sea. He knew that a harp was out of the question, so his yearning grew for a violin.

The tides took out the years.

Poor though the young man's folk were, they saved hard and one Christmas night he came home with snow in his hair to find the whole family grouped round the fireside, awaiting him. There on the hearth, laved by the flames, lay the rose-red heart of his deepest dreams: a beautiful, polished violin, curved and winy like the waves of the sea; intricate with the fragrance and flowerings of some forgotten forest, it seemed so old. The craftsman had caught the minutest details of sea-work in the wood and had waxed them to perfection. The strings ran over its surface like the silver moon-bridge that crossed the firth when the moon was full. It was a miracle of metamorphosis, an instrument that might have come out of the sea itself.

He picked it up and gazed at it with a glad face.

The following day he went to the house of the old music teacher at the west edge of the village, not far from the church. He asked him if he would teach him how to play.

'Listen,' said the old man, 'anyone can play with fingers and brains

200

and a knowledge of the notes. What I can teach you can be learned in a single day.'

The young man did not understand. He persisted in begging the master for a musical education and at last the old violinist gave in and began to give the boy lessons.

After a time it became evident that the eager young pupil would never be an outstanding success.

'It's no use,' he cried despairingly.' I can't make it produce the sounds I want from it—the sounds of the sea!'

The old man nodded and smiled a sad smile.

'Just as I told you, my boy. You see, anyone can play with his fingers, but how many play with their souls?'

'Then how can I learn to play with my soul?'

The teacher shook his white hairs.

'That you may never learn,' he said. 'But if ever you do there will be a heavy price to pay, and the day may come when you will wish yourself back here, paying me the few pennies I charge for the sake of a pipe or two to sweeten my age.'

Uncomprehending, the young man walked down to the sea, his violin clasped to his heart.

'Old men are so absolute,' he thought to himself. 'Anyway, there's nothing more he can teach me now.'

And he carried on practising day after day.

Until the day he fell in love.

That was the day he saw the girl who walked on the sands. When he saw her he forgot all about his violin for a time.

She was sixteen when he first set eyes on her as she followed the lines of seaweeds and shells with her bare feet. The moment he saw her the last fragments of his boyhood fell to the ground like a flower forgotten. Over its fading petals a strange new melody throbbed like the sea.

Nothing else mattered to him now.

Her hair was coarse and lovely as a wind-torn wood, her straight nose had the strength of a tower, her lips were a slender scarlet thread, sweetened by a special sadness that vanished when she laughed. Her forehead had the sweep of a snow-filled field, and her breast was a strong white curve. But it was her eyes, he thought, that were her most remarkable feature. They were wide with an undefined yearning that made him shiver. He longed to satisfy whatever it could be that her strange longing intended.

'How strange,' he thought to himself, 'that she should have lived so close to me for all these years and I have never properly seen her until today.'

Ah, strange indeed. For what is that mysterious affinity we call love, which, if not created in a single miraculous moment, will not be crafted by decades or by the labours of generations?

It was then that the horrified realisation reached down into his heart like the cold hand of the executioner.

She was unattainable.

In her indescribable loveliness she was a being he could never hope to come near. She was merely an ideal, a melody he could never play, one that he would always hear in his heart alone. Other young men would walk with her, some of them holding her hand perhaps. He himself would never know what that felt like. No, but he would hold her hand in the quietness of his own heart. For the rest of his life, in the secret places under the stairs, he would keep it warm with his love, and there he would caress the tips of her white fingers with his hopeless longing.

From far off he heard the notes of a violin sobbing in someone's throat. He recognised the melody at once—it was the language of the heart. Yes, he was fast and fallen in love and there was no cure. He resigned himself now to a life of watching and listening, a passive presence on the outer rim of her circles of friends; and though he had always been a somewhat solitary young man, yet he courted the company she kept, simply to be near her.

Whenever she spoke he was stirred beyond reason—she touched words with her tongue and they trembled like dewdrops on webs in the early morning mists. Her mildest gesture struck him to stone and he pictured it for days. She slanted her head to the sky and became at once an enraptured saint. He watched the thoughts pass over her face, sad and glad, like shadows racing over the fields, like shards of sunlight sweeping the sea. She had merely to walk along the village streets and the houses bowed to the processional she made, the trees touching one another's fingertips to form green arches for her as she passed.

Only the church bell never boomed for joy.

And when she walked homewards he followed her, to marvel for the thousandth time that so humble a dwelling could house such a goddess. Bricks and mortar would never be the same again—she transcended ordinariness. Wherever she slept and woke, wherever she lived and breathed was a temple. She had transformed the whole world for him from bronze to gold.

Yet she never knew that he loved her so, never glanced at him for a moment—and if she happened to meet his eyes by accident she looked away at once with a mixture of shyness and scorn.

His heart began to ache for her.

That was how he took to standing outside her house in the long winter nights, his music sobbing to the stars, his fingers shivering on the frost-filled strings. The wind wept on the sands to the sound of his pain; the tides swung in their chains and moaned in tune to his misery.

'They can hear me,' he shouted aloud to the planets, 'the whole universe hears me and knows that I am in love! When will she ever listen to me, oh, when will she hear my song?'

The windows of her house stayed hard with light, the black harbours brimmed with his sorrow, the days died for him, and the nights passed like other people's weddings.

In time he had played so hard in the great winter whitenesses which fell that year, that one cruel night his fingers cracked and the drops of blood spattered on the snow, hot golden gore wept from his heart's pain. His tears froze on his face. Gradually the violin grew heavy as a gravestone hung with webs of frost. The once supple strings changed to a brittle rainbow of white ice, the death of sound and colour. And by midnight the instrument had turned entirely to stone.

Cradling his treasure in crackling arms, he staggered a few steps in the snow and laid it as carefully as he could on her doorstep. Then he walked wildly to the graveyard on the hill and for a time he was lost in the bulky black shadows of the church.

He returned carrying something inside his shirt, next to his breast. All the stars watched him as he went down on his knees again at her doorstep. He reached inside his tattered shirt and took out his gift—laid it gently across the petrified violin. It was a single stone rose from a lover's tomb, a white sculpted rose from the kirkyard.

'A memorial to my love,' he whispered, 'and an elegy to my art.'

And he walked home desolate, his eyes hard and glittering as the stars.

In the morning the girl opened her door and saw the violin laid stiffly on the doorstep.

Her eyes filled with tears.

She could see now what had been happening all this time. She looked down at the instrument, itself its own memorial now, stone against stone on the whitened sill. It had no more tongue in it than the dumb step she trod on every day of her heartless life. She dropped to her knees, picked up the stone rose that was laid so poignantly across the strings, and gazed at it. It fell heavy on her hand, like a broken heart. Her tears began to fall. One of the drops splashed on the violin and she reached out instinctively to brush it away.

It was as she did so that she saw the miracle. Just where the teardrop had landed the icy stonework was dissolving like salt and a tiny circle of polished wood was widening in its place. The petrified song of the forest was returning. A cry of delight shrilled from her through the blinding curtains of her remorse, and as the hot scalding droplets rained harder out of her eyes, she could see that the reversal was now complete. The stone rose too, that had never lived at all, was suffused with a blood-red fragrance. She kissed it and placed it in her bosom.

The she rose to her feet. The violin was now gleaming again—burnished and bright as the winter air. Still in her nightdress she ran through the snows till she came on bare feet to the house where the young man lived. She knocked breathlessly with tingling fingers.

When he answered the door his eyes were as pale as the last stars of morning. But when he saw her standing there, her feet bandaged with snow, holding out his replenished violin, his face lit up again with a mad joy. They looked at one another with recognition and fell into each others arms. They had found what they were looking for; they were in love. He bent down and kissed her bare blue feet. She had come to him, a penitent, bearing his violin like a candle in winter. He forgave her his heartbreak in a burst of love.

They walked hand in hand down to the winter sea, her blind feet frozen on the frost-bound pools of the shore. There she sat down on a rock between the young man and the sea, to watch him play. He faced the waves, gripped the bow, gathered the violin to his heart, closed his eyes and struck the strings.

At once the sea shivered and shook: the vast salt strings of the ocean trembled into song. The girl had heard the song of the sea from her childhood, but never till now had she heard it crooning the true song of love. She sighed. Her young body thrummed rapturously to the sounds of the new world.

For all around them now the world was awakening for them, shedding its whiteness. Pure as crystal ran the notes from the strings and the streams around the sea-girt village threw off their fetters of frost and bubbled with laughter. The bow drew gentle whispers from the polished shell and the spring breezes rustled round the coast, green fields fluttering like sleeves in the bright winds. A profusion of grace notes, a bouquet of colourful flourishes—and a crowd of flowers proliferated in the meadows, thronged the ditches and bewildered the banks and braes.

All this time the trees had stood like empty staves, broken black lines etched against the chill white manuscript of the sky. But now the young man was filling the staves with the green and golden leaves of his notes. Crotchets and quavers brought forth oak leaves and copper beech, and the lime trees poured fountains of luminosity into the brimming sky. There the birds swooped on the young musician's notes. A pure sound stuck in each feathered throat and the songsters sowed them like seeds, fluting over the fields.

Deeper now the player plunged, deeper into the scale of sounds, lingering on the lowest notes. The sun sank and bled; darkness swept the sky—a black wing. Yet still the girl sat on and on, silvered by stars, ravished by music. And when the moon rose, a golden-cloaked harpist sweeping the strings of the firth, she thought that she would die of ecstasy, caught in that madly beautiful duet: her lover and the harpist moon.

Night deepened. He plucked the strings with practised fingers and still more stars pricked the sky. His fingerpoints scattered the constellations like fields of celestial corn. Only when dawn blossomed over the sea, a dripping rose, did the young man lay down his violin with a pale face and look at his lady. She knew what his look meant. Through the experience of loving her he had mastered his art. She drank his eyes that were full of the sea, kissed him, and took him by the hand. Wordlessly they walked along the shore, hand in hand. The world was all before them—a world filled with their love. But not the world itself would separate them now.

They went through fields and woods; they sat by hedgerows and streams; they wandered the lanes and byways of their green and carefree earth. Most of all they wandered between sand and foam where the surf whispered across their dreaming feet. They would never forget the sea, where they had first seen each other through the eyes of love and art. And in their long love's day they drank from one another's mouths the elixir of their undying love.

It was a pure uncomplicated love. A love of eyes and lips and hands. The violin separated their bodies, a golden flame, a sword of chastity. Yet it was the violin that expressed the soul of their emotion, and everybody saw how much more beautifully the young man played now that he walked and talked with the young girl.

'You are fortunate,' the old music teacher said to him one day. 'She has made you play with your soul. Not many have that experience in this difficult world.'

The young man scarcely heard him. Every day produced new melodies, new murmurings and nuances of emotion. She had become a kind of symphony which he understood more and more deeply with every day that passed—but which he could never finish playing.

Ah, but nothing lasts forever, the sea whispered to the young lovers as they sat one day by the shore, hand in hand, gazing into each other's eyes. Nothing in the world of men is forever, murmured the changeless sea. Make haste, make haste, they heard the urgent little waves whispering as they met. You are young, but time is passing. You cannot sit by an eternal shore all your lives till you grow old and die—pretending you are gods. There are other melodies to be learned.

So the young man picked up his violin and began to play again, but this time with a faltering hand. Not the pure notes of old but a series of sounds fraught with a thick and turbulent excitement. The girl heard the music and her body ached for her young man. At the same time fear flooded her eyes. Her lover's hands fluttered and plunged frantically, his playing became undisciplined and wild, and the strings buzzed with questionings and doubts. He suddenly flung down his instrument and ran his fingers wildly through his hair. It was no use—the music kept coming, in his head, in his groin, a blind murky melody, as irresistible as wine.

The girl began to kiss him passionately. For the first time in their love he cupped the chaste chalices of her breasts and bent his lips to drink. His mouth burned—they were goblets of snow. She let her hands run over him, to tell him that he was a man, that the day had gone forever when they could love with hands and lips alone. The song of the earth was tumbling into that of the sea, filling it with its darker music.Trembling they tore off their clothes and the tide rushed in and swept their flimsy garments from under their naked feet. They drew closer. Deep in their loins the violin unlocked a long forbidden chord. It burst like a rose.

It was then that they heard the awful beating of the black bell. They looked up. Behind them on the clifftop the kirk was bombillating like a gong: an iron blossoming in the sky. The priest was a bird of prey on the skyline, the entire congregation a black huddle at his back; the gray wail of psalm went up and the strange new music faded and died. The girl saw the danger.

'Never mind them, my darling,' she pleaded, 'play our own music, my sweet, and leave them to their sober joy. They can only play in one key—the key of eternity, the music of the dead.'

Her lover listened to her for a moment and looked at his violin, silent on the sands. The kirk's tongue clanged again, insistent and harsh.

'Never fear them, darling boy,' she urged him desperately now, 'we have a music greater than all the tongues of praise. Finish our symphony, I beg you!'

But the young man had not her strength. He turned on his toes and ran into the sea, madly striking out for their few clothes that the foam was bearing away. He brought back what he could to cover their nakedness.

'Here, put them on again,' he said.

They dressed in a cold wet silence and took their way home, shivering.

And that was the start of the death of their love.

From that day onwards the young man grew colder and colder. He who had yearned so hotly for the possession of her heart, his own heart gradually froze towards her, and he played to her less and less, and with less and less passion—until one day he ceased to play at all.

And then he left her.

He played his violin to other young girls and he went back to the purer safer melodies of the past. But something of that first beauty never came back to his playing, and everyone commented on how it was not quite the same calibre as it had been with his first love.

He never saw her tears, for she was too proud to make a monument of her grief. She stole softly to the sea and asked it why he had done this to her: the sea shrugged and sighed as it always does. She asked the stars: the stars, as always, made no answer.

So the greatest love they had ever known was allowed to die—and the sea listened and the stars looked on. But for their special children, these two young lovers, they could do nothing. They were fated to love apart.

Thus the world passes away.

Soon after that the day came when they left their sea-splashed village, the young man and the young girl. They travelled to palaces of learning, in distant cities, far apart, and like two pebbles thrown into separate pools, they gathered round them circles of friends that widened with the years, hiding them from one another more and more, masking the painful memories of the past.

He had long ceased to play his violin. He became in time a doctor of old philosophy, an unknown soldier in the war against ignorance. His comrades became the books and people of the past. Indeed he scarcely lived in the present in any real sense.

At first he did not know what had happened to her. Till one day he heard that she had married. A pang went through him as he remembered what had nearly been his. But he went on with the gray art that living had become to him. Not long afterwards, on a visit to his village, he saw her in the street, near to one of their old haunts. There was a man with her, and a tiny child. He smiled at her—a pale smile. But his heart inside him snapped at the stalk. He knew that like the great betrayer he had cast a pearl away richer than all the world.

It was then that he asked for the hand of another lady, and she accepted him gladly. In time they too had children—and so the two young lovers of the world's youth went on as they had for years, living their lives apart, hardly daring to recall those sad golden days when they had loved one another so deeply.

One day in the emptiness of his heart, he remembered again the girl of his dreams, and his unplayed violin. A great emotion took hold of him, so great that he could hardly stand. He had moved to a city far away from his old home, but he travelled back there that very day, taking his violin with him. Down he went, past all the old familiar places where he had held her close and whispered to her the thoughts of his heart. He reached the rock on the shore where she had first told him that she loved him. Taking his violin in his arms he faced the sea, gathered up his memories like fallen petals, and started to play.

The old wood and strings that had been dumb so long burst into a sudden bouquet of sounds so sweet, so piercing, so fragrant with remembering that the sea drew in its breath with a deep sigh and the surf rushed up the shingle and over his feet. He never heeded it. Life had saddened the young man, young no longer now, and experience had matured his perception of things to such a degree of poignancy that he knew he was playing with the accomplishment of a master. He had at last achieved some kind of triumph over time and death.

From that day on he practised his lost art so well that he became famous as a performer of his own compositions. People came to hear him play. He travelled round the country answering requests for performances. He earned a golden reputation, he was accepted into the magic circle of art.

He prospered.

By this time the silver had entered his beard. The day came when he was invited to give a recital in his old sea-town home. He travelled there at once, for he was always glad to be visiting the old places of his youth, and in his busy city life he was in perpetual winter exile from the sea, his ancient love. Travelling home always saddened him too, but lately he had come to feel that it added a special quality to his compositions which it would be foolish to deny.

He took up his position in front of the small gathering of people and started to play as he had done a thousand times before. He was only a little through his first piece when he saw her sitting among the people. Deep in his heart an old tune began to beat, a salt sweet lament, savage as desire. It entered into the melody he was playing, unheard by the other listeners except for the girl, who knew him so well. She could hear in his playing one of their fondest melodies—a sweet tune, but embittered by the minor chords of longing that could not be untwisted from their hearts.

And so he appeared to her again, like a poem familiar yet far off— the white in his beard mere spray from a beating sea that could be flung off in a moment of desire. And she remembered. And she remembered.

He played of love and heartbreak, of separation and of the widening years; he played of true love and false love, and of love reached by compromise and reasoning and regret. Love withers and dies, mourned the C string. Nothing is forever, nothing is worthwhile. No, no, no, sobbed the E string. The heartbreak of true love never ends, never loses its worth. And what is true love, pray? demanded the C string. And the answer came, plangent and pure on the E—First love, first love, first love.

And they saw the anguish in each other's faces, flickering behind the taut smiles. The music reached its climax, their hearts leapt together out of their breasts, like two doves meeting in the high arches of a lofty hall.

Afterwards they met in private and for the sake of old time, as they thought, they walked hand in hand to the edges of the sea, where they had stood as lovers so many years ago.

The stars shone softly down on them, the sea stopped its breathing and listened to their talk. They talked of the old days, when they were young, and when the violin too was in its youth, the young man's art. There was no doubt that experience and age and suffering had improved his playing immensely, but they recalled the tunes of their youth best of all, when the violin had thrilled their strung hearts with the knowledge of love.

It was not long till they stopped their talking and dared to look into each other's eyes. And there they saw what had never gone away in all these years—their love for one another. Their breaths met and intermingled.

They kissed as naturally as wave meeting wave. It was as though the years in between this and their last kiss had never existed. They ran their trembling hands against one another's bodies.

'You haven't changed, my love,' she said. 'You feel exactly like the same as when—'

He kissed her once more.

'And you,' he said, 'you still look the same. And you will always look the same to me, always sixteen.'

For a time they were innocents again under the stars, all their years of experience in the making of love fallen away from them. It was not long however till passion flowered again between them: a red rose in the night, a dark root that had lain undisturbed for a quarter of a century while the tides ebbed and flowed. The scent from that forgotten flower spilled out among the stars. Their breathing quickened.

'I want you,' she breathed, 'oh I want you, I want you, my love.'

Her body told him it was true.

It was then he confessed to her that she was the first girl he had ever kissed.

'But,' he said, 'since I wedded another you are once again the first I have kissed. And I have never been unfaithful.'

'Nor have I,' she said, 'I have never broken troth.'

They looked at one another with infinite sadness.

'Let us not be unfaithful to one another,' he said at last, after a long pause. 'To spoil this perfect love of ours would, after all be untrue.'

'Then,' she whispered, 'after we are dead, let us meet here together on the shores of this quiet sea, where we first fell in love.'

The stars stole quiet glances at them, the sea brimmed respectfully the notes of the violin filling the firth. First love, first love, first love. Be true one to another, be true, be true.

Again they looked into each other's eyes with hard and agonized longing.

But they heard in their hearts the gray old tongue of the church bell, tormenting the star-struck sea. They saw the priest on the hill, that black bird of prey, brooding over their naked yearnings. They thought of their families and their friends. They thought of everyone except themselves.

And so they parted there on the shores of that sea. He left her forever, the girl who would have given him her love.

And they went back to their lives.

After that day people noticed that he gave fewer performances on the violin, and when he did play he no longer seemed to be able to summon up the old magic. It was said of him that at last the well of his artistry had run dry.

In the course of time he stopped playing altogether, and day by day the violin grey grayer and heavier, like stone. And indeed, in time, it reverted to stone, just as it had done many years before, when he had despaired of his love.

He became a bitter old man living alone on the shores of his native sea, to which he had returned in his twisted age. The sea failed to bring him the solace he had sought in it—the sea that had symbolised for him the girl of his heart, the mystery of their love. The years broke over him in white waves and fell away. At last he was an empty shell left stranded on a rock by the tides of life. No-one cared about him.

And in the end he died.

But someone remembered that he had been a violinist, and paid the sexton to carve a violin, in white marble, on his memorial.

'And,' said the withered old woman who came to the sexton's door—for it was she—'see that a rose is carved on it too. A rose laid over the strings—for he was also a true lover.'

And she went back to her last years—a nameless number in that vast army of the earth's women, whose children leave them in the end in pursuit of their lives. A woman whose ancient breasts were seen no more by any man.

And in time she too died, as people do.

One summer's night that was full of stars, two young lovers were standing by the harbour wall near to the sea's edge. They were very much in love.

Not far from these lovers, who stood there in all the fullness of their flesh, two shades met at the mouth of the tide. They were as insubstantial as the lacework of the sea.

One shade spoke to the other.

'I was wrong,' he whispered over and over again.'I was wrong, I was wrong, my darling love.'

'What is it you are saying?' she sighed. 'I cannot understand you, I cannot hear for the salt is in my ears.'

The sea breathed urgently and the white whispers of foam ran under the stars.

'That night,' he said hoarsely, 'that night under these same stars—

it would not have been impure, my darling, it would not have been impure.'

'I know that now.'

The sea seethed and sighed.

'I know that now, too late, too late.'

'Nothing, my love,' he murmured, 'nothing that might have taken place between us could ever have been said to be impure—for we were true pure lovers.'

The sea voices made the two young lovers on the pier pause in their kissing.

'Two true pure lovers, true lovers, too pure.'

The white surf churned and chafed at the stones of the beach. One of the sea voices spoke again. It was a girl's voice floating on the waves, wild with regret.

'We listened too hard to the voice of the priest on the hill,' it said. 'Thou shalt not, thou shalt not, thou shalt not.'

'Thou shalt not commit adultery,' he groaned, as the sea ground the shingle.

And at the sound of the weary sea-voice the stars stirred in the sky.

'My dear and only love,' he whispered, 'Our whole lives were an adultery—after we parted. We committed adultery the day we married apart. That was the real impurity, the real sin. And it was my fault, my fault.'

He reached out with fingers of spume to touch the memory of her breasts. The sea swung and soughed where they were and two waves clashed and mingled and separated again.

'Ah yes,' she cried, 'we denied one another the purity of our love.'

The tide was chewing fiercely now at the shore, closer to where the two young lovers stood on the pier, forming an arch beneath the stars.

'I should have fought for you, I suppose,' she added, with the bitter taste of salt in her throat.

'And I should have conquered fear.'

'Too late, too late.'

Too late, too late. Shut in by the bolts and shackles of society at first—and now by the foaming fetters of the sea.

The two young lovers by the harbour wall broke off their kiss again.

'What was that?' whispered the girl. 'Is there somebody down there, do you think?'

'No, no,' said her young man, 'it was just the sea talking to the sand. It was just one wave whispering to another, that's all.'

The two waves met again and ran with each other to the shore.

They reached the beach together and their reunion was a froth of whispering and syllables that disappeared forever into the sand.

'Oh, is that all?' said the young girl on the pier. 'I thought something was going on down there.'

Her young man closed her eyes with his kisses.

'There's nothing going on down there, ' he said, 'only up here.'

The archway closed again, its point a tender kiss.

'Down there are the dead and the drowned, that's all.'

And the last words of the two dead lovers were gathered as echoes into the ebb.